The Weight of Air

a novel

April D. Jordan

TODD LARSON, EDITOR • BILLI-JO LOTT, CONTRIBUTING EDITOR

ISBN: 978-1-4834-8150-0 (sc)
ISBN: 978-1-4834-8149-4 (e)

Library of Congress Control Number: 2018902345

Lulu Publishing Services rev. date: 05/02/2018

This novel is dedicated
to the *wonderer* in all of us.

Amy, thank you for your love and laughter!
To all of my family, big and small, you all make me proud.
Hugs to each of you, always!

Special thanks to author Dave Eggers for his well-wishes.

"Love what you do and do what you love."

— Ray Bradbury

CONTENTS

Part I   Avery

Chapter 1   More Honest Than Lies 1
Chapter 2   Blackberries and Bleeding Snow 5
Chapter 3   The Girls 10
Chapter 4   She Came Calling 17
Chapter 5   Little Bird 22
Chapter 6   Rest Stop 29
Chapter 7   The Mailbox 36
Chapter 8   Renewed, Healed 43
Chapter 9   Need a Light? 48
Chapter 10   Better than Good Enough 57
Chapter 11   The Passing of Time 64
Chapter 12   Afterthoughts 73
Chapter 13   Close Quarters 81
Chapter 14   Lost and Found 87
Chapter 15   Making Space 92
Chapter 16   Torn 100
Chapter 17   Anchor 109
Chapter 18   Fonder Heart 118
Chapter 19   Dust and Distance 124

Part II   Gabrielle

Chapter 20   Returning 135
Chapter 21   Discovery 142
Chapter 22   Like Being There 157
Chapter 23   Full Circle 169
Chapter 24   Retribution 179

PART I

Avery

CHAPTER 1

More Honest Than Lies

Just leave it alone. Walk away and keep your hands to yourself, my little-kid voice mocked my mother's. *Put your hands in your pockets and leave them there,* I told myself over and over again. I was the kind of kid that needed convincing, reminding. I wasn't bad — just a slight bit shy of good.

In the dark, damp house the smell of summer rain clung to the window screens. The sky was gray and muddy. *No chance of playing in the yard this morning,* I thought sulkily. My five-year old fingers picked at one another — anxious, a busybody, always on the move. I was constantly nagged about biting my fingernails and my mom threatened to dip them into hot pepper sauce to end my bad habit. "Does that really work?" I wondered aloud. Highly doubtful.

Leather, our dog, hovered near the crooked little doghouse my dad had built soon after we had moved into our home. She was a rescue, I think. The doghouse's shingles matched those on our rented place in upstate New York. A mix of every dog-breed under the sun, Leather got her eccentric name from me when I was three. The name was my "bright idea," my parents always reminded me once I was old enough to realize how ridiculous it sounded. But I reminded them in return that it had been their "bright idea" to let me name her.

We lived on Broadway Street, the artery of a town with nothing. Surrounded by farms, lakes and mountains, it appeared so empty and

1

vacant, from a child's perspective. My graduating class hit a whopping eighty-six students — a big group that year. I grew up to appreciate Deer Lake, but it took a bit of growing up to do so; every country kid wants out, but most of us try to get back in one day.

Later in life, a college friend asked me jokingly what my "porn" name would be. "What the hell are you talking about?" I quipped with a tinge of *What the hell did you just say?*

"You know, if you were a porn star, your name would be your dog's name and the first street you grew up on," she razzed me.

"Seriously?" I reacted, realizing her question was in jest. "Well, shit, I'd be a very talented Leather Broadway, then!" Important to share, my path never did lead me to porn.

The rain now coated the windows like syrup and dripped down the panes slowly and steadily. I watched the sinister storm-clouds puff, snarl and stir overhead. As I peered out of the window, my reflection stared back at me. I had never seen that before — never really noticed my own eyes looking back at me, not even in a mirror. An eerie feeling of mischief settled into my stomach and my palms started to sweat. The room was unusually quiet, given the chaos that always lurked. I had never been alone like this before. Where were the girls, my sisters, the babysitting kids? There was no one.

Dad's matches and cigarettes sat on the end table next to the ashtray I had made for him in art class — the pinnacle of all elementary school art projects in the seventies. My, how things have changed! The red-and-black-patterned carpet and wood-paneled walls seemed to be smiling at me, beckoning me to do something stupid.

My mother's words resounded in my tiny head, *"I'll trust you until you give me reason not to…"* My sisters and I had this mantra memorized. Those words blanketed us every time we left the house. They were a pretty strong deterrent most days, but not today. Not today.

The book of matches, now in my hand, was held in a tight fist so my sisters wouldn't notice if they suddenly appeared in the living-room doorway. I pretended I was creating an illusion, about to begin a fabulous magic trick.

"Wallah!" The matches mysteriously appeared from my hand with a quick twist of the wrist. The magic trick that never happened would have been a hit, I'm sure. However, the task I set out on was far more spectacular…in fact, downright memorable!

I remember watching my mother, whom I adored, hemming the living-room curtains earlier that week. After hanging them, she kept commenting on the length and wishing they were a tad shorter. The bottoms of the curtains licked the floor each time they were drawn open or closed, and already a dusty sheath was collecting at the foot of each drape. *I could help,* I thought. *I could fix this little problem.*

I used to watch my mom make these pretty plaques for relatives by burning the paper edges of a beautiful picture, or poem, and then lacquering them to pieces of marbled wood. She got the idea from a magazine. To me, they were works of art. Mom would carefully set the edges of the paper on fire and then ever-so-precisely turn and angle the paper to direct the flame along the edge, creating an antiqued border. Delicately, she would extinguish the flame with a soft blow of air, so as to not ruin the picture.

Careful not to make a sound, other than the whispering strike of the match, I crept close to the curtains and buried myself behind them. A veil of sheen cloth bellowed in front of my face. I peered through their opaqueness, wondering if I would see anyone coming into the room just in time to stop me.

No one came.

PPPssssstttttt! The match struck, and an orange flame balanced between my thumb and forefinger. My eyes, big as saucers, stretched the outer limits of my brow. I had never lit a match before. Fast and hot, it started to creep toward my fingertips. I panicked and looked up, praying someone would come into the room to stop me, to help me. But it was still, quiet — not a soul other than my own.

"Oh, my God! Oh, my God!" I heaved out loud, choking on my own throaty breaths.

An oscillating fan blew in my direction and the show began. One curtain flashed and hissed. Then multiple panels intertwined, and the fire crawled up toward my waist. I cried and ripped them away from me just before they had the chance to rake against my skin and ruin my favorite cut-off shorts. I could hear the rain hitting the window hard now, as if the whole world suddenly amplified. How I wished it were raining inside to fix what I had done, to help me undo this fire, to erase my stupid idea! *Shit, my mother is going to kill me!*

I looked up again, hoping for rescue from my disaster. Steven, one of the kids my mom babysat, appeared stunned and bewildered. One foot clumsily stepped on the other, his red Chucks grass-stained at the toe. His mouth dropped open, gaping, as he stared at the blazing curtains. A scream of utter thankfulness shot from my mouth like a dart when I saw my mother rush into the room behind him by only seconds. She grabbed the curtains and ripped them to the floor.

The rod, crooked and bent, clanged near my feet sending the clay ashtray flying off the end table. A cancer rocket had been launched. I had never seen my mother so strong and determined. The curtains flailed as the fan swished by us and they danced like snakes on that red-and-black carpet. Mom stomped on them ferociously to extinguish the flames. Her arms rose up in the air and twisted while her knees pumped up and down. It reminded me of a beautiful African dance that my mind had recalibrated into slow motion.

Stillness overcame us all. Not a word was said. Tears rolled down my face. My mother's chest rose and fell quickly as she wiped the side of her mouth with the back of her soot-stained hand. Steven stood still, his mouth agape in shock. The fan hummed, and ashes swirled into the air like little gray snowflakes — some fell to the floor, others clung to the ceiling. The fire was out, the rain pounded, and thunder cracked far away. All I could do was point at Steven.

I came to know my mother's wrath that day as I stood by muted and petrified. I watched, stunned, as her bare hand spanked his butt. I remember him crying, and I just stood there unable to speak up. Too inept to step in and stop what rightly should have been *my* punishment, I became numb all over. I cried, too, knowing Steven was helpless, knowing I deserved to have the piss slapped out of me, but I didn't have the courage to yell, "Stop!"

Again, my breath was stuck in my throat and I choked on my snot. Steven's eyes closed, squeezing every last tear to the floor and he sat down after a couple of whacks, defeated. I knew I would never stand by and watch something unjust unravel before me ever again. I learned that day that I needed to be better than cowardly, stronger than weak, more honest than lies.

CHAPTER 2

Blackberries and Bleeding Snow

When I was in first grade, I walked to school but not alone. My mother paid an older girl, Suzy, to walk me to and from my elementary school. I don't know how my mom or dad found Suzy, but I think she was a fifth-grader who lived down the street a ways. I overheard my dad call her a "bruiser" once when he was talking to Mom — Suzy was tall, kind of burly, and had curly black hair. They trusted her, funny enough, though she was a stranger.

Suzy would walk far ahead of or behind me and chat with her older friends; I was more of an afterthought. I knew she considered herself too "cool" to walk near me, a little first-grader. Not much of a personality permeated from old Suzy. She wasn't a mean girl, nor was she nice to me — indifferent, I suppose. If I had run into the street and been hit by a car or abducted by a stranger (my mother's greatest fear), Suzy likely would have felt badly. However, I guessed the extent of her sympathy would have culminated into a shoulder-shrug and a somewhat-sorry, "Ohhh."

Upstate New York winters were harsh, and Mom used to bundle me up prepared to survive the Arctic. A thick scarf my nana had crocheted would be tangled double-time around my neck. My green mittens were sewn together with a long string that used to thread through one arm, across my back, and down the other arm so I wouldn't lose them. I think my mom made those. The wind juggled the snow with the strength of a giant helicopter-propeller against the desert sands, lifting it off the ground and creating whirls of small snow-tornados. Navy blue moon-boots protected my feet and shins from the damp and cold, causing me to trip from the bulk of each step. I was such a dork in those boots, like a lost astronaut trudging through the snow. Bouncing weightlessly on the surface of the moon seemed so much the opposite of these cement blocks attached to my feet.

The afternoon looked stormy but no flakes fell. The town seemed quiet and still while I walked home from school this day. The wintry sky was neglected, crayon-gray, and dreary. Suzy was not with me. I was alone and I quite liked it — what little girl wouldn't appreciate the chance to walk home alone, free to do whatever she wanted? I tripped on my own two feet shuffling down the snow-covered sidewalk, and I noticed, even then, my own lack of coordination in those goofy boots.

Our neighbor's house was a small, dingy shack that sat about thirty-five yards off the road. I don't remember the woman's name but I remember how incredibly old she seemed to me. She had stringy white hair pulled up into a bun, precariously nestled on top of her head. Her skin was thin as rice paper; blue veins ran across the tops of her frail hands. She used to pick blackberries along a barbed wire fence that divided her yard from ours.

"Hello," I would utter shyly, unsure of how she might respond on the hot summer days when I would catch her plucking the dark berries from the thorny bushes. She seemed to ignore me, but maybe she never heard me. The sound of her voice never left her mouth, not even in a hush. I remember gazing at her cracked, fragile hands and thinking how much those thorny bushes must have stung brushing up against her lucid skin. Her stained fingertips looked as if they had been dunked in black ink. Her head would cock sideways, always shaking a bit — quick, twitchy bobs — and her watery blue eyes would connect with mine. I wondered if she had ever been hugged in her life or if it hurt her face to smile. Did she feel alone in that tiny house so far from the road?

The neighbor-lady wasn't scary but something about her was so vacant and hollow. Her steps were shuffling doses of aging humanity.

One tiny step in front of the other, it took her twenty minutes to walk to the mailbox at the edge of the road and back to her front porch each day. In the summers I would tuck down on my belly in the tall, honey-colored grass burnt from the sun and watch her. Her red flannel robe wrapped around her body two times over, even in the June country heat. Her frame was as thin as a pole. Her ankles were purple and lean, like the branches of a tree, and met her slippers like sticks in the mud. She focused on the mailbox with fierce determination and I marveled at the intensity that radiated from those aged blue eyes. I would count the steps and pauses of her slow, methodic gait.

I tried to imagine what the neighbor-lady must have been like as a young woman. Had she been as determined in her life as she was to reach that stinking mailbox? Perhaps, when young, she traveled to faraway places without a map and drank red wine with lovely women on balconies overlooking European towns. Perhaps she farmed land with her bare hands and watched as the changing seasons reaped the rewards of her labor. I wondered if she had ever been married or raised children. Maybe the neighbor-lady had a cat named Bella and she danced late at night in the quiet of her living room to Vivaldi scratching from an old record-player. I imagined she liked her coffee with cream and sugar and read the newspaper in the glow of the morning sunlight streaming through her dingy kitchen windows. My little girl self-surmised, "It's sad that I don't know these things." Actually, it's *not* sad that I don't know these things, if someone else does. That is all that really matters in life — that someone knows you...the real you.

The wind blew in my face and literally ripped the breath right out of my lungs, startling me out of my daydream. I gasped and turned my head but it only made me trip again on my hulking boots. The snow overlaying the ground kicked up and meandered its way down the back of my jacket stinging the skin of my neck like prickly needles. The scarf around me writhed, blowing the fringes like little fingers waving at Old Man Winter. As I passed the neighbor-lady's house, I looked to see if maybe I would see her dancing in that living room or notice Bella the cat balancing on a windowsill the same way I had imagined.

Alongside of her house, as if the snow had begun to bleed, I saw red draped over the drifts. It was far from me, far from the sidewalk I was walking down. I was almost home, so close. The red was so bright and seemed so out of place. It did not move; it did not flow like a river. My eyes stood still in their sockets but my legs kept moving forward in an effort to simply pass the foreign scene and safely arrive at my front door. Tipped off-balance, my upper body met the ground in a swift, awkward plunk. *What was I looking at?*

The bloodshot color among the polar white snow was familiar to me. Warmth crept into my body, and my mouth started to salivate, as if I were about to vomit. Salty, wet fear coated my tongue, and I swallowed hard. The scarlet snow...it was the neighbor-lady's robe, red-and-black plaid. Flannel, I suppose. The snow was not bleeding; the snow was crying and cradling her frail body. There she lay, still and lifeless in the snow.

An inconceivable pressure exerted itself upon me as my young brain finally realized what my eyes were taking in. The weight of air, magnified by some scientific miracle, was exponentially and miraculously increasing the earth's gravitational pull on me. Every molecule in the sky was landing on my back as I remained sprawled in the snow on my belly. The heft of the neighbor-lady's frigid happenstance constricted my lungs, creating a pain similar to my organs collapsing in on themselves.

"Oh, my gosh! Oh, my gosh!" My words were snatched up by the wind and stolen away quickly. No one heard me; no one noticed the neighbor-lady. Had she been in the snow a long time? How sad. How permanent. I tried to imagine her dancing when I passed by the stillness despite the crying snow that day, but my little-girl heart broke at the realization of what I was really looking at. She was gone. Life no longer wove through her body. She was still, but no one else was noticing. In reality, *who* she really was would be but a figment of my imagination.

It didn't seem right to not know her name. *Neighbor-lady* was impersonal, unkind. Isn't our name the one thing we usually hold onto in life? I decided she deserved this dignity even if I had to name her myself. To me, she would be Breya, the old lady next door who died on her long trek to the mailbox on a harsh winter's day...the lady I knew only in my mind's eye as a lover of life long ago, who had become lonely while living just fifty yards away from a house filled with laughter and love...my own. We would have invited her over for dinner had we known her better (or at all, really). We should have cut down those bristly blackberry bushes that separated our worlds. We should have carved a place for her in our lives and then I wouldn't have to make up a name for her.

I was the first to find Breya in the snow. I could tell she was face-down, which made the distant scene all the more frigid and still. I was too petrified to get close to her on my own, so I ran home. The cold air spun tiny icicles in my nose and lungs. My legs were rubbery from the running, and the snowdrifts pushed me off-balance as I cut through the front yard to our porch. The screen of the storm door had not been changed, and a torn piece of the metal scraped at my coat and mittens as I fumbled to get the rusty door open.

"Mom!" I yelled from the door. "Mom! The lady next door is in the snow! She isn't moving!" My words rang through the house finding their way to my mother in the kitchen.

"What? Don't be silly. I'm sure she's fine," my mother responded, as if I were making up the entire scene.

I looked back out the front door and through the torn screen. The snow was falling hard and my little body shuttered with the thought of the icy blanket covering Breya like a winter comforter. I closed the door and went upstairs to change my wet socks. Breya now mattered to me more than ever, but the irony was that it was too late to ask the questions that had always made me curious about her. The day turned into night, but no one went out to check on Breya. Everyone assumed she was at home alone, in the stillness, as usual. After all, when you are a child, your voice is a subtle sound that often gets shushed and dismissed. So my message fell on deaf ears that night.

Breya was discovered in the following hours by the grown son I had not even known she had. My mom and I never revisited Breya's death in conversation. The guilt of not checking on Breya haunted my mother, I believe, for the rest of her life. That winter we both learned the significance of really hearing people, of listening and absorbing their words, their message, their sentiments. We were changed.

CHAPTER 3

The Girls

Years had passed, and my gawky teens had come and gone like an express train. Throughout college, I returned to my upstate home to be with my family each winter and for the summers. Along the quiet roads the trees seemed taller and the homes uncared for, as if time had taken a toll on the place and left wrinkles on not only the tender faces I recognized but also the barns, silos and fences that traced the roadside in the foothills of the Adirondacks. I used to think that only people aged but now it was glaring that even the earth aged. Even my little farm town had grown old. The mountains escalated closer to the sky, every pine tree reached taller into the clouds, and the oak and maple branches stretched across the landscape filling voids where green hillsides could once be seen between them. And, as obvious as the passing of time was, looking out onto the hills and pastures made me realize that I was unchanged in many ways — as if a lifetime had passed me by while I was away at college. My dad would laugh and say, "You act like you've never been here before."

Not that I didn't know my own home, but I never appreciated it as much as I did when I returned as an adult. Now it was familiar but different, as if I were a visitor returning to a place I had a recollection of but could not place my finger on. Perhaps that was what it meant to grow up — the world reinvents itself anew, and the things you once understood can be viewed from a fresh perspective, through a different lens. Had I become wiser? Maybe it was less about being wise and more about just being forgetful or unappreciative of the beauty that had always been around me as a child. Whatever the reason, I was now grateful to be home in the country and proud to have grown up in that quaint little place where people knew each other and waved to each other at the IGA store. The very aspects I once thought made this place simple had become special to me.

My sisters were younger; one was in college, and the others still lived at home. We fought incessantly when we were growing up, but we loved each other like crazy. However, the five of us did endure a phase when we couldn't stand to be in the same room as the other. After hearing us whine and complain, Mom would shake her head and say, "You are each other's best friends, and you don't even know it!"

What she didn't know was that we *did* know it. We always knew it. But when we were young, we annoyed each other and fell between patterns of wanting to avoid each other, then laughing together and sharing secrets. Poor Mom never knew what she was in for. As we became women, our love for one another grew deeper. Each of us knew blood was thicker than water. We had each other's backs. We always did and we always would. We were "The Girls."

I was the oldest, Avery. We confused the hell out of our teachers and neighbors, because there were so many of us and we all looked alike. Nobody got our names right, and when my parents were angry and yelling at one of us, inevitably the wrong name would fly out of their mouths. It took three or four tries before the right one balanced on their tongues. Most people just referred to us as "The Girls," sort of a small-town moniker, since everyone knew us in Deer Lake.

My parents were good people — loving and always treating us fairly. They supported us, motivated us, and taught us. Our home was full of humility and affection. Though tiny, with one bathroom in a house full of girls, we did all right. My dad loved to hunt and fish, so we were a combo-platter — part tomboy, part girly-girl. Dad was a gentle giant, tall and thick like a football player. When I was a toddler, we would rock in a chair my papa (his father) had made. Dad would play with my tiny toes as I perched on his lap. Notes softly puffed from between his lips as he closed his eyes and sang Beatles songs. I could recite the words to "Can't Buy Me Love" and "Eight Days a Week" before I knew how to spell my name.

My mom was funny and sweet, though she would probably never describe herself that way. She never had a lot of confidence; she was quiet and preferred one-on-one conversations. So she would marvel at her five confident daughters who believed they could take on the world by storm. Baking was her comfort; the smells of sweet breads and cakes would fill the house most Saturdays. A cinnamon, butter, glaze and sugar aroma beckoned for anyone passing by to drop in for a bite and a cup of hot coffee. It was that kind of place, our home — always lots of food for extra guests and friends, with enough leftovers to feed an army. We did not have money to waste but I always knew we were rich with the things that mattered most.

Mom was strong and loyal. It's funny how much clearer you *see* your parents once you are grown. You come to realize how the mundane things you took for granted as a child required time, planning, and commitment, necessitating selfless acts of love often mistaken for obligation. Mom and Dad gave often and complained little.

Of all of The Girls, I was the one who sought new places and adventures once I was in my twenties. Before I left for the Peace Corps in South Africa, my cousin asked me, "Aren't you afraid of what is out there in the world? How can you just go?"

I remember looking at her and saying with all honesty, "Scared shitless! But that's why I know I *need* to go."

The easy route never impressed me much while growing up. I guess I knew that the easy path would teach me little about the world or myself. I remember falling once when I was nine after running down a dirt path in the woods. My plan was to run fast down a ravine and then jump over a creek that flowed over some rounded rocks. By the time I got halfway down the path, my upper body was moving faster than my legs, and I went ass-over-teakettle before I even met the water's edge. I was scared then, too, but I went for it. I tried. Sometimes the scrapes are worth the trying. Lessons are often found in our failures, though they can feel like small car accidents. Scraped and bruised, we dust off our knees, dab our egos with alcohol (which might sting like a bastard!) but we recommit ourselves. Most of life is about commitment, isn't it? Yeah, I was scared, but the learned lessons would outweigh the fear. I knew I would leap far enough one day and I would be better for taking the chance despite the outcome.

My sisters were both similar to and different from me at the same time. Kate was funny and could make anyone laugh. I loved to watch her bust a gut, because her eyes somehow got swallowed up, leaving only small slits below her eyebrows. She would crack up at her own jokes — they were pretty funny — and sooner or later anyone within earshot would die laughing, too. We shared a room when we were little, and sometimes we would crawl into bed together when we got scared. The modest double-bed was pushed against the paneled wall, so one of us would be on the inside and the other would be on the outside.

We later found out that we had the same theory, but we never told each other until we were grown. The person on the inside felt a sense of safety: in the event that someone broke into our house to *get us*, the sister on the outside would be grabbed first, essentially warning the inside sister with a scream so she could get away. Needless to say, neither one of us ever wanted to sleep on the outside of the bed! No one ever did come to get us, not even the bogeyman. Our *alikeness*, Kate and I, was in our wanting to be near each other to feel safe.

"Adorable" was the adjective typically used to describe Kate as a little girl. I was sick of hearing from the older kids on the school bus, "Your sister is so cute!" But she was, and I knew it. I was like a troll next to her, with my big 1980s glasses and the short haircut my mom hacked up.

My mom was not a hairdresser, so why did she insist on cutting my hair? Money. Convenience. "It looks good!" she would convince me for a short time, encouraging me to try a perm. "Aunt Candice can let us borrow the rollers and she can show me how to do it!"

Mom did learn how to give a perm, with which she transformed me into Little Orphan Annie in the third grade. It took me eight months to grow that disaster out. But my mom was so proud, and she thought it looked "so pretty." My reflection in the mirror did not know whether to make fun of me, to burst into fits of hysterical laughter, or to cry from self-pity. I pretended to like it, preserving Mom's happiness, and inadvertently encouraging her cosmetology experiments until the dawn of middle school. Then it had to end.

My sister Alexis — Alex, we called her — was the rebel. She didn't give a shit what anyone thought. She was a good kid with her own idea of what she wanted and how to get it. Constant clashing with my parents resulted. Yeah, we both did stupid stuff but we were smart enough not to get caught. Our *alikeness* was embedded in our wanting to make it to some teenage party and sneak back home so no one would be any the wiser.

I was too old to hang out with Alex. In fact, when I left for college, she was only in seventh grade. We were not close enough in age to be sister-rebels together as kids. Yet we channeled the same teen-energy in our adolescences, smoking and drinking with the cool kids. The only difference was, I would have been mortified if caught. A fiery spirit raged within Alex that brought her close to the edge of tragic consequence time and time again, but some elastic moral fiber always managed to rip her back to safety before a woeful ending was ever realized. Thank God! This tightrope walking always scared me, though. One step away from disaster was not far enough for my comfort.

One time while visiting home, when Alex was sixteen and I was twenty-two, it was discovered that we had both picked up the habit of smoking — you know, one of those temporary fixations you latch on to, trying on a different skin, if you will. We drove around blowing smoke out of the car windows with the radio blasting and feeling free as birds. With our forearms propped up in the open window frames we sang harmony to the Indigo Girls while wearing our cheap sunglasses and chewing peppermint gum to mask the smell of the smoke. We knew that smoking was really just a short-lived bonding experience for the summer and we would kick the habit by fall. We did, and time would prove that a bad habit now and then is really just a part of life.

Sister number four, Jess, was studious and innocent — and so giving and kindhearted. When we were little, she would save her weekly allowance of $2.50 and end up spending it on my mom. She would surprise her with flowers, usually carnations from the grocery store, or a candy bar. How many kids do that? She was special in that way, and still is. When I got my first apartment in Arizona, Jess rode cross-country with me, and I paid for her plane ticket back to upstate New York. We thought we were the shit in our cut-off jeans, ponytailed hair, cruising in my new Hyundai. It was a cool sports car — electric blue — my first adult purchase made in 2000. It required my dad to co-sign so I could get the loan. I knew nothing about life at twenty-five, but my ignorance made me refreshingly courageous.

Our *alikeness*, Jess and I, was couched in our nerdiness. We both worked hard and were interested in academia, always striving for good grades. She was naturally much smarter than me. I had to work my ass off to get decent grades. I wish I could say that our likeness was rooted in that generous, giving spirit, but that would be unfair — not because I'm not gracious, but because Jess is so much more so than me. I guess that's how I know we love each other, us Girls. We can see both the good and the bad in ourselves, and in one another, and not be afraid of it. We embrace the truth, and we help each other to accept the flaws that are a part of each of us. Sisters are mirrors unto ourselves.

The baby of the family is Leah, and she milked it for all it was worth. We coddled her more than we should have when she was growing up. We were the crutch that propped her up when goals seemed too lofty to consider. A life-plan was not her language and she was more of a take-it-one-day-at-a-time kind of girl. In all fairness, she did have goals — just no design to reach them. Herein lies our *alikeness*. We were both goal-setters; I was simply more inclined to sanction my goals with a blueprint, due to the type-A part of my personality, I suppose. Are there other types? If so, what are they? No one ever mentions type B, C or D. Maybe I'm a type L and don't even know it.

Leah had talent I adored! She could look at someone's face for no more than a minute and draw every shadow that cast a silhouette of that person's life story. Pencil, charcoal, pastels, oils...it did not matter. Leah had a gift for drawing the very soul of a person as if it were charmed out of them and lulled onto a page or canvas by merely looking into their eyes. Her gift was hers alone and it was her imprint on the world. Her pictures and paintings, her treasures, were never shared but stacked in our attic. At least they would be preserved and un-cracked by the sun or undamaged by the flicker of light that cast through the windows and down the hallway of the old house we grew up in. If only all of us had a safe place to resort to when life was harsh, when the sun was too bright, or the winter too cold. Her pictures, those unseen works of art, would be safe from judgment and criticism in the attic, along with the life goals Leah would one day decide to embrace.

Looking back at some of the things I endeavored brings a smile to my face, knowing only now how bold and brave they actually were. Yet, at the time, these things seemed ordinary, like natural forays into adulthood.

CHAPTER 4

She Came Calling

The passing of time had caused the blackberry bushes at the edge of our yard to grow thick and tall, weaving in and out of the wiry fence. I could no longer see Breya's house from my parents' yard and it had been years since I had thought of her laying face-down in the snow that wintry day when I had passed by her as a child. I tried to forget it — not her, just the bleeding snow. I actually thought of Breya many times over the years and wondered whatever happened to Bella, the cat I pretended she had. I imagined the wallpaper in her home curling at the edges and yellowing over time. Her son likely put the place on the market, but I don't remember my folks ever talking about any new neighbors over the years. Even the dingy green Broadway Street sign had fallen crooked at the end of the street— either no one cared or no one noticed.

It was just before dusk one evening in late September when I was home for a long weekend visit with my folks. Manhattan was where I lived but Deer Lake was *home*. My sisters, who still lived nearby, always coordinated their plans so we could be together when I came into town. Before they rolled in for a family dinner, I wanted to go out for a walk and take in the country air. The city of New York offered few opportunities for such quiet and tranquility.

I pulled on my fleece and gloves. "Ma, I'll be back in a few!" I yelled back toward the kitchen and then headed out the door.

A deep breath filled my chest and I took it all in. The mountains were dotted with the rusted hues of red and orange autumn had ushered in. The smell of burning leaves wafted in the air. It was apple-picking season. I drifted down the road in a meditative fog letting the serenity carry me. No path, no compass, no worries; I was home. As I kicked pebbles while meandering down the cracked pavement, the sky started to turn both purple and pink as the sun finished setting. Wisps of clouds seemed to point me in the direction of Breya's home. I wondered if it was still standing. Perhaps a family had moved in and turned it into a fixer-upper after all.

Clearly no one was living there. The house appeared abandoned, crooked, and bent from neglect. The gutters sagged; weeds could be seen growing out of the left side of the roof's perimeter. I had never seen grass sprouting from a rooftop like that and it was sad for me to see what seemed like a world turned upside down. Breya's old tin mailbox, stained and rusty from the rain, still stood at the end of the driveway, its sun-faded flag upright. Out of curiosity, I decided to open it and peek inside. Surely nothing would be in there but I felt compelled to look anyway.

I took off my glove and tugged on the miniature arched door. It creaked and crumbled a bit as I pried it open. A brittle letter sat inside and the cold of the metal against the side of my bare hand startled me. The letter seemed as frail as the old house staring at me. I gripped it tightly, careful not to let the wind snatch it out of my hand. My gloves, pinched between my forearm and side, fell loose to the ground, and then flopped and tumbled down the driveway — an unnerving wave goodbye from the fluttering fingers.

The handwriting on the front of the envelope appeared as if each letter had required a great deal of concentration to form. The ink was blurred from water droplets over the ages and it took me a moment to realize it was my own name I was reading. *Avery* was scribed in careful print, perfectly centered on the weathered envelope, which had no stamp or return address. Could this be a letter from an old friend who had come back to town and mistaken my childhood home for this one? Maybe it was just a "hello" from an old classmate who had dropped by when no one was home and thrown a quick note in the wrong box. That kind of thing happened in the country. Shit, half the neighbors didn't even lock their doors!

I zipped my coat tightly under my chin and walked up the long drive to Breya's porch. The stones crunched under my boots and the air grew colder as I inhaled the brisk dusk of fall. I sat on the porch's edge, just one step up off the ground. The paint was peeling from the siding and what used to be white was now the color of egg-yolk. The dark green shutters were faded and the curtains were closed in all of the windows facing the road. They looked like eyelids on the face of the napping house. Behind me, a swing dangled by metal chains from the porch ceiling, eerily swinging gently as the wind pushed it side-to-side. Creaking back and forth, it appeared to have a mind of its own, a yearning to be in motion. My attention drew back to the enigmatic letter in my hands. I slid my finger under the lip of the envelope, gliding it across the stale paper to open it at the seam.

The letter inside was handwritten and dated 1996. It began:

> *Thank you for finding me, Avery. My life had been one of great thrills and adventures, as you guessed it might have been, but it was also lonely and desperate. I watched you walk by my house many days, and Bella and I would secretly wave to you...*

What the hell? This question reverberated in my mind, literally banging around in my head. My heart was like a sunken weight buried within my chest, burrowing its way deeper into me with each word read. My body became light and my heartbeat actually pulsed against my skin so I could count the beats against my nerves. The letter continued:

> *I waited for someone to see me as you did for most of my life, to ask the questions you asked, to wonder where I had traveled and what I had done. Few people ever did. But even from a distance, you seemed to see me. You wanted to know me and I could tell you even grew to respect me. I liked the name you chose, Breya. And for all of these years I found it curious that you chose a name with such significance behind it, the name my parents also gave me.*

How could this be? I wondered. This letter, written fifteen years after I had found Breya in the snow that wintry day, made no sense. Was it a cruel joke my mind was playing on me? No one else knew my wonderings about her life, my curiosities about her. How did she even know? How could she? She hardly spoke a word to me when she was alive, and she never returned a smile — only a glance. Those watery old blue eyes seemed to want to say more but never did. Now I was fracturing inside and my mind and heart were splintering apart at the realization that this letter was now being held in my twenty-eight-year-old hands long after Breya's death. The prospect felt stupid — delusional, even.

I returned my gaze to the letter in my hands and watched it tremble as I read further:

> *Avery, there is more to this life and all that comes after it than you could ever understand. I have watched over you and my attention has cloaked many decisions you have made, both good and bad. Perhaps, our souls merged the day you saw me in the snow. You saw me and now I see you. I am but a guidepost without judgment. Your story is yours to write. It is in the wonder that you will discover much about yourself, those you love, and the things that you will dare try. I have not left this place and my story, too, continues to be written.*

The stillness of the evening grew disconcerting and the purple sky now hovered in a mantle of dark grays. Like lanterns unanchored by gravity, a few stars caught fire above me. I could see the glow of my parents' porch-light in the distance. I lit a cigarette; my old habit had returned after Jax and I had broken up. The match lit a protective circle around me for a brief second, and I inhaled sharply on the cigarette. ChapStick soothed my dry lips, as I sat back down on the porch for a minute. *What to do? What to do with my thoughts, this letter, this situation? Am I losing my mind?*

I shoved the letter back into the mailbox as I stomped past it on the way home. I didn't want it. I didn't understand it. If I ignored it, perhaps it would be less real.

Entering my parents' place I was greeted with hugs and kisses, smiles and laughter. The Girls had all arrived. Mom was in the kitchen finishing up a roast with carrots, potatoes and onions — my favorite. I knew I looked a wreck despite my attempt to be jovial and spirited, and I knew my sisters would see through it. They would know something was amiss.

My dad came out to the kitchen and gave me a bear-hug. He always gave my neck a squeeze and kissed my cheek when he first saw me. "Cold!" he exclaimed. "How long ya' been out there?"

"Just a bit, Dad. Just walking around. Thinking…"

"'Bout what?"

"Old times. People I used to know."

"Well, they're all here. Things don't change much. You ought to go visiting tomorrow and catch up with old friends. You know people love to see you!" He pulled out a chair at the dinner table and motioned me to have a seat.

"Yeah, they're all here," I trailed off as I sat down for dinner.

CHAPTER 5

Little Bird

Looking out of the window of my SoHo apartment, my reflection stared back. I remembered seeing my eyes meet my own, just as they had done that day I lit the curtains on fire as a kid. I had left Deer Lake a couple of days ago, trying to forget the letter I hadn't the strength to claim. I practically convinced myself I had never read it at all. Neither my sisters nor my parents noticed the change in my demeanor while I was home for the weekend, which somehow supported my ignorance and denial. Here in the city I could allow my hectic life to swallow me back up and continue working without hesitation or acknowledgment of that evening. Maybe it was some sort of daydream — some delusional ideation of a connection to Breya I had longed for as a child, perpetuated by the guilt of finding her dead and never calling for help. Whatever it was — a fictitious letter planted in my mind by guilt, maybe — I chose to ignore it. This method worked pretty well for me as an adult: ignore the things I didn't wholeheartedly embrace and they would eventually just go away.

It was now a Saturday morning and I was sitting at the window of a café I treasured. I would lean my back against the exposed brick, cozy up to the bar at the front window with my steaming cup of pure relaxation, and stare at the passers-by on the streets. *How do they manage to make a leaf float whimsically on the surface of a latte with the flip of a wrist and the twist of a spoon?* I thought. Black-and-white photographs depicting scenes from around the world adorned the walls in worn, antiqued frames. Paris, London, Bangkok...all emanated a bit of culture and added to the ambiance that would have otherwise been warehouse restoration, circa 2004. This bundle of bagel-joy used to be part of a textile plant. The photos somehow made the café sexier while still historic and charming, cozy and simple. The brick looked abused and worn from the years and the heavy machinery that had likely shaken and quaked inside this place.

I played a game I used to play in church as a girl. I would sit in the front pew during communion, kneeling and looking at the shoes of the parishioners as they walked back to their seats after sipping the wine during communion. I would then look up at their faces to see if the shoes matched the personalities of their wearers: sometimes they did, sometimes they didn't. I did the same thing in this little café from the comfort of my stool. Looking through the slightly steamy window, I propped my feet up, took in a deep Saturday sigh, and felt the warmth of the sun penetrate the glass and cast itself upon my body. I was at peace.

A brown leather pair of shoes with cracked soles strolled by. Red wool socks were peeking from beneath the bottom of the jeans, slightly rolled up to the ankle. He was a bearded guy with a guitar on his back and dark sunglasses. A tattoo of a mandala decorated the back of one hand, his sleeves were pushed up above a watch with a wooden face, and colorful bracelets of string and leather cuffed both wrists. *A match.*

Next came yellow high-heels and white leggings with polka-dots stretched up to the thighs of what I was guessing might be a twenty-something woman. She donned a navy-blue miniskirt, a white flouncy blouse, and a fur vest. Gaudy beads dangled from her neck. Big glasses pushed up under her bluish hair, which framed a face that appeared more forty-ish. *No match.* I could observe the shoes and faces for an hour or two before becoming bored.

The book I was reading sat idle beside me as I people-watched for a while. The sidewalks always buzzed, but on an early Saturday morning it was distinctly different from any other day of the week. The entire city slowed down just enough for those of us who lived here to get a sense of the shift in momentum. It was subtle but glorious. I sipped my latte in a way that made a slight slurping sound, it was simply too hot to be any more polite than this. The slow burn as it settled in my stomach was soothing, causing the thermostat within me to rise two degrees. The clock on the bank across the street was a few minutes slow, fitting for the Saturday morning slow down. Only two other people sat at the window on a stool as I did and they were buried in what seemed to be an outdated past time: reading the newspaper. The smell of baking croissants teased me and lulled in a passer-by here and there from the street.

A tap at the glass snapped me out of the delicious daze I had fallen into. *Holy shit! It's Jax!* an internal dialogue ensued. *Be cool, deep breaths,* I encouraged myself. *No big deal. Yeah, he's the love you've been missing for the last month, but keep it cool.*

I could have called him but I never did. It would have been an affront to my independence. I wanted to appear *laissez-faire,* as if seeing him were really no big deal at all. I thought everyone wanted to appear this way, yet inside I was doing a dance, jumping up and down, and high-fiving the shit out of someone who wasn't even there to receive my boundless joy.

Avery, I told myself, *a slight smile will do; not too aloof and certainly not too excited.* This little pep-talk felt appropriate and responsible, actually. It had been a while since Jax and I had last seen each other, though his shadow cast upon each moment of my day, the way all lovers do after their goodbye. Jax and I had been together for a year and had recently split over our egos. Neither of us was likely to admit that, but it was the truth.

I had a job curating pieces at the art gallery nearby and he was an architect in Manhattan. Which meant we were both creative, stubborn, and moody. Together, we were self-centered and arrogant, but we also found grains of vulnerability in one another that we never shared with anyone else. I disclosed thoughts to him that I never allowed myself to share with another person. He did the same in the quiet of the mornings after we buried ourselves in the blankets of sweat and honesty. We fell in love and loved hard, but we also loved gently and innocently. With him I became a child, engulfed in the innocence I thought had long left me. Wonderings about who I could become, or where I might travel, all came to life again when I met Jax. Imaginative recklessness.

He smiled through the window of the café with one hand tucked inside the pocket of his faded black jeans. Still in his tracks, he studied me for a moment, as if I were a puzzle missing a piece. My intuition was to pretend I didn't notice until the urge to nod, inviting him inside, had already tipped my head. We had not spoken in a month since walking away from each other — a slow walk we knew we were never fully committed to. We never actually said, "Goodbye" or "It's over," but we both sensed the need to just go — go on without each other. Where to, neither one of us knew. We never made fighting routine — in fact, we hardly ever even disagreed. But, again, our egos and the need to be right outweighed any quiet resignation we feigned.

The minute Jax came into focus, my heart raced, and I wanted to wrap myself around him. *Play it cool,* I coaxed myself. I could tell he wanted to touch me, and as soon as we were close enough to reach out to one another, he grabbed my waist and pulled me close for a hug. His scarf smelled fresh and clean, like his skin, and his worn leather satchel was strapped across his body. His dark hair had loose, lazy twists, and his olive face was brushed with a five-o'clock shadow. He was seriously the most striking man I had ever known — not just because of his looks, but also because of his kindness and humor. On Jax's index finger was a plain silver ring his grandfather had given him, signifying that Jax had a sensitive side very few people had the courtesy of knowing. I felt lucky to have been one of those people.

"Sit," I sputtered, backing up onto my stool and gesturing to the empty one next to me. The steam from my latte was fading, the cup was nearly empty. "I'll grab another, if you're staying." This was my way of asking him to without really saying the words.

"Ave, I've passed by this freaking café every morning for a month, hoping I'd see your face in the window." Again, our egos would rather have us waste time and energy searching for a meeting of chance than pick up the phone and call one another or send a text. "I've missed you a *little*, not a lot." He smiled and winked.

"Same." My voice strained, working to prevent the tears from pushing against my stubbornness. "Same," I repeated. My heart was growing inside my chest, pressing against my lungs, shortening my breaths. He was like air to me, and my body was gasping at the thought of suffocating in his absence; so discernible to me now, but obscure only minutes ago.

The café seemed quiet and the only people now in the place were the two of us and the barista behind the counter. The voice of Adele pushed through the speakers, adding to this affection-inducing moment. Jax stood between my legs, facing me, and pushed in against me. His corduroy jacket with patches on the elbows was a rugged, intellectual statement. We loved books, debate, and a challenge. He was my challenge. I knew that, no matter how much I wanted to be in control around him, I was frenetic; my heart was a bit feral.

As we walked toward my apartment, our strides were in sync, and we moved with a shared sense of urgency. There was no invitation, no conversation about rekindling the *us* we once knew; we just strode the familiar path to my door. The sidewalk grew thicker with people as the city woke up and the day waned on. Our eyes darted between each other and the river of faces that came toward us. I tripped slightly and his arm tightened and cradled my back. I sensed he wouldn't let me fall as long as he was close enough to reach me. This was what I knew about Jax — and loved. We couldn't get home fast enough to let ourselves fall into one another. It had been over a month, and I unquestionably missed the way he had looked at me and made me feel like the most important person in the world. My inhalations shortened at the thought of him once again touching my skin, the weight of our bodies against one another. He was my beloved, my friend, all I had come to cherish. Circumstance brought us full circle, right back to the place where we stood toe-to-toe, eye-to-eye.

Only blocks away now, we smiled at each other, knowing we were back together. Our souls were somehow intertwined, as if we were one being. *Were we ever really apart, as in broken up or separate?* Physically, a month had passed, but he had occupied the far corners of my mind every day. I could feel him trembling as our bodies now touched, hip-to-hip, walking. Finally he leaned down and whispered in my ear, "I love you, Little Bird."

These were his words. I was his *Little Bird*. I missed hearing his voice say that to me and now they sounded like a sweet lullaby retrieved from storage. His hand fell away from my waist as he raced ahead to unlock the door. He winked again as he looked over his shoulder at me and stepped off the curb to run to the front stoop across the street.

The world fell silent.
The screaming of brakes pierced my heart.
Numbness seized my body.

My eyes were fixed, static.

My body locked with paralysis.

Detained by pure terror and disbelief, I stood still, stupid, stunned. Others ran toward the taxi that sat sideways in the road. The hum of an engine churned and a driver's head lay limp against the steering wheel, motionless. Another car with a smashed front end screeched to a halt against a metal light pole. The lady inside, blinded by hair flung across her face, was hysterical. I could see her mouth open, screaming, as tears and blood ran down her neck, but I couldn't hear anything. I was still, stupid, stunned — and now deaf.

No one noticed me. No one came to me. I stood in shock and terror on the sidewalk and watched the scene unravel before my blurry eyes. I gasped and focused on the apartment door across the street — the door Jax was rushing to open so we could walk through and start to put the pieces back together again. The door, the fucking door, was right there. I could see it from where I was standing. The door seemed to stare back at me and I fell to my knees hard enough to crack my kneecaps. I was breaking. Every part of me was shattering into fragments of what *used* to be instead of what was *supposed* to be. My chest was so tight I thought I would choke to death in that moment.

My feet stuck in what felt like setting cement. They could not move me forward, and, as much as I wanted them to, they could not move me backward either. I wanted to see my Jax, to get to him but I could not move at all. Fear was wrapping around my body like a python, starting at my ankles, twisting around my calves and thighs, and now tightening around my arms and chest. I started to hyperventilate, and a woman my age with long, black hair clutched my hand. She, too, was stilted and arrested with emotion, but little did she know how connected I was to the catastrophe that was spilling onto the street and sidewalk before us. Her eyes locked with mine and a familiarity struck me for the briefest of moments. No, I didn't know her, but I desperately wished she were a person I knew. Though we were strangers, her hand held mine tightly, and we clutched onto each other for an immeasurable amount of time.

The horn from the taxicab where the man was unconscious against the steering wheel suddenly burst in my ear like a needle to a balloon. My body was precipitously thrusting forward, free of the cement and python, as I lurched into the street to find Jax.

"Jax! Jax! Jax!" I screamed in a frantic pitch I didn't recognize.

Seeing his shoe lying in the street, I ran toward the darkness, where I sensed his body was becoming one with the ground. A crowd of people huddled around him, and I saw only his legs. Total stillness and chaos were enveloping everyone all at once. I couldn't part the people to get to him.

"Move! Help me! Help him! Help him!" a mantra fired from my mouth. But no one heard. This army of unsuspecting people and neighbors were shielding me from my last glimpse of his life. They were robbing me of my spirit, but they had no idea they were doing so. People leaned over him, some bent down close, trying to help.

"Move! Fucking move!" I sputtered through gurgles of rage and disbelief.

Like a game of keep-away, they unknowingly blocked me from seeing and reaching Jax before his last breath was sipped from the air and taken into his chest. By the time I got to him and could see his face, he was gone. And the inexorable silence returned. Lights flashed, but with no sound of sirens. Police officers and paramedics ran past, shouting, but I couldn't hear their words. Just like the day I saw Breya in the snow, the pressure all around me was increasing without calibration. The weight of air, the sound of death, was absolutely deafening.

CHAPTER 6

Rest Stop

I lay on the bed, staring at the sterile white curtains that framed my window. The ceiling fan was still, yet particles of dust flittered in the path of sunshine that sifted through the pane of glass where the curtains parted. Eight months ago, Jax had died. I felt bitter, angry that he had been taken from me. I was sure everyone who suffered such a loss experienced this stranglehold, too — a vise grip squeezing tighter and tighter around reality. As if trapped in a straitjacket, leather straps buckled around my torso, I was screaming and flailing trying to rip it away from me. This anger, this pain, this feeling of utter rage coursing through me was overwhelming. I clenched my fists so tightly my nails pierced my palms and my jaw cracked. I was lost, but I didn't know how else to be. Everything had become temporary.

My sisters called but I ignored the phone. I couldn't pretend to be all right and I knew that was what they wanted to hear. They wanted me to feel stronger every day and say, "I am coming to terms with my loss," which I was precisely not doing. My parents left messages almost daily. I returned their calls, but always when I knew they would be at work so I wouldn't have to talk to anyone.

My body ached. Who knew that sadness could actually plant physical pain? It was as if the sadness inside of me were growing in my abdomen, akin to unrelenting weeds. I was scared and alone in a place of utter darkness. The taste of loss lingered in my mouth, and I couldn't wash or wish it away. I tried to do so by singing songs Jax and I had loved and by reading aloud letters he had written to me, but my own voice annoyed me. Broken and beaten, my soul was scraping against my chest, trying to crawl out and away from me.

An empty fridge stared back at me when I opened it, its light much brighter than I remembered. The cupboards were bare. My stomach hurt, growling from hunger, like a dog when cornered. My leave of absence from work was ending soon, and I needed to get my head on straight. In two weeks I would have to go back to the art gallery and assume my avant-garde disposition. *It's all so fake at times, phony bullshit,* I thought. I loved the role art played in the human condition, how it could inspire and move people to talk and debate. But I never appreciated the assholes who believed that art was meant for *some* people and not for *all*. Close-minded attitudes like that bothered me. Art was for *everyone*, taken in differently by every eye, I believed. I needed to bemuse myself with art these days; it would be a means to get on with life. I realized this to be true.

My priorities had changed over these months, though. Maybe I could ignore Jax's passing — just pretend it never happened — and perhaps it would be less real, much like the letter I had found and refused to acknowledge in Deer Lake. Would I have to pretend Jax never existed at all? Could I make myself believe I never really loved him? Should I hang onto his memory, the love, and imagine he never even died? I began to question myself over and over again: what was the right way to allow, or tolerate, a loved one's passing? The questions kept coming, and I had no answer. Not one.

My sanity was wavering. The four walls of my apartment seemed to close in on me. Devon, my best friend, was banging on my door pleading with me to answer it. She was persistent and had been stopping by at least three times a week, despite my indignant disregard of her. "I'm not leaving, Avery!" I heard her shout through the door. "Open the door before I bang it down! Pushing the world away will not make it *go* away. Come on!" I could tell she was growing weary. My heart sank at my selfishness. I could hear her sigh. Her voice cracked, "Open the door, please." She was crying — for me, at me, with me.

I brought my hand up to the door and pressed against it, as if searching for a heartbeat. I touched the cold brass chain and slid it aside with a clank. Devon must have been sitting, defeated on the other side, because I heard her scamper to her feet and sniff hard. As I unbolted the deadlock, the doorknob turned slowly in my palm. The open door released a vacuum of despair that had built up in that tiny apartment, and suddenly my eyes dilated and took in the light that came with Devon's presence. She fell into me and we hugged each other. This was the first hug I had given or received in months. I had locked myself away, taking on every pain as if it were only mine to own.

My place was a dump — I knew it. Sitting across from Devon on the couch, I became self-conscious about the mess: wrappers on the floor, my hair disheveled, dishes balanced in a pile like a game of Jenga. She didn't seem to notice, or maybe she didn't care.

"What took you so long?" she asked me, as if to chastise and tease me all at once.

"Dev…" I started through wet eyes.

"I'm here." She folded her legs underneath herself and sat opposite me in an armchair. I sunk further into the couch, though I really wanted to extend my hand to her.

"I just can't imagine the simple things without him," I began, face full of tears. "I don't want to, anyway. And in here, I could convince myself that I wouldn't have to imagine those things. In here, in this apartment, I could imagine life was just on pause and Jax would be back, ya' know?" My delusions were comforting, despite my coherent understanding of their foolishness.

I saw that Devon was crying again, too, as a tear slipped between her lips while others rolled under her chin. Maybe she was hurting for me, or perhaps she was feeling sorry for me. It seemed to make sense to me, the life-on-pause theory, as I heard it coming out of my mouth, but I could tell Devon's patience was thin and she was exhausted. The last eight months were not just my pain but also that of my friends and family, and I compounded it with my hiding out from them. My denial was reckless, but only now was I able to see this. I needed to apologize. I knew that with that apology I would find my strength, my will to accept the loss of Jax, and the courage to leap over that creek. I was afraid that the acknowledgment of death would also give way to its permanence.

Death's undeniable presence in my life might create a darkness in me that would likely forever loom inside my thoughts, permeating the flecks of happiness I chased.

I thought back to that time I had fallen trying to jump over the creek when I was a little girl, and the time my cousin had asked me if I was afraid of what was out there in the world. I had told her I was scared, but that was why I knew the world must be full of great moments waiting to meet us. The truth is, if I had the chance to answer that question all over again, I would tell her that sometimes the easier path might teach us just as much about the world and ourselves as the difficult path. For now, I wanted the easy path.

"On this day, even the easiest path would take courage, strength, and resilience," I whispered to myself. Devon just looked at me and smiled.

"Mom? Are you there?" I inquired into the phone after the answering machine picked up the call that evening.

"Yes, Avery, I'm here. Oh, my God, it is good to hear your voice!" she said with unrestrained concern. Her tone weakened as emotion softly welled within her.

"Can I come for a visit, Ma?" I asked, sounding timid and nervous. I did not have to ask to come home but I always found it polite.

"Ave, just come home," she said tearfully.

Together, we just sat silently on the phone, allowing the space between us to catch our tears. We cried in hints of tiny gasps and breaths and sniffles to soothe our hearts. Everyone needs their mom when they are hurting. No matter how old one gets, there is a comfort between a mother and a child that no one else can fill. In the quiet between soft sobs, we loved each other with unwavering commitment. There was strength in knowing she was my mother, my protector, no matter our ages.

The next morning, I packed up my hunter-green Jeep and headed north to Deer Lake. The drive would take six hours after meandering through the foothills of the Adirondacks. I grew up just ten minutes west of Vermont, so either way you looked, mountains cushioned every view. My favorite music was ready to go and plenty of snacks and drinks were thrown on the passenger's seat. I was a snacker when I drove: Snickers, chips, bananas, gum, water, Pepsi. I started with a coffee in a Thermos to kick off my caffeine binge and rolled out of the city high as a kite at the prospect of soon sitting in the peaceful countryside. It was too windy for the Jeep's top to be down, even though it was an early July day. But I opened the windows so I could smoke a cigarette and have the breeze pull the smell off of me. I figured I would arrive at my parents' place around noon.

The Girls were coming, too. They always did when I came home, which I loved about them. We were like a pack of wolves — always together and fiercely protective of one another — only much nicer, far funnier, and without a sense of direction.

I worried about a barrage of questions, though. *Would they tackle me with a thoughtfulness I would find too asphyxiating?* I wondered. I have a serious issue when I go home with my parents treating me like a kid just because I've been away so long. I don't think they will ever grow out of this as long as I live far from home. Weirdly, my excitement was turning into panic. Perhaps they would just carry on as usual and avoid the questioning. My mind let it all go as the road mesmerized me into a calmness that sustained me for the next few hours of the trip. The summer months had painted the trees and grass a vivid green, which soothed me further.

After a while I had to stop to use the restroom, so I pulled off an exit I had been to before. My body stretched as I stood outside the Jeep and reached for the sky to twist the stillness out of me. My neck was stiff, and I was growing bored. I had the attention span of a gnat, Devon always told me. Friends — they'll be honest, if nothing else!

The sun was heating up and I rolled the top of the Jeep down for the rest of the trip. A cigarette was pinched between my forefinger and middle finger, and I blew the smoke upward, as if this would somehow assist the environment or the lungs of those around me. I sat on a curb, stretching my legs out, one crossed over the other.

"Can I borrow a light?" a woman's voice asked as she walked up beside me. She wore black leather boots, each with a leather strap buckled to the outer side. They were scuffed, worn in. Skinny jeans fit tightly around her muscular calves. I was curious to see if the boots were *a match* to her face, but the sun blinded me from seeing it; only a silhouette loomed above me. The surroundings were wooded — mostly pine trees. Cardinals flew in and out of the dense woods like flares streaming through the branches. The forest was so thick the tree limbs seemed to braid together in a weaving of pine-needles and sap so tight the woods became a darkroom. Imagine if inside were the black-and-white photos of everyone who had walked its trails — a museum of life.

I snapped back to the moment, shook off my daydream of the photos hung by clothespins deep in the forest, and turned toward the woman. "Sure," I smiled as I reached upward to hold out my lighter to her.

She took it and lit the cigarette that was dangling from her mouth. "Wallah!" she murmured as she flipped the lighter closed. "Thanks!"

This woman seemed confident, bold, independent. I could sense the adventure inside of her and her urge to move forward into the world. Perhaps her picture was hanging in the forest museum I had just imagined. I could see her face now as she leaned over to pass back the lighter. *A match*, I registered. I sensed that I knew this face and long dark hair, but I couldn't place her. *God, she's gorgeous. Have we met before?*

"Wallah," left my lips, repeating her expression with a nod, hoping to see a smile in return. But she was a bit hard at the onset, the kind of person who didn't give her smiles away. I understood that they had to be earned. Only with familiarity came softness, I could tell. She started to pace and look around at her surroundings. A drag from her cigarette brightened the tip to a searing red. A soft, white smolder slowly drifted from her mouth, easing skyward, creating a smokescreen between us.

"Where you headed?" I asked her, hoping to get another glimpse of her face. I could not place her, but I had met her before, I was sure of it now. *What is her name?*

"Upstate," she put it frankly. "Going home," she added in a way that suggested she had a long story to tell but not enough time to share it. This was not to assume I was privileged enough to hear it — after all, we were strangers who had just stumbled upon each other. She seemed friendly but distant. I respect that in a person, wishing I possessed more of that quality, rather than giving my trust away so easily.

"Avery," I blurted my name, trying to exude a confidence I could own. "I'm going upstate, too. I grew up there." We stood together, looking toward the woods, while the hum of the highway buzzed behind the trees.

"Yeah, I know," she smiled. This comment caught me off-guard. I looked up to meet her gaze, but she had already turned away from me.

"Do I know you?" I asked her, figuring we must have gone to the same university, or maybe she grew up in a town nearby.

"I know *you*," she smiled slyly.

I guessed we were acquaintances, but I couldn't imagine forgetting her face. I couldn't put my finger on it, but I knew those eyes — iridescent jade. "I'm sorry, I can't place you," I said to her.

I always feel so horrible when I meet someone I've forgotten. Her eyes stopped and looked at mine long enough to carve a memory, one that would not be forgotten, into my mind. Her hair, long and dark, fell down her back in waves. The breeze flitted against the strands at her shoulders. Soon her back was turned to me again, and she was walking toward her beat-up truck, the encounter over.

"Thanks," she yelled over her shoulder. "I'll see ya'…"

I just shook my head, unsure of what to say or what to do. *Bizarre.* "See ya'," I instinctively yelled, a bit confused, and finding it rude that she had let on that we knew each other but walked away without putting the recognition into context.

Will I? Will I see her again? If so, where? Who the hell is she? These questions taunted me for the rest of the drive and I remembered the soft scent that lingered after she had walked away, as if a second self had walked three steps behind her, like a shadow stuck in the moment. In just moments, this woman was crawling into my thoughts in a way very few people ever had, and I could tell I wouldn't be able to push her out easily. Perhaps the power of intrigue was haunting me more than her actual essence. Whoever she was, I became compelled to move toward her, yet I had no idea where she was going, where she came from, or where she was at that very moment. So I pushed harder, and soon the thought of this woman, this stranger, fell away from me, forgotten, as I continued driving down the highway, headed for the towering mountains ahead.

CHAPTER 7

The Mailbox

I pulled into the driveway of my parents' place and sat there with my seatbelt on for a while. The ride seemed longer than usual; my legs stiff and heavy. I turned off the engine and listened to the ticking that followed as the Jeep cooled down.

My breathing insinuated that I was preparing for a moment of anticipation. I wondered what this visit home would be like. It was my first time seeing everyone since shortly after Jax's funeral. My folks insisted I stay with them the week after, and Alex stayed with me for a few days in December. But since then I had been huddled up in a self-protective cocoon. What if I couldn't articulate my feelings while I was home? Would my parents and sisters find it natural, or dramatic and selfish? I hadn't brandished the fortitude to put my thoughts and feelings into words for the past eight months. It was time. It was time to find the words.

"Call a thing a thing," I once heard a life coach say on television. *Call a thing a thing,* I encouraged myself as I opened the front door with some hesitation, only to have the doorknob yanked right out of my hand from the other side.

"Avery!" my dad shouted with excitement as he swung the door open and revealed his warm presence. "Hon, how was the drive?" He took my bag off my shoulder.

"Good, Dad! Real good!" I hugged him warmly and my eyes welled up when I smelled his Brut cologne. My arms barely fit around him as I squeezed and felt his warm heartbeat through his chest. "Love you," spilled forth as I cried against his worn flannel shirt. "I really love you."

The hugs kept coming. My mom, dad and sisters all passed on their strength and support by merely sitting in the same room with me. Our outer thighs touched as we bunched up on the couch, sat in chairs in the den, and reminisced. My mom held my hand and made me tea, black with sugar. We talked and cried, told stories, and shook the sadness out of our bodies with jokes and old memories that made us laugh until our cheeks hurt.

Kate reminded me of the time she and I had hidden in a tree and shot spitballs at the kitchen window until Mom got so frustrated she ended up accidentally pouring the milk for her cereal all over the counter, missing the bowl completely.

We recalled the time we had chased Mom around the yard with a garden hose on a hot summer day, spraying each other, until someone was pushed into the pool.

We laughed about the crazy things we used to do out of sheer boredom or for no other reason than to get a rise out of each other. Once we had hidden a bucket full of grasshoppers in the pots-and-pans cupboard just to watch Mom unravel at the sight of them jumping all over the place when she pulled the door open. Like little firecrackers exploding, one here, another there, they hopped and jumped about turning Mom into a screaming lunatic! She hated frogs, so you can imagine the field day we had with that little nugget of information as kids.

Jess cracked up at the time Dad had gone barreling through the sliding door, thinking it was open, only to bounce off the screen door hard enough to tear it right out of the frame.

Leah and Alex grabbed a tissue to dab their eyes from laughing so hard. It felt so good. It had been a long time since I had laughed like this with my family — with anyone, really — long enough that each bout of laughter built up within me was exhaled an octave higher with every story shared. This kind of hurt felt right. A healing was happening as we sat together, remembering days that had passed. It's funny how the simplest of things can leave such lasting impressions.

We spent the evening together in this way. There were no scary questions, no need to explain myself or my feelings about Jax's passing or my plans for the coming months. On this night, I would not have to verbalize my loss. It would have been impossible to wrap it in words to contain the grit of the matter, anyhow. My family understood that we would have to let the water flow under the bridge and allow the paper boats to float away. The water under this bridge was due this honor, was owed this understanding. We all understood that the paper boats would come floating by again in time.

The next morning, I woke up in a room I had once stayed in for a period of time as a teenager. The same afghan covered the bed and I could see that a watermark formed a circle on the ceiling tile above me. If I squinted one eye, it looked sort of like a face smoking a pipe. Nostalgic for Papa, I could smell the cherry tobacco he used to pack into his own pipe. The curl of the mahogany that turned up to his lips was so vivid to me, as if I had just seen it yesterday. He would gently hold the black stem between his lips as he drew short, quick puffs, sucking in the flame of the lit match held to the end of the pipe. I loved the smell!

He also used to listen to Hank Williams crone through the static needle of a record player. "Mmmm," I sang, recalling these moments. It had been almost ten years since my grandpa had died. It didn't seem possible.

When I was little, I would spend the night at my grandparents' house some weekends just for fun. I remembered the smell of the sheets on the bed, crisp and somehow different from the fragrance of my mom's sheets. My grandma cherished an old cast-iron frying pan, swearing it made the world's best fried eggs. Admittedly, I never tasted any quite as good. My grandparents were very faithful people, spiritual in nature and practice. Hell, my grandmother even told stories of times she had actually spoken with the Hail Mary!

I was fascinated by her devotion and wondered if God had literally summoned her to be his conduit here on earth. Was their relationship one that was earned or destined? Were their conversations real, or aberrations created by hope or faith? I don't know, but I can say this: every time she retold one of those stories, I sensed God in those moments. I felt Him through her. And not a single detail of her stories ever changed. Lies — now *those* details tended to change over time, so my gut told me Gram was the real holy deal!

As my eyes refocused on the stained ceiling tile in my old bedroom, my body stretched beneath the covers in a moaning twist. My dad could have replaced the tile easily enough; I wondered why he hadn't. The smell of coffee permeated down the long hallway to my room and put a smile on my face. *Who's already up and about?* I thought. *It's only seven a.m.* I stayed still and let my body melt into the mattress while an old fan stood in the corner of the room and creaked each time it turned and passed over me.

The lilac bush outside my window brought back more childhood memories of those summer days that began with its sweet scent. As an adult, I thought of the day I might plant one in my own backyard. The purple buds scraped against the side of the house and window-screen, chaffing the perfume of the bushes into tiny remnants left in the squares of the window screen. Their summery perfume lingered into the first month of fall.

Slipping on my jeans and a white T-shirt, I headed down the hallway, hoping to grab some coffee. Happiness was pushing me into the day.

In the kitchen I poured a cup and noticed that the timer had been set on the coffee-maker. No one else was up, and the house was quiet, as all of the sleeping heads still rested on their pillows. The sun reflected off the countertops — the day was just waking, too. My mind drifted to the outdoors as the birdsongs carried into the kitchen through the open windows. I shook my head at the notion of leaving windows open in the country and how different my regard for safety was, now that I lived in the city. Scribbling a short note, I grabbed my cup of coffee and headed out the door for a walk.

The screen door opened with a creek. It would have banged shut behind me, potentially waking someone up, had I not caught it with my hip just in time and then slowly sliding away into the fresh stillness of the July morning. The roof on the porch was new and the lopsided sag I had grown accustomed to was gone. Our sidewalk meandered through the front lawn and up to the driveway — a slight incline that made it a slippery disaster in the wintertime. Over the years, the cracks in the cement walkway had grown slightly wider, and patches of grass had found their way up between the fissures. I watched my feet pass over the crags and headed up to the quiet country road our home rested on.

Breya's house called to me. I thought of the letter I had found in her mailbox with my name on it so long ago. The house lured me and suddenly my walk had a direction. *Was it real? Had I made it all up?* I questioned my lucidity. It seemed absurd that I had even considered such a thing. *What would have come of it, if it were real?*

The road cornered and rose slightly up a hill. The coffee jostled in my cup, requiring concentration to avoid spilling it. I took a couple of sips, blowing it off to cool it down. Breya's rooftop came into my sight, the tiles looked more worn than the last time I was there. *There it is,* I said to myself, affirming that the house was still standing.

The mailbox met me at the end of the driveway by the road. A deep swallow took over my throat, while nervous blinking possessed my eyelids. I stared at the box's flag, which again stood upright, as if to wave down the mail-carrier and alert him or her of a letter waiting to be sent away. As I gave the front of the house a once-over, I noticed the slight movement of a curtain in one of the old bedrooms on the second floor. I blinked and looked behind me, as if to receive some kind of recognition from someone else that what I had just seen had actually taken place. Of course, no one was there to confirm my vision and I whipped my head back toward the house. All of the curtains seemed still, as if frozen in a time-capsule. Surely, the fluttering of a drape was nothing.

Now all seemed motionless, vapid, as if baked by the summer sun. The metal mailbox was heating up, warm to the touch. The house numbers affixed to its side, black stickers with gold trim and embossed numbers, curled and chipped. My fingertips brushed away a leaf that balanced unsteadily on the wooden post and I fumbled for the lip of the small door. Opening the mailbox, I bent at the waist to peer inside. Cautiously, I reached in and jerked my hand out, as if bitten by a ferocious animal burrowed in the back of the tin capsule. My hand touched something brittle, its edges rough and dry. A letter sat inside, just as I had dreamed it to be, or seen it once before.

The same letter, still here? It made sense, I guess. I had stuffed it back inside, I just didn't expect it to still be there — or, more honestly, I half-expected the mailbox to be empty, as though the letter had never really existed at all. Initially, I chalked the eerie note up to an emotional response regarding all of the trauma that had seeped into my life in the months prior. *If you tell yourself something long enough, you start to believe it,* I thought. I had come to believe the letter was fictitious, a mental domino trailing sorrow.

A denial of sorts was clawing at me once again. The envelope inside the mailbox was sealed. The writing on the front had my name printed on it just as I had remembered it — but sealed? Again, I looked around, as if this joke must be the creation of another, and surely they were watching just to see my reaction. Not a peep, not a soul stirred. I was alone.

"Funny!" I yelled. "Very funny!" Stillness stopped time.

Looking more closely, I could tell the envelope was not the one I had previously opened, however, and my hands began to quake. Instinctively sipping my coffee to wet my dry mouth, it now tasted bitter. Tearing open the envelope and grabbing for the folded paper inside, my fumbling fingers were holding a new message:

> *Avery, you came back. I waited and worried about you since the*
> *loss of your love. I have seen your heart break and watched you*
> *put the pieces together. It will take time. It always takes time.*

These were Breya's words again. She was talking to me through the ink that had long dried on these pages, from beyond the boundaries of death. My faith told me Breya had moved on, but it never explained a possibility such as this. *Where was she? Somewhere between the sweetness of heaven and the pains of hell?* The moment was surreal, ubiquitous. The letter went on:

> *There are no fears, no worries. My days have been filled with*
> *new moments among people that breathe and laugh and live. I*
> *am here with you — sometimes close enough to touch. It was*
> *my hand that reached out to you when Jax stepped off that*
> *curb. I squeezed your hand and felt your existence vanquish*
> *for a brief moment when he hit the pavement. You stood still as*
> *stone. I watched you stare at your apartment door, Jax on the*
> *pavement, and I felt you buckle inside. Death was deafening.*

My eyes swelled with tears as the words turned to still-shots of that fateful day. Suddenly, I heard the noises and sounds that had banged against my ears during the accident. The sound of the metal crunching beneath the power of two moving objects colliding, the echo of glass exploding, and the shivering cries of sirens all came streaming into my consciousness. My ears rang and bled. I was back there, and I sensed Breya's hand in mine, as if the scene were unfolding before me again. She was the one who reached out to me, the stranger who held my hand when I felt so unequivocally alone. It was her hand in mine. She was the familiar kindness I needed in that moment of utter despair, disbelief, and disjointedness.

> On that day, I was the woman who held your hand. We are like butterflies, Avery. Our souls float in and out of one another and continue to help the world keep spinning. We continue to weave new stories, build new things, and create more problems to solve. The complexities of the people and the world are limitless. Some of us move on, while others come back to pass on knowledge and legend; morsels of life collected over time.

Breya's words seemed foreign to me, made up. There was no explaining her presence during the accident or how she *knew* the experience I had thought was mine alone. She had been there with me in some way. For Christ's sake, she knew my thoughts! *No way,* I reasoned. *No way, it can't be.* My lips twitched. *Can't be. No way!*

Pacing moved me left, right, back and forth. I stood in Breya's yard with the patchy grass underfoot. I put the letter in my jeans pocket and stared at the house once more. This time I would keep the letter but I doubted I could make any real sense of it. I thought of the times I had imagined Breya's adventures as a young woman and hoped I would come to know more about the life she had lived, or the many lives she had lived. My fear was turning into something else as I stood there in the yard. I didn't know what or how to name it, but I was no longer scared.

"Where did you come from, Miss Breya?" I mouthed to the morning sky. Or, better yet, "Where did you go?"

CHAPTER 8

Renewed, Healed

During those days with my family, my heart was cradled, renewed, healed. It reminded me of the time I went trekking in Nepal after two years in the Peace Corps as a volunteer. I was determined to make a political statement to myself as a young independent woman in her twenties, that I could navigate the world alone. Unyielding in my determination to seek an adventure after my stay in South Africa, I wanted to choose my every decision, from the moment I woke in the morning to the moment I fell asleep at night. I decided to hike the alternative route to the Annapurna Circuit and go to the base camp of Mount Everest. Some of my Peace Corps friends had done the trek trying the Annapurna route, so of course I wanted to try the less-traveled path to the base camp. I hired a Sherpa named Pemba to at least ensure my safety. I was brave, but not dumb.

Those days were grueling and hard, hot and cold. The vastness of the mountains arched around my entire view, becoming a panoramic cage of rice fields, ups and downs, mountaintops, and ravines met by streaming rivers far below. The stirring water beneath the mountainside paths appeared as glass, sunbeams reflecting on its surface. So small among the etched rice fields in the sides of the rolling peaks, mortality felt staggeringly real.

Farmers in flimsy two-dollar flip-flops pushed past me on the three-foot-wide trail I trudged over with my giant backpack in tow. My boots seemed so unnecessary — indulgent — as I watched the small men basically dance up the side of the mountain with practically nothing on their rough, cracked feet. Blisters canvassed my heels but my resolve to move forward toward the trail's end sustained me for many days.

The sun beat down on Pemba and me relentlessly; no shade unless the angle of the sun moved to the other side of the mountain we were trekking up. I could see peak after peak replicating in the distance. They never stopped, and by my own admission I had signed myself up for a seemingly insurmountable task. I remember the sheer amazement of encountering town after town dangerously balanced on the side of each new alp. Civilizations, handfuls of people who called these tiny places home, lived here among the clouds in Nepal.

At the start of the trek, seven hours outside of Katmandu by bus, we had now walked five days from where the roads literally ended. Yes, the pavement actually ended, and the driver waved goodbye, shooing us out the folding door. Schools, temples, and shacks nestled among the trees stood half-cocked and lonely.

A boy wearing a Michael Jordan sweatshirt passed me, smiled, and waved. "'Ello, American!" he shouted through a jagged grin. Three of his front teeth were missing, and I guessed his age to be eight or so.

"Hello!" I returned with great zeal. Turning to Pemba, I added a muffled, "Really? Michael Jordan? No shit!" I couldn't help but laugh out loud. The reaches of America, its influence, blew me away at each turn.

Another Sherpa passed by, carrying a giant basket on his back, with a cloth strap pulled across his forehead to bear the weight as he climbed the trail. "Excuse, excuse!" he said when he saw my blond hair from behind. I remember stepping aside, and he, too, smiled, exposing his yellowed teeth. His eyes were encased in wrinkles, and his skin was darkened from the sun and chapped from windburn. He stopped to chat with Pemba, and they shared a cigarette. God, I wanted a drag, but I understood the cultural indignity it would bring me, a woman, to now be alone and smoking a cigarette. Instead, I inhaled the smoke and pretended the cigarette was pursed between my lips.

"Try," Pemba said to me, pointing to the basket the other Nepalese man was carrying in his muddied orange flip-flops.

"Naw!" I replied. I did want to try though, so they showed me how to hoist the basket on my back and place the strap across my forehead for support. I bent my knees and strained, lurching forward and upright, as if to stand up. The basket did not move at all. The little man laughed, his leathery face scrunched up in another grin.

"What is in here, Pemba?" I asked, curiously looking inside the basket. In the quiet of this countryside, headed to various towns scrolled into the side of Mount Everest, a fifty-year old man in flip-flops danced steadily on the side of a mountain to bring glass bottles of Coca-Cola to the people of remote Nepal. *No shit,* I thought. *The far reaches of America.*

My trip ended after nine days. Suffering from food-poisoning, I had to call the trek off early. I could keep nothing down, my stomach was in wrenching knots, and an unbearable thirst consumed me. Coincidentally, I kept meeting up with a few trekkers by evening at each stop, and we became trail-mates. Often I shared a room with a nice guy named Andy from England. He was tall and unassuming — the only reason I was comfortable sleeping beside this strange but kind young man. We were about the same age, and my mom was from England, so I sensed some sort of kinship toward him. Something told me I could trust him.

In my time of total sickness, it was Brad, a cute guy from San Francisco, who ended up helping me through an afternoon of puking my guts out. He offered me a Snickers "for later" — a rare, sumptuous treat while trekking — and rubbed my back after I threw up in incessant heaves. I was dehydrated and couldn't keep anything down. Churning, gurgling, bubbling, my stomach twisted in pangs, as if wrung like an old towel. I had never felt so far from home as I did in those moments.

Pemba walked me to the local *doctor* in the town where we were sleeping for the night. The health center was a one-room shack with a countertop and four raw wooden cupboards. I sat on a medical-type bed for an examination by the doctor, who wore a dirty white coat. Anxiety tingled at the back of my neck; the hairs stood stiff. Dried blood was smeared on the wall above a garbage can. Chickens were running around outside the shack past the open door. Their random clucking was so foreign to me, yet in the context of the moment it should have made complete sense. It was I, not the chickens, who was out of place.

I wanted to stand and yell, "Hell, no!" but I knew I had no options. To say I was freaking out would be an understatement! I wanted to run far away from the shack-doctor but was too weak and too scared. Thank goodness Pemba stayed to translate as the doctor listened to my heart and my breathing and asked the details of my sickness. Dr. *Shack* suggested giving me a shot for the dehydration. It was like being at the auto-body shop back home: you never know what they're talking about, or if the repairs they suggest are even necessary. But what the hell are you supposed to do — risk driving down the highway and losing a tire? So you trust. We all trust.

While carefully copying down the writing from the side of the vile that was in English into my journal, Dr. *Shack* was about to pierce a newly opened needle into my arm. *Flick, flick,* he tapped the side of the saline-filled tube and chuckled as he offered a test-squirt into the air. I prayed, trusted, and puked again.

Returning to the hostel, I saw that the wooden shutters remained closed, keeping the sunlight at bay from my very small bedroom. The other hikers had moved on, making me a memory in the wake of their up-and-coming adventures. The quilt smelled of the wood fire the innkeeper had kept burning to warm the hostel. I imagined that, when I next looked at myself in a mirror, I'd find myself besmirched with black soot. Thick smoke had coated my hair, sweaters, and backpack, as if all had been pulled from the embers.

The innkeeper was a small, round woman that moved about with a baby snuggled at her bosom with what I would call a Nepalese Björn. It was simply a piece of blue cloth decorated in a daisy print that crossed her chest and cinched around her waist, serving as a baby-hammock at her front. Amazed, I watched her sweeping, cooking, and bending to stoke the fire with that sleeping baby attached to her body. How did the baby not wake or, better yet, slip right out of that baby-hammock like a wet fish whenever she bent over? Neither one seemed bothered, encumbered, or phased by the other. Momma did her thing; baby did his.

Pemba and I trekked to a nearby town hoping to arrange a flight off the mountain. After two more days of hiking, I had fallen too far behind my timeline to complete the trek and catch my flight back to the States. Slow as a still picture, we came to a landing strip in the grass big enough for a small engine plane seating six people plus the pilot. I flew out alone and remember how funny I thought it was that the flight attendant held a plastic tray from the 1970s I remembered seeing at garage sales while growing up. At first I didn't understand what the cotton balls on her tray were for when she offered them to me and the two other passengers on the plane. The dumbfounded look on my face gave me away, and she gestured that they were intended for the ears. "Oh," I said, embarrassed, quickly stuffing them into my ears. She smiled, nearly getting stuck, her hips wedged between the single seat rows on the left and the right.

The engine roared and we started down the pseudo-runway full of bumps, rocks, and holes in the grass. We were actually driving off the side of the freaking mountain. I said the Lord's Prayer and did the sign of the cross as we lunged into the air, shaking and rattling in the tin-can plane. This was by far the scariest part of my trek toward self-discovery. I will never forget the awesome size of Mount Everest from that plane window. After taking off and circling around to fly beside it, I was not looking down on it, but rather gazing at its midsection. Here we were in a plane, flying, and only halfway up to its peak.

Mammoth, grandiose and magnificent she stood. In that moment, I knew I was finally headed home after two and a half years in the Peace Corps and a long walk in Nepal. My effort to find myself had fallen short, yet I was renewed by the awesomeness before me. In this time away from my family I came to know myself separate and apart from them. During these years away I had found my identity as an adult evolving into something more than just who I was taught to be. I found myself, and I liked her.

And now my life was circling a new venture of discovering independence after losing a best friend and love. Pieces of me were reimagining the weightlessness that came from soaring above those clouds in Nepal, wondering if they were a stairway with the potential to lead me back to Jax somehow.

CHAPTER 9

Need a Light?

My long weekend with my family was exactly what I needed, and it helped me remember who I was, where I was going in my life, and what I wanted. They gave me the compass I had lost. On my drive back to the city I pondered what these things meant to me at this juncture in my life. I guess it was more than remembering where I was going — it was about charting a new course for myself, one that suited me now at this point in time. I was ready to hit the reset button and get on with living, even if living resembled prickly agony at times.

As my Jeep darted past the tall pines of the Adirondacks, I contemplated how I would define myself, and I decided I needed to think about what I wanted and what would make me happy. A woman with a career, I also wanted to take the time to relax and enjoy reading, writing and painting more. Traveling and exploring cultures and people far away from the familiar rhythms that guided me each day needed to be a priority for me again. The radio filled the small dome of my Jeep as I thought about these things and I took a swig of the Pepsi jostling in the console.

What about love? I asked myself.

Love seemed to be one of those things that would either happen or not. There was no planning that type of thing, no way to predict or time love. It showed up whenever it wanted and in whatever form suited the heart, I supposed. In the back of my mind, the thought would burrow itself for the rest of the drive back to the city. Like a silkworm swathed in a cottony cocoon, it would lay still and dormant until least expected. Then, it would crawl into my inner ear and whisper, "Keep your eyes open."

Only an hour and a half had passed but I needed to get out and stretch. My back was aching, dull and low, so I pulled into a rest-stop and shut the engine off. It was a dreary day, feeling much later than it actually was. I stood up and twisted, sending little pops up my spine, relief throughout my body. A deep breath filled me. The air smelled like rain, and only a few other cars were pulled over. Leaning against the bumper for a minute with a cigarette between my lips, pondering my self-imposed questions, I grappled with the reality that I would soon be stepping into this changed life — fully functioning, as opposed to pent-up in my apartment — once I reemerged in Manhattan. *Yeah, I got this,* I encouraged myself. My head bowed in an unconvincing gesture toward the ground, as if nodding in agreement.

"Hey, you again!" A woman's voice crept up behind me, shaking me from my thoughts. A hand, the shade of brandy, reached around with a soft flame balancing on the end of a match. "Light?" she asked.

"Nice timing," I replied before pivoting around to face this mystery woman who had met up with me again on my return trip. "If I didn't know better, I'd think you were following me," I said, half joking. She sat down on a curb at the front of where I had parked and outstretched her legs onto the pavement. "I'm Avery," I stammered, self-consciously, thinking about how windblown I must have looked, my hair in a knotted ponytail.

"Hi, Avery. Gabrielle. Can't believe we've run into each other again. What are the chances, right?"

"I know," I issued forth in an awkward laugh. I'm sure I rolled my eyes as I said it. "Where are you headed? I'm getting back to the city. Manhattan. I just visited my family upstate for a few days."

"Me, too. I mean, going back to the city. I'm from there, but I jaunt out to the country now and then to write and take pictures. I'm a photographer, an artist, dabbling in freelance projects to make ends meet."

Gabrielle's hair framed the sides of her face, falling in front of her chest in dark waves. Her eyes were as green and piercing as I remembered the first time we met, but it was only now that I actually was seeing her fully. Her face was uniquely beautiful, like the people in Calvin Klein ads. The chemistry of her origin was embedded in her long fingers, high cheekbones, shiny hair, tall stature…and those eyes. I tried not to look at her as if I were studying her, but I couldn't help my captivation — almost as if I were netted and struggling to escape, but the more I tried to move the more tangled I became. She was talking, but I was half-listening, trapped in my own inner discourse.

I had never looked at a woman like this before. Sure, I was able to recognize beauty and sex appeal, but this was different. This was *sensual.* I tried to shake the thoughts out of my head, coughing, standing to try and recalibrate my mind. *What the hell?, Avery?* I scolded myself. *Get your thoughts together!*

"…And now I'm hoping for a showing at the end of the month," Gabrielle trailed back to my ear.

"For your photographs?" I had to ask to realign myself with the conversation I had pretended to listen to for the past minute. *Okay, she was hoping to show her work at the end of the month,* I explained to myself. "So, do you have a space or a date?" I asked her, since this was my kind of work, too. "I curate artwork for the Hive in SoHo," I shared with some hesitation. "There's a fantastic opportunity coming up, and we haven't yet settled on the artist who'll be on display. You know, not the artist, but the work." My words were clumsy, as if I had just come from the dentist. My smile was crooked, my lips unable to properly keep the words from spilling out.

"I've been there — the Saffron exhibit was really moving," Gabrielle shared as a compliment. "You collaborated with Gloria and Xavier to get the pieces, right?" She looked genuinely impressed, causing pride to swell inside of me.

"Yeah, that was me. It took two years to bring it all together, but it was pretty touching, right?" I asked, needing more affirmation from her that the exhibit was worth the effort and time. Those two years had been full of ambition and encouragement from Jax. He was integral to that exhibit by the sheer nature of his support. Exuberance had filled my pores as I tried to establish myself in New York among the artsy types while planning for that show.

I was mostly made of grit, really, but the sediment settled more in my soul than at the surface, like most artists I had encountered. Gabrielle, for instance, kept her shirt unbuttoned just between her small breasts, while mine was always buttoned just above them. She wore cheap chains around her neck in a tangled mess of various lengths that likely grew more tarnished with each shower. Each day I carefully chose a 14-karat white gold necklace to match the outfit I was wearing. A skeleton-key tattoo discretely lay hidden on my right shoulder blade, while Gabrielle proudly showed off a tattoo of a hummingbird on her left forearm and kept her sleeves pushed up to her elbows. Today, her boots of scuffed brown leather swallowed her jeans as they met her ankles. My shoes always looked clean and new, as if chosen especially for that day's journey, prepared with great care. Yes, my grit was on the inside, while Gabrielle's was on the surface.

"So, uh, we both have a lot of driving ahead," I stood up with a burst, since my thoughts kept wandering off-topic, tugging me into some dark rabbit-hole that left me wondering what Gabrielle might do at the end of her days. I still could not place her, but I was mortified at the thought of asking where we had met.

"Um, yeah," Gabrielle replied, caught off-guard by my abrupt ending to the conversation — which truly had become a monologue, since I resorted to head-nodding as I became lost in thoughts of her: where she came from, how she held a wineglass after her third drink, and what she looked like in just an oversized T-shirt. "Yeah, I guess we should hit the road." Her voice was feminine but deep, soft and resolute. "It was nice seeing you, Avery. Maybe we'll bump into each other again."

Something about leaving Gabrielle in that moment felt unfinished. *Shit, what if I never see her again? Why did I hurry a goodbye?* Something about her was tunneling into my self-consciousness and luring me to her. Amenable to trying new things, still, I never found myself looking at a woman the way I was seeing Gabrielle. Though hesitant, I couldn't just let her walk away.

"Do you wanna catch up for dinner in a couple of hours?" I finally asked her. "We can take a break before we hit I-287. There's a little diner at Exit 15. Nothing fancy, but it'll give us another chance to stretch and talk more about art and your show."

"Sounds good," she said while already walking away. She turned back around and smiled. "I'm in the black beat-up truck." She pointed to her truck and swung its door open.

"Of course," I said in a whisper.

We took turns leading the way as we barreled down I-87 toward I-287. At times, Gabrielle was in my sights; at other moments, my mind wandered to work and getting back to the gallery. Real life was about to unfold itself as my leave of absence from the gallery was coming to an end in days. I was ready. I was able. I was grit, too.

In the rearview mirror I looked up to see Gabrielle in the lane next to me but lagging behind just enough so I could watch her. She was swaying to some music and leaning on the window-frame. I imagined the sounds of Sade or something sexy that could slink into a person's bones, physically moving them by its smoky flavor and tenor. The outline of her body in my mirror was captivating: one hand propped on the steering wheel, her fingers tapping to the beat. Her long, wavy hair moved in the wind, as if she were Medusa in a shabby truck. I hit cruise control, because the distraction of Gabrielle made it impossible for me to keep a steady speed. A beautiful, exhilarating stride came back into me. I could feel it without even walking.

The road signs flagged us for our exit. We had been driving for almost three hours, and I had to go to the bathroom so badly. When we finally reached the diner, the air was getting chilly, and I grabbed a jacket to throw on. Gabrielle was wearing a black biker jacket with eroded creases crawling up her back like vines. Her left sleeve was pushed up, revealing the feathers on her tattoo. I thought of Jax and how he used to call me "Little Bird." Uncanny. *Grit on the outside. Got it,* I chuckled to myself as I got out of my Jeep.

"I gotta run, Gabrielle!" I shouted to her as I darted inside the diner. "Grab us a seat!"

As I stared at myself while washing my hands, the bathroom mirror reflected the dinginess surrounding me. Someone had written *Everyone is beautiful* with a magic marker on the wall next to a florescent-yellow sconce. "I suppose they really are," I said out loud with sincerity. My hair was a mess, my skin soft and fresh. Country air does do a body good. I splashed cold water on my face and was thrust out of my driver's haze. I wiped off the awakening gently with the rough, sandpaper-like paper towels falling out of the dispenser. "Whew," I blew out a puff of air to clear my lungs and relax myself. My body was starved — for food, laughter, affection, brilliance, creativity. Yes, I was going back home — my adult home. Everything felt different before even arriving and the anticipation was boiling inside of me. Only two hours away from the city.

Gabrielle coolly put up a couple of fingers to flag my attention, and I slid into the booth she chose beside the window. It was getting dark, and the car lights blurred through the steamed-up glass. The rain finally started; small droplets clung to the windowpane. Gravity gently tugged them toward the ground, leaving squiggly trails behind, carving riverways into my reflection in the glass. We sat across from each other. My body was both on edge and relaxed, as if I were sitting with a friend who had amnesia. It seemed as if there were things we knew about each other, yet the reality was that we were strangers. Drawn to her in a way I had never experienced with anyone else, I wondered if this intrigue was only coursing through me, or if Gabrielle acknowledged it, too. I was so very ordinary next to her and she seemed amazingly exceptional.

"Do you know what you want?" she asked, raising those green eyes above the menu.

"Hhhmm? Um, yeah, I'll go with a cheeseburger and fries." I cleared my throat and managed.

"Thank God you're not a salad girl!" She smiled teasingly. "So what were you thinking about while you were driving?" She settled into her spot and wiggled out of her jacket. A ring of turquoise stones wrapped around her middle finger. I hadn't noticed it before. "I kept thinking about these covered bridges I was photographing," she ventured. "They were actually in Vermont. About twenty-five of them still stand. Most of them were made of wood in the 1920s. I wonder if life really *was* simpler back then?"

She stared off into the distance.

"Life is complex," I reasoned. "If people are involved, so are emotions, feelings…a complicated tapestry, for sure."

In a sweet, sensitive way, Gabrielle asked, "How did complexity disappoint you, Avery?" Our eyes locked in a gaze that seemed to drag the very breath out of my lungs. I was not ready to share the weight of my life with her, not now, not yet, not even with a familiar stranger. "I have a bad habit of asking questions that strike a cord," Gabrielle said apologetically. "I didn't mean to go too deep."

"Oh, no. It's nothing," I tried to smooth over my awkward silence. "I've just been adjusting to some changes. Let's say things have been more complex than simple in recent months. I'm sort of redefining myself, you know, as an artist, as a woman..." Tears rimmed my eyes; suddenly vulnerability was encasing me like bindings enveloping my entire body. Shit, I was about to fall apart in front of a stranger at the first test of getting it all back together! I sighed and smiled through the tears swelling in my blue eyes. I dabbed them with a napkin and tilted my head, as if to say to Gabrielle, "It's all good. This is my heart washing away the silt left over from a lost love, and it feels good. It feels right. I'm ready to let go." I couldn't share these words with her, though. It was all too much. We were supposed to be having a cheeseburger, not a damn therapy session.

"Hell with simplicity," Gabrielle said as she squeezed my hand. "I was never really drawn to the easy path." *Did she just mention the easy path?* my mind taunted me. *That was my thing...avoiding the easy path.*

"When I was young, I had to take care of my mom," she continued. "She got sick when I was eleven and my dad was never really in the picture — you know, in and out, holidays and stuff. He walked away for real, I guess, within the year. Haven't heard from him — not a Thanksgiving, not a Christmas." She looked out the window as the words trickled out. "God, my mother was something else! Lovely. She was a dancer, and I grew up in the Bronx. She used to carry three jobs, though — you know the story — but she did it with such grace! I remember watching her stretch one leg on the radiator in front of our eighth-story window each morning. She'd turn on music — all kinds — and scoop me up in her arms when I was little. She'd twirl, sing, sway, and dance around our apartment. Sometimes we'd both put on white tights and she'd teach me foot positions. She ripped up the shag carpet and sanded the hardwood floors all by herself to create a dance floor that helped us to glide and shimmy. She shellacked them herself, and our landlord flipped when he found out. She always made up her own rules."

I looked up at Gabrielle, as if to suggest that I had a feeling she was the same as her mom.

"What?" she asked smiling.

"Like you?" I asked, cementing my assumption that she, too, made up her own rules.

"Maybe," she hinted. "My mom got sick with cancer and struggled with it until I was twenty-one. Fuck, nothing prepares you for losing someone you love. And so it was, she was gone after fighting for five years. She was in and out of remission. I took her to the ocean and we slept right on the beach one night in South Carolina. My mom danced in eight more shows in those five years, and I saw the strength of her body come and go, and come and go, again and again. Cancer was a tease, really."

Now Gabrielle's eyes grew wet and I reached across the table to touch her hand. She turned it over and opened it up so our palms touched. It felt naked and raw to touch in this way — so soft, her hand warm against mine. "Maybe we can only *do* deep," I said, trying to cut the tension now passing between us through our joined hands. *Should I let go, pull away?* I wondered. The moment was intimate, odd, yet soothing and comforting. I guess nothing was wrong with finding support from one another as we shared stories, right? *Exposure breeds vulnerability,* I reminded myself. A safeguard had been established inside of me backing me up into a place of capitulation, surrender, and trust.

"Heavy," Gabrielle said, having no idea that this type of emotion was going to surface. Her hand pulled away from mine and a tinge of longing overcame me. "Let's get our order in, huh? So tell me about your work," she encouraged in an effort to find a topic more neutral. She cleared her throat and readjusted in the booth. We both resorted to a few rapid blinks to keep our eyes focused on one another.

We laughed over our greasy fries and burgers and found lighter topics to toss back and forth as we ate. Work at the gallery and her photography was the common thread that wove us together. Art. We were art. I gave Gabrielle my card and told her to call me if she wanted to show me her material. There might be potential for a showing if she was good enough. I already knew that, if she called me, I would find a way to make sure she was just that. The rain's soft pitter-patter faded as we sat in the cozy diner. The sky was a bit pink, like a flock of flamingos intersecting with swirls of gray wisps, as if brushed onto a canvas.

We paid our checks and walked back to the parking lot. Separate vehicles forced us apart, and a piece of me worried I would never see her again. I wasn't brave enough to ask for her number or a way to contact her, but I watched as she slid my card into the back pocket of her jeans. I wanted to put my hand against her cheek, smell her hair, before leaving. I had no idea where this need came from or why these thoughts were writing themselves inside of my mind. Gabrielle and I gave each other a generic hug goodbye, and I snuck in a silent breath to take her sweet scent with me. I couldn't help asking myself, did *she* wonder if we'd see each other again? Did *she* care if we did or didn't?

"Gab!" I stopped and yelled. "Did we meet before this weekend somewhere? The first time we bumped into each other, you said you knew me. Seriously?"

"Yeah, Avery, I've seen you before," she said over her shoulder as she walked to her truck.

"I don't remember," I said, trying to sound unaffected, unimpressed, untouched.

"I know," she said while winking and rolling my business card between her fingers. "It was nice listening to the rain with you."

I jumped into my Jeep while Ingrid Michaelson's remake of "Creep" swam all around me. *I don't remember meeting Gabrielle, ever,* I laughed to myself, thinking she was just messing with me. I put the top back down, said a little prayer that the rain wouldn't return, blared the music, and sped the whole way back to New York City.

The lights ahead beckoned in the distance through my windshield, welcoming me back home. *I never did like easy,* I reminded myself. Yes, a new me was arriving to carve out a different place in the world, I had decided.

CHAPTER 10

Better than Good Enough

It was Monday morning. The sun shone through the sheer curtains that dangled at the sides of the windows, half covering the blinds. Sunbeams, striking against my hardwood floor, radiated up the walls. One ray cast itself against the mirror, sending a blinding shower onto the bed, as if to set fire to the sheets. Part of me wanted to roll over and go back to sleep. Another part of me wanted to rush toward a tall glass of cold orange juice and a bagel.

On this morning, fear made me feel inadequate, out of control. I felt neither strong nor wise. I realized I was afraid to walk in my own shoes. Perhaps they wouldn't fit me as they had before. I was afraid that, with each step into this new chapter of my life without Jax, a blister would form, a callus would rise, causing me a new kind of pain. The unknown was always scarier than the predictable. I knew my work, however. Immersed again, it would make me feel useful in ways that made me shine from the inside out, like swallowing a light bulb in the dead of night.

As I sat up at the edge of my bed, I decided that today I would walk in my shoes and press on, even if faced with insignificant details forgotten in my time away from the gallery. *After all, pressing on is what women do,* I thought. Suddenly, courage was pushing outward inside of my abdomen, inflating me with energy. Any thoughts of doubt about returning to work were ones I did not want to own! My brow furrowed, trying to make sense of how those thoughts had even crept inside of me. With utter determination, I decided I would make them go away.

"Hell with doubt! It's Monday!" my voice bounced off the walls of my bathroom as I took my shower. My internal turmoil was squashed, and the shower rinsed all of the bullshit down the drain in a swirling whirl of Irish Spring and Pantene.

I was careful to walk around the grimy grates in the sidewalk for fear my high heels would get chewed up in-between the metal crosshairs. I weaved to avoid the thick crowds, bobbing in and out of them as they both charged at me and drove me forward through downtown toward 8th Avenue, Penn Station. The train-ride had lasted less than ten minutes, and the walk took nearly twenty. Humidity thickened the air like most July mornings and the shop owners were spraying their stretches of the sidewalks clean.

Joey, a short, bald man wearing a white apron, stood at the corner with a cigarette stuck to his bottom lip. "Hey, Avery! Morning!" he shouted with a crooked smile, careful not to let his ciggy slip away. He sold flowers, and he was my favorite constant when walking downtown to the train station each day to the gallery.

It's funny how certain people become a part of your day over time. They make an impression on you, or just become part of the scenery by nature of their presence each morning or afternoon. You come to look for them, as I did for Joey, because they remind you that life is made up of patterns and tiny circuit boards connecting people in some distinct or maybe very ordinary way. Sometimes I imagine this is part of God's plan. He plants these habitual moments and familiar people into our lives so we can pass on a kindness, a simple smile, a wave, or a "good morning."

"Hey, Joe!" I shouted back over the brouhaha of the bustling cars, passing people and spraying water. "You're my brightest spot!" I shared with a wink, and kept moving.

Joey was probably old enough to be my father and I wondered if he had any children. For in reality he was an outsider who decorated the backdrop of my life. If we were caught in an elevator together, we wouldn't really know two things about each other. Maybe that was what made our meeting each day special — *not* knowing one another, respecting each other from a distance. What if knowing him, the real substance of him, would have been a letdown? Or vice versa? Shit, I would have had to find a new route to work, or look in the other direction when I passed the sunflowers and orchids. I liked the Joey I didn't really know. In this way he could be as wonderful and gentle as I imagined him to be.

"I like you, Joey!" I shouted as usual.

He blew me a fatherly kiss.

On the train, a collection of quibbling flutters awakened in my stomach. I was nervous on this first day back to work. I could practically feel the breath of those standing next to me, and I stretched my neck and rubbed each side of it, as if to wipe their germs away. No one made eye contact on the train. Most sat in a coma with headphones on or stared mindlessly at their phones or tablets. Some read, others chatted. I just relished in the stillness as we whipped down the tracks in the darkness of the subway. While standing, my knees bent slightly, and I gripped a railing to avoid falling as we jerked to a stop or achingly turned corners. At times I felt like a surfer riding waves on a beach I couldn't see or smell.

Spring Street flashed against the wall in a blur as the train slowed to a stop. The platform suddenly burst with people in a daybreak fog; commuters jostling to get on and off the trains. The stench of urine stung the back of my throat, and I breathed through my nose until I got to the top of the stairs emerging onto the sidewalk. The SoHo streets welcomed me as if I had never been away. I joyously sauntered toward the Hive. *I got this,* I said to myself in a way just short of convincing.

The Hive had come into its own, as a gallery, only eight years ago. The building has stood since 1969, built just after the Stonewall riots in Greenwich Village, arguably the most pivotal uprising in LGBT history. The building was totally renovated in 2014 to emulate the contemporary world and project the name it carried. The Hive symbolizes a safe haven in which community members can live and be a family, a place where art can tell everyone's story, be it of joy or pain.

As I approached the Hive, its intricate honeycomb structure perched above the treetops, perilously balanced among the other urban spaces, orchestrating a rumbling in my body once again. Nerves. I always found it beautiful, unique, and stunning. At night, each section of the honeycomb glowed with the light from inside the gallery. Pitching outward, the illumination escaping through the hexagon-shaped windowpanes became the life-force of every artist who had privileged the walls with their work. From its ceiling rafters to the hinges on each door, this place projected each and every human emotion.

I purposely left extra early this morning to avoid the many hugs and welcomes that would fall on me as I entered the space. Attention like that always made me uncomfortable, like getting a new haircut and anticipating all of the "ooohs" and "ahhhs" that would follow. That exact moment, being the center of attention, was like being in the eye of a storm for me. I could hear my heart thumping in my ear. The office area was quiet and still. As I approached my door, the click of my high heels kissed the wooden floors. *Clack, clack, clack, clack* echoed off the high cathedral ceilings.

My desk was just as I had left it — neat and organized. The stainless-steel shelving and glass desk were postmodern, matching the décor of my apartment and the rest of the gallery. My phone's message light was blinking, but I had checked my messages while away, so I figured whatever voicemail awaited me now had been left pretty recently. I began to play back the messages through the speaker so I could also thumb through some proposed prints that had been awaiting my feedback for a showing in the fall.

"Avery, it's Corey. Hoping we could grab a bite to eat this week. Call me."

"It's Mom. Just wanted to say I'm thinking of you. Love you."

"This is Dr. Gavin's office, reminding you of a cleaning at 2:30 p.m. on July 26th."

"Ave, hope you made it back all right. Dinner was nice. Hope we can listen to the rain again together soon!" Gabrielle's voice filled my office, making me suddenly aware of every little thing in that space — the hum of the air-conditioner, the buzz of the light-baluster above me, the tapping of a bee's wings against the window. "Hhhmm," I muttered, seeing the irony in that bee. Gabrielle's message was the sweetest way to start the day. *She called. Nice!* I suddenly wished I were in my Jeep with her sitting in the passenger's seat, her long legs propped up on the dash with the seat resting back.

Seeing the stack of work awaiting me, I puffed out my cheeks and strolled over to the table beside my desk. I had so much to catch up on, including selecting the premier artist of the approaching exhibition this October. The PR would be rushed, but doable.

The gallery board and the resident artists had already filtered through a stack of submissions, but I was fortunate enough to make the final call. These submissions had been due three weeks ago, but I was only now taking a look. Though we were prepping for the next event, we hadn't yet visualized a theme. This time we were hoping the vision would come to us through the selected artist's work.

To avoid bias, I always resisted the urge to look at the artists' names on the back of the prints. You know, everyone has their favorites, but we wanted to dig deep into the annals of untapped work to find someone new, fresh, and unbridled by any expectations of what art *should* be. I was particularly driven instead to first recognize art that spoke to me and drew on the social underpinnings of our times. Perhaps that meant I was looking for a likeness of oppression, creativity, happiness, and suffering. As I shuffled through the deck of prints like cards, one stuck me like a pin — sharp, poignant, profound.

Mixed media captured the glare of piercing yet ghostly blue eyes. Tears welled in the inner corners, rimming with what appeared to be cobwebs, rolling down wrinkled, weathered cheeks. This face, these eyes...for a second I knew them. I set this image aside, realizing it had caught my attention in a way no others had. Like a massive hook sunk into my abdomen, I was being reeled toward it, even while trying to consider the others in my hand.

Another image leapt off the matte board and grabbed me, this time around the throat. It was difficult to inhale, as if watching an old film lodged in a memory I had only dreamt, not truly experienced. The same woman — that startling face — was now middle-aged. Balancing a glass of red wine between her thumb and forefinger, she bent over a balcony railing in Paris. A wrinkled map lay at her feet. The same woman was on the next print: her long, tattered dress was dirty from kneeling amid strawberry plants, and her hands were plunged into the soil. She looked so tired. The landscape was bright with the golden colors of changing leaves pressed against a blue sky. Her ghostly blue eyes cast down toward the dirt. Her knees sank into the soil beside a woven basket with a soiled rag tied to its handle.

The following print portrayed a room with the same woman dancing alone, her framed arms holding tightly to a partner who wasn't there. Her head leaned to look at a record-player on an oak table near a brown leather sofa. Her legs were long and graceful, with a pointed right foot just above the floor. The same clear blue eyes held the oceans. The rhythm of the moment somehow penetrated the print and filled me as if I were in the room listening to the music myself. A soft sway turned into a subtle swoon, while the voice of Nina Simone came to mind and left my soul heavy and rich, begging for an encore.

The last in the series was the same woman, abused by time and overcome by age. Wrinkles melted onto her face, but her beauty was undeniable, her eyes duller but still blue. She sat by herself at a kitchen table, and a cat was perched on the windowsill in the background. Steam from her coffee cup rose up into the foreground, creating a haze I was peering through just to observe the print. A cast-iron frying pan sat on a stovetop with a blue flame underneath it, while a silver toaster on the counter caught the old woman's reflection.

Thrill undulated through me, realizing I had found the work, the artist. I didn't know the artist's name — never even looked. But it didn't matter to me. I was more confounded with the subject matter and why the woman depicted over time seemed to have existed in my own mind and memory. Damn, it was as if I could have photographed, painted, created these pieces myself, but had not! Undeniably, a sense of ownership over these prints possessed me. Immediately, I was regulated with the same protectiveness a mother has for a child. A primal instinct emerged from me for the precious few moments I stood alone in my office, and I cried for the sake of relief and the return to my work.

A knock at the door jarred me from my reverie. I hurriedly stacked the prints on my desk. "Figures," I choked, wiping my eyes delicately with a tissue. I turned toward the door and shouted, "Gimme a sec... Come in!"

Ahmed, my assistant, popped his head into the doorway. "Hey, you! Glad you're back! Running to deliver the seventy-two-by-thirty-six to the framers. Be back in a couple of hours. Call if you need anything!" He blew a kiss, threw his satchel across his back, and slammed the door shut.

The artwork had found me, I believed. The pieces spoke to me, really — and who was I to ignore them? The art was far beyond good enough; it was remarkable! In fact, it was a life preserver protecting me from dangerous waters and keeping my body afloat. These were the works that would sustain me, focus me over the next three months, as I doggy-paddled my way back to safe harbor. My days would be filled with bringing the woman depicted here, and this artist, to the vanguard of SoHo. Yes, a place to direct my focus while getting back in the saddle.

CHAPTER 11

The Passing of Time

The first week back at work was a whirlwind that left me dazed some evenings, but feeling accomplished, too. I paced around my apartment while the city's nightlife stared back at me one Friday evening. Happily staying in for the night, I found comfort in slicing cheese at my countertop on a wooden cutting-board my mother had given me when I first moved into this apartment. The heel of a loaf of French bread poked out of the end of a brown paper bag. I laughed, wondering why the bag never covered the whole damn loaf. Not surprisingly, that end of the bread I typically cut off and just threw away, for it was a sponge of New York's exhaust fumes, in my eyes.

The first time I had tasted a Shiraz, it was dry, even harsh. But now that my taste buds had evolved a bit, it rolled around my mouth, allowing me to savor the hints of berry, wood and pepper. The plum burgundy painted the inner corners of my lips and warmly tickled the back of my throat. The deliberate, lascivious tone of Emilie-Claire Berlow filled the apartment with lyrics I couldn't understand. She was a French singer I once heard while listening to Pandora. Her sexy voice melted me. The more I sipped from my glass, the more the music swirled into the rafters of my loft and channeled through my body. I danced slowly, twisting my hips and sliding in sock-feet. It felt so freeing.

Lighting another candle, I stood, gazing out the window onto the buildings at eye-level and below me. Each lit window was a tiny sparkling dot of life, sprawling across the landscape. I wondered about Gabrielle, where she might be, what she might be doing. I was hoping she would contact the gallery again, but all was quiet. A week had passed since our meeting at the diner, and I hadn't afforded myself the time to think about anything but work, so I hadn't called her back. Now was the first time she had tunneled her way back to the forefront of my thoughts. I gently pushed Gabrielle to the edge of my thinking, instead making space for my closest friends. Now I was regretting not joining them for an evening out. For a moment, I wanted to be not looking at the lights but standing in the glow, shoulder-to-shoulder with Devon, Amy, Corey, and all of my closest friends.

Corey and I never did get together for dinner this week, though his messages were a nice reminder of the sweet people in my life. His invitation was left open, and I didn't have it in me to fake my enthusiasm for a date I'd been avoiding for months. He was kind — adorable, even — but my heart was just not into him.

Our friendship had begun three years ago while hiking one weekend in Olympic National Park in Washington State. Devon, Amy, and I were hiking through Hoh Rainforest. Sitka spruce surrounded us, towering overhead, as the bright green counterbalanced the rocks in an area called the Hall of Mosses, where our two hiking groups converged.

While we stopped to take pictures and refill our water bottles from the chilled river at the rainforest's entrance, Corey stumbled upon us. He, too, was awestruck at the scene Mother Nature had presented us. His friends and my friends all just stared at the trees blanketed in the striking lime-colored moss. Wet with the dew of the morning and glistening as the sun shone through the trellis of branches, a surreal mist hovered above the ground. Crisscross, the sun broke through the tree limbs, casting shadows at our feet.

"Amazing," Corey said, his eyes wide. A smile glued to his face.

"Amazing," Amy repeated in confirmation and agreement.

Our groups hiked on together for the next few hours and we came to learn that we were all from New York, some from upstate, others from the city. How funny it was that we met nearly 3,000 miles from our homes instead of at Walgreens while picking up a bag of chips or cough-drops! The world is a small place.

Corey and I ended up as walking mates, since we could walk two-by-two for much of the morning. The trail was narrow and damp, caking the side of my boots with mud. Corey was easygoing, his demeanor much like that of a brother. I felt safe with him near us, and his friends — a mix of two girls and two guys — all carried with them a serenity that was calming and appreciative of life in general. We laughed and walked, parting ways later that afternoon after exchanging contact information.

Since then, Corey and I have met on occasion for coffee or drinks. The friendship has always been one of respect but void of intimacy. Exchanging book recommendations and travel adventures never amounted to anything more than conversation and laughs. Lately, however, Corey was calling me more frequently. He left messages on my home and work phones with the careful concern of a friend while I was visiting my family.

His increased frequency of contact left me guessing that he was starting to see me in a different light. I didn't want to encourage any kind of relationship other than a friendship, so I kept a bit of a distance from him. Yet Corey was a good person, tender and patient. After Jax's passing, the delicate balance life had once offered me had gone off-kilter, my equilibrium unleveled. Corey was the equalizer I needed, and his elixir of humor didn't hurt, either!

The music from my apartment started to ricochet off my memories, bringing my thoughts back to the present. Now Etta James swooned in the background. The bottle of wine on the counter absorbed the glow of a nearby candle and cast a shadow on the hardwood floors. The outline of a miniature man appeared to stand motionless before me, looking up at me, reading my mind. Embarrassment caused my cheeks to flush as I realized I was thinking of Gabrielle again.

It was as if my mind created a frame that zoomed in on one-half of her face. She was driving, staring straight ahead through the windshield of her truck, window down, her hair blowing wildly around her. Her arm was propped up on the door, and a reflection of her hummingbird tattoo on her forearm was displayed in the side-mirror. Her hand ducked and rose with the wind, mimicking a small dove, as she drove down the highway, occasionally moving up against her face to wrestle the hair out of her eyes.

The frame in my imagination widened, and I could see her other arm outstretched across the front seat toward the passenger's side of the truck. She was reaching for something, but my daydream — night-dream, actually — could not extend past the divide of the front seat's vinyl midsection. I wanted to call her, hear her voice, but my rational brain couldn't make sense of my longing for her beyond friendship. It was the opposite of the Corey effect — sensual and new.

"What is she reaching for?" I shouted out loud, raising my hand to offer a pretend-toast into thin air. Biting my lip, I stared at the zebra-like lip-prints on the rim of my glass and blew out the candles. I wished that those prints belonged to her, that she had been here to share the evening with me. I wanted to know the force of her body pressed against me, close, dancing slow enough for our mouths to hover at a slight distance from each other, yet close enough for the heat of her breath to feed my own.

"What is this?" my thoughts spat out in the lonely space of my living room. They took me by surprise. I had never embraced a woman, nor thought about doing so, before meeting Gabrielle. The emptiness of the room, and now the darkness, enveloped me, crawling up on me like a toddler scampering up a mother's leg. The scent of the freshly blown-out candles lingered while the smoke swam on the light, streaming through the giant window. The city lights were bright enough to guide me across the floor and down the hallway to my bed, where I fell onto my back, staring at the still ceiling fan. I wanted Gabrielle beside me. I could sense her presence in the room. Closing my eyes, I constructed her silhouette in my thoughts.

Sleep swept me away with the help of too much wine, and the morning came quickly as my alarm-clock jolted me out of my dreams. *Why is it that the alarm-clock is always just a hand's width out of reach?* I thought as I groped for the 'snooze' button. There was no need for the alarm on a Saturday, but I'd forgotten to turn it off before falling asleep last night.

My head hurt. I was thirsty. I recalled my mother jeering me with, "The grass never grows under your feet," her less-than-subtle way of telling me to slow down and enjoy life. But I could feel something shifting within me. I was tired of the eternal race toward something I could never capture. Not that I never captured what I was *chasing* — success, a thrill, whatever — but I always set my eyes on a new prize once I arrived at the one I was after. So the race never ends, if you will, because the thrill is never fully realized. What is a person to do after she has climbed the proverbial mountain? I mean, once you're at the top and have taken in the vista, what's next?

I'm looking out and around, and I feel lost, I thought. For the first time, I'm unsure of what my next move in life will be. Do I pick a new mountain and climb toward a new finish line? Should I just walk down the one I'm standing on, consider my goals achieved, and pocket the memories? What if I just catapult myself off the top of the summit, seriously, open my arms like wings, and glide on the wind to someplace new? I want to feel alive, but in a different skin. Maybe I'm bored, or nearly fascinated by something just a tad out of view. This has to be my midlife crisis, but it appears to be arriving a decade too early.

Saturday lay before me with no agenda. It was early, since the buzz of the clock had been set for a workday. I wanted to ignite the feeling that had filled me when hiking through the Hall of Mosses, the tranquility that had drifted in and out of the trees. Though I was enjoying being back at the art gallery, Manhattan was more like a thumbtack, pinning me into place, than anything else; my body restricted, my mind taken hostage. I wriggled in a fictitious struggle with no one but myself.

My own initiative began to feel like chains. It was a bastion of motivation that I now wanted to melt onto the floor, off me, out of me. *Mom, you're right,* I admitted. I thought I was ready to return to work but now I just wanted to walk away from it all. Panic crept between my skin and nerves, teasing my sensibilities. *Doesn't grief have an expiration date?*

At the risk of sounding like an asshole, I wanted to move on, or back, or whatever goddamn direction I needed to move in, to feel like myself again. Reasoning rocked on a fulcrum, daring to be pushed. Perhaps the answer was out in the woods, where the quiet could help me reconcile with the world and regain perspective. I was still thirsting for an awakening, a way out of the loss, after all. Grabbing a bag, I shoved some clothes, my wallet, food and water inside. The zipper snagged as I yanked it shut and dashed through my loft. I needed my cell phone and then I'd be off. Where to, I do not know.

"Come on!" I yelled — my usual go-to when pissed and hurried. My cell was nowhere to be seen. "Goddamn it!" was as articulate as I could be upon realizing I had left it at the gallery. Lurching for my keys on the end-table, I slung the bag over my shoulder and took off out the door.

The elevator ride to the lobby was like watching paint drip down the side of an old can. A slow roll was carrying me downward, with long pauses on four floors. A ding pinged as the doors separated down the middle, allowing its passengers the opportunity to separate, fanning into the lobby. I took a hard left and navigated a small hallway down to the parking garage. This level was partially exposed to the street, and the air and sunlight snuck into the dampness between the columns that upheld the ceiling. My stomach was aching and gurgling with both excitement and hunger.

I jumped into the Jeep, opened the glove compartment, and retrieved an apple from the day before. I grabbed its lumpiness, bruised from banging around in there for a day, and sank my teeth in. I clenched it in my mouth as I drove onto the street, one hand on the steering wheel, the other clicking the seatbelt. Surfacing from the underground lot was like a chick breaking an egg's surface, cracking it open from the inside, emerging into the world.

Music flung from my speakers and sprayed itself like confetti onto the New York streets as I darted through them. Vitality rushed through an abandoned Manhattan, pronouncing itself in the form of speeding veracity. Six a.m. flashed in blue from my dash. The Jeep's top was already down, and the wind ripped through my hair, interwoven with the dirt of the city and the grime that settled to earth every Saturday morning. The evening rituals of the night before always held the secrets of the people, but by morning they were falling to the ground like dust that could be cleaned and swept away.

The Hive could be seen from six blocks away, its intricate windows reflecting the rising sun like a stained-glass monument. Managing to find a parking spot was usually like hitting the lottery but at this hour it would be fine. *In and out,* I told myself as I parked, jogged up the stairs to the treetop doorframe of the gallery, and unlocked my office door. Sure enough, my cell sat there, right beside my laptop, awaiting my arrival and retrieval. *In and out* came back to mind as I laughed, recognizing my wanting to be back on the road. In one motion the phone was in my palm and my body had swiveled back toward the door.

Like a propeller, my arms twisted and my legs set me in motion past the stack of prints that had engrossed me this past week. The fall exhibit flooded my brain, while the pictures that had captivated me were staring back from my circular table. I howled in pain after banging into the table with the fierce momentum of my knee. The stack rocked, and half of the prints floated to the floor, shuffled in a random pile at my feet. Upside-down, sideways, a mishmash of beautiful art sprinkled onto the carpet. It was offensive to see the prints being mistreated due to my own clumsiness and haste.

"Shit!" My knees involuntarily buckled, and I fell to the floor with fingers fanned out, wildly trying to grab the prints still floating downward. Bending quickly to scoop up the images, as if the floor could devour them whole, my fingers wove them into a messy pile and carried them safely to the tabletop. One slightly bent corner gripped my attention and I tenderly pinched it between my fingers to straighten it back out.

Originally the prints had no order, at least not as submitted, but I now saw a logical series unfold. The sequence of a lived life seemed to radiate and connect each print to the next — the life of a woman with ghostly blue eyes, aging and moving through life with a simple elegance that told where she had been and what she had experienced. I arranged the scenes like a puzzle with the scrutiny of a detective working a crime scene, one moment leading to the next. A story, the passing of time, was so evident — an artistic timeline of life.

Was this presumptuous of me? Who was I to know what the artist was thinking? I didn't know the artist, but I knew the woman whose life was captured in these photos. Breya and I were meeting eyes. For the first time since girlhood — or maybe for the second, since she had somehow held my hand while I had watched a car careen into Jax — Breya was before me in these photos. My lip quivered. Tears fell onto the table, beading on the surface. Splashes of disbelief and confusion condensed into tiny pools. The pictures, now neatly ordered, were stacked like a centerpiece on the table. A heavy, weighted gasp inflated my chest. My arms propped up my face, my elbows resting near the fallen tears. A sigh released itself from my lips.

I didn't know what to do with this moment. The lights were turned off, the phone I had come for rested in my hand, and my mind was vying for my full attention, but I was distracted, fractured from focusing on any one thing. My heart extracted old childhood memories of walking past Breya's house and times about her life I thought I had *created* to quilt together a story about the woman she might have been.

I climbed into the Jeep and leaned across the front seat to put my phone in the glove box when I saw a card without an envelope leaning against a pair of my cheap sunglasses. The card seemed so out of place. I hadn't noticed it while reaching for my apple less than an hour ago. Written in black ink and familiar penmanship:

> *Dear Avery,*
>
> *My history unfolds like any other's story. My narrative has been captured by you, in thoughts, and by another, in spirit, through artistry. Nestled in the emerald green of the park you once visited, I came to better know you through a gentle friend who speaks of adventures and travels over coffee and wine. I move with you and around you in small moments, for bits of time, only to encourage your own will and direction. In Corey, my support is offered and unwavering.*

Pulsing, the blood pounded at my temples. My neck grew hot and tight. I strained to squeeze my left shoulder, though my palm was trembling and sweaty. I put the card gently back into the glove compartment for safekeeping, glanced into the rearview mirror for running mascara, and started the engine. I could not read another letter from Breya and fully absorb it moments after realizing it was her image in those photos inside my office.

Decidedly, my destination was chosen. The weekend called for a quiet cabin a couple of hours north. My cousins were away, but a standing offer had been made some time ago. Mystified, the road led me away to try to clear a pathway of meaning. I would revisit Breya's card later, but first I needed to process how pictures of her had made their way to my gallery.

CHAPTER 12

Afterthoughts

Leaving the cabin after just a couple of nights there, I left my cousin Jenna a note, locked up, and hid the spare key. The time away was ideal, but the truth is, as I slept, hiked, and ate, I wondered. Constantly, wondered. The solitude just brought on thoughts that further befuddled me. No clarity was found, little guidance gained. Wisdom was lost on me, while little room was left for rationalizing the photos of Breya or the card she had written. I have always been spiritual, having grown up in the Catholic Church, but I veered away as an adult — not from spirituality or faith, but from organized religion. But what could explain this, the messages from Breya, the pictures, too? Frankly, I wondered if I was losing it — that is, losing my shit.

I had to see the prints in my office again before I could confront my detachment from sanity. I pulled up to the Hive now in the evening and again jogged up the staircase to the gallery's main door. My hands trembled as I struggled to find the keyhole. The main lobby pressurized with an eerie calmness as I strode toward my office door. I cracked my neck from side to side, preparing myself for sour twinges of insanity to start flushing through my arteries. *Do crazy people know they're crazy?* I wondered. *Should I be this self-aware?*

I didn't know if I would feel better actually confirming that it *was* Breya I had seen in the prints, or that I merely *imagined* I had seen her in them. Either way, the fortuitous letters were still boggling all reasoning, scrambling all rational reckoning.

The stack stood as a small vertical tower in the middle of the round table. The photos at the top were just as I remembered them — vivid, unmistakably the Breya I had known as a young girl, the same Breya I had found face down in the snow in a red flannel robe. Not only was it Breya frozen in these photographs, but it was also the life I had imagined her to have so many years ago. I began to rub my leg out of pure frantic confusion, and my feet started to fretfully shake beneath the chair. *Who took these? How? When?* All washed over me. "I don't get it," I whispered into the cramped space. "It can't be."

When I turned the first photo over, the artist's name and logo stabbed at my eyes: a hummingbird balanced upon a tree branch beneath a name, *Gabrielle C.* The second photo was labeled the same way, as were the third, fourth, and fifth. I was flipping each one faster than the last, creating a motion-picture booklet as I had done when I was a little girl, making drawn stick-figure people appear to run in my tiny spiral notebook when the pages were turned quickly. Gabrielle, Gabrielle, Gabrielle, Gabrielle flashed again and again. *I have to talk to her, find her,* was all my mind could muster.

Each print carried the contact information of the artist. Unbeknownst to me, Gabrielle had actually been in my life, waiting for me to discover her long before our encounters at the rest-stop. And all these times I wondered what she might be doing, who she was, and where she lived, though her phone number sat idly within my reach.

So now what? Do I run to her or away from her? Do I want to understand the inner-workings of this production? Scared and confused, I felt myself coming undone at the witness of what I had thought were my made-up childhood memories of Breya. Now they were warping into a reality, making my life a tragedy that would end with me becoming far out of touch with reality. *I'm crazed. Am I crazed?* "I give up!" I barked out. "I give up!"

I wanted to let it all go, to set these photos on a raft and shove them away in a ball of fire. But I couldn't do it — not all of me, anyway. I couldn't bring myself to surrender to the uncertainty just yet. I needed to find Gabrielle. Tears merged in the corner of my eyes, and a quick, hard sniff magically dried them out.

Unaware of the time the evening had claimed, I was controlled by my determination to arrive at the address printed on the photos. By now I had them with me in a folder inside my bag. My Jeep dashboard clock read 11:58 p.m., but I could have cared less. I couldn't describe my thoughts — in all seriousness, I didn't trust them at this point, anyhow.

A blank stare overcame me as I drove toward the Bronx, but I could still see the road, the bridge and the lights. *I suppose I'll know what to say when Gabrielle answers the door,* I decided as I pulled the Jeep against the curb into a parking spot, got out and approached her door. *The buzzer on the stoop should be ringing inside her apartment, but I have no way of knowing until her voice comes through the speaker,* I thought as I rang the doorbell repeatedly, totally out of touch with the amount of angst this would probably stir inside of her.

BBzzzzzzzz. BBzzzzzzzz. BBzzzzzzzz. BBzzzzzzzz. "Come fucking on!" I shouted into the darkness. *BBzzzzzzzz. BBzzzzzzzz.*

"Oh, my God, who is it?" Gabrielle's voice streamed through the intercom. "Is everything all right?" The panic I had just created pulsated in me. I could tell she was startled, disoriented, sleepy, alarmed.

"Gabby, it's me, Avery," I said trying to exude more self-control to lessen the anxiety I brought to her doorstep.

"Who? Avery?"

I was now crushed, embarrassed *and* crazy. "Avery, with the Jeep. We stopped for a burger on the two eighty..."

The door's lock clicked as she buzzed me in. *Should I run or walk to her apartment door? Fuck it!* I ran, but I paused to catch my breath before knocking on her door, still having no idea how to confront this situation. Yesterday I was practically envisioning our bodies wrapped around each other. Now I was trying to harness the will to ask what these pictures meant and how she could have possibly taken them.

"Oh, hi," I sputtered as she opened the door, chain still on. *I don't blame her — crazy lady she just met a little over a week ago, buzzing the shit out of her doorbell at midnight. Chain on makes sense.* "Sorry to bother you, Gabrielle, I know it's late." My voice sounded higher than usual. A soft trembling tickled the back of my throat. My panting softened.

"Damn, Avery, are you okay? What is with the frantic wake-up call?"

The lock slid to the left, and she opened the door, more or less pulling me inside.

A deadbolt locked behind me. She was standing in her underwear and an oversized sweatshirt fell off her shoulder. I could tell she had been asleep; her hair was tussled, and her eyes squinted under the glare of a flickering kitchen light. She pulled out a stool at the island, and we sat across from one another, similar to the way we had sat in the diner. I was trying to take *her* in. She was real. She was here. We were sitting together. The same little bird on her forearm was exposed as she dragged one sleeve toward her elbow.

"What? What is it? I, uh..." Bewilderment settled in her eyes, an awkward silence hunkered down between us. I put the folder on the counter. She glanced down at it and then back up at me. The silence ballooned. I gently slid the folder closer to her.

"Look," I said timidly. Pounding thumped through my whole body, every breath stilted and shallow.

Gabby reached inside the folder, pulled out the prints, stared at the photos, and then back at me, as if to say, "Yeah?" Then she said, "My submissions. Yes, these are mine." Her hands shuffled through each print, and then she neatly stacked them on the bar.

I could tell she was waiting for me to explain why the hell I had come to her place in the middle of the night and stormed the freaking buzzer to show her her own photos.

"I don't get it, Avery," she said. "Why so late? What is happening here?" By now the sleep had fully left her and she was baffled — and probably a bit pissed off! But for some reason, she didn't show any anger; instead, she held my hand and peered into my face. "What, Little Bird?" she asked.

I reflexively pulled my hand back. "What did you say?" I asked her as my head whirled and my eyes started to tear up. I rocked for a moment and wrapped my arms around my torso, as if comforting myself with an inward hug. Shaking my head, I asked again, "What did you say, Gabrielle?"

She stood up and moved toward me. "Ave, how can I help you?"

Her body moved in-between my legs as I perched on the stool and she held me as I had just held myself. *Hadn't we been like this before? No, we hadn't*. I sensed Jax, not just in her words, but in her full being. My mind reeled — a part of me wanted to shove her far away from me, and this other part of me wanted to hang onto her for dear life. I wanted to hold her before any other remnants of Jax appeared. *Little Bird?* I twisted my shoulders left to right slowly, forcing Gabrielle to relinquish my arms back to me. But I then resigned myself to her — to whatever this was — and wrapped my arms around her midsection. Her long hair was now pinned beneath my arms at her back. We stayed like this for a while, until our hearts started to beat in time with one another. I felt safe amid my emotional mayhem.

I didn't want to let go and confront either the photos or my complete compulsion for her. Neither choice made sense to me. But I couldn't hold back my nagging curiosity. So I finally asked, "Gabrielle, who is in these photos you submitted?"

"Someone my mother used to know. Why, Ave? What has you so worked up?"

She walked to the cupboard and took down two glasses. The crackle of ice breaking free from the tray rebounded off the walls, and the cubes clanked sharply against the glasses. She poured bourbon into each but I knew my stomach wouldn't be able to handle it. Gabby handed me a glass. I considered taking a sip, but the smell alone was too biting for me.

"Breya and my mother were friends," she said. "Long time ago, though. They actually danced together for a while, trained in a downtown studio at one point in time. My mom adored her! Used to talk about how they would audition and prep each other for different tryouts around the city. Gosh, I think they were even roommates for a while after traveling to Europe one summer. Why do you ask?" Gabby sipped her drink and sat back onto her stool. Our knees straddled one another's — mine, then hers, then mine, then hers.

"Your mother lived with Breya?" I asked, stunned by what I had just heard. "They must have been close. Dear to one another?"

"I think my mother saw her much like an older sister, a mentor. They backpacked and spent time on the Eurail when my mom was in her twenties. Again, Breya was older — not sure how much older. I remember pictures, and the stories that clung to each one. Mom kept a shoebox under her bed like a treasure-trove. They were cherished, and once in a while those pictures became my bedtime stories. Like the time she and Breya stowed away on the train to Brussels because Breya's pass blew out the window. My mom would smile while telling me this, and I could see in her eyes she'd gone to another place — you know, whichever city she was telling me about."

"What else? What else do you remember?"

"France. My mother loved France! It isn't my favorite place, but she would tilt her head and close her eyes when she described the food, the smell of the coffee, and the leather bags both the men and women carried. Her and Breya once hitchhiked to the Alsace winery in the Rhine valley, I think in the south. They found a room with a small balcony and plotted their next destination on a tattered map my mother used to keep in the back pocket of her jeans. Is this too much detail?"

"Not at all," I said, motioning for her to keep generating particulars.

Gabby smiled, reliving these stories as though her mother was sitting right there with us in the kitchen. "Breya shared more photos of herself over the years when she and my mom exchanged letters and Christmas cards. In fact, even after my mother died, Breya continued to write her but addressed the letters to me. She couldn't let the friendship go, I suppose."

I nodded. "I get it."

"I still don't get your intrigue, though, Avery. Why are you here? I mean, I'm glad you are, I've been thinking about you. But I don't get you showing up at this hour with the pictures. What is it?"

I shared my narrative, how I had seen Breya face-down in the snow when in first grade, and how I had imagined Breya's life: the dancing in her living room, the balcony, the strawberry fields, her alone in a kitchen with Bella the cat. "Your photos ripped something out of me that I was afraid would be lost for good, Gabrielle. I thought I was losing my mind when I saw Breya looking back at me in your work. Not only was it her face, but they reflected her experiences as I'd constructed them, too. I feared that I somehow became the architect of something vapid, utterly made up, but now it all seems much more lucid, less threatening, in a way."

My drink instinctively met my mouth. Forgetting it was bourbon, I took a swig and twisted my face, forcing it down my throat. A track of fire lit my esophagus into flames.

"The photos came from my mother and Breya, Avery," Gabby said. "Yes, I added my own touches — the artistry. I re-envisioned what was already there, but the core of each one hopefully remains intact. So you're saying you knew Breya, too?" She seemed perplexed. "I never knew her myself — I just knew of her through Mom's reminiscence. I thought by using these photos it was a nice way to remember my mother and their friendship. I recall my mom saying Breya had moved upstate when I was real young. She was your neighbor?"

"Yeah, for years," I stammered. "I didn't really *know* her, Gabrielle. Maybe something changed in her. To me, she was the old lady next door. She kept to herself, but I later learned she did have a grown son. I had no idea she really was so alive at one point in time." I purposefully took a drink this time and stabilized myself for the smoky after-burn. "So you having the pictures makes some sense, Gab. But how the hell could I have known of the experiences they captured? For Christ's sake, am I clairvoyant?"

This question was rhetorical — I was certainly not clairvoyant. My crazy-scale tipped slightly less toward insanity, yet the balance I was praying for was still out of my line of sight. Maybe this was all I could handle for one night. Pushing the stool back with my upper legs, I stood, walked the glass to the sink, and cleared my throat. "I should go." I picked up the folder of photos and put it in my bag.

"It's late, just stay," Gabrielle offered. I knew she was trying to be kind but there was nothing left in me to extricate. All of my energy had been mined.

"I can't." Opening the door to leave, I could feel her move up behind me and place a hand over my shoulder, flat against the door. She stopped it in mid-swing, leaving it ajar by just inches. Then she lightly pushed the door closer to closed and slid off the chain. I turned. We were face to face.

"Be safe," she whispered near my cheek. Her breath carried the slight vapors of alcohol, yet it was her perfume riding atop of it that made me feel intoxicated. "Let's make time to meet tomorrow. Breakfast at the little coffee shop near the Park Place stop off the '1' train. It's about halfway between us. Seven a.m.?"

Her hands were on my shoulders, as if to keep me at a distance, far enough away to look into my eyes and close enough to pull me back in for a hug. Our arms now took each other's body in closely; one hand cradled the back of my head. "It'll be all right." Her left arm extended and reaching for the doorknob tendered a glimpse of the hummingbird imprinted on her skin. I ran my forefinger down the length of her forearm and nodded in agreement.

"See you in the morning," I said shyly.

"Sweet dreams."

CHAPTER 13

Close Quarters

I was awake most of the night listening to the white noise of a fan on my dresser. The air-conditioner was on but the sound of the fan usually helped me fall asleep. Recalling the unraveling of the evening, I mentally tried to separate the fragments before me. Breya knew Gabrielle's mother. They were old friends, roommates. Breya was my neighbor. Breya and Gabrielle's mother kept in touch over the years, sharing pictures and letters. I never really knew anything about Breya, but everything I dreamed about her happened to be true. And Breya was leaving me letters from beyond the grave, as if she were a guardian angel.

Gabrielle conjured feelings in me I had never felt, never knew existed. She called me "Little Bird." Where did that come from? Had I mentioned to her the affection those words revived in me? I didn't recall saying anything at all about Jax to her. I hadn't. How uncanny she used the same term of endearment! She was allowed, though it would never feel as if she really owned it to me. Maybe I would never hear it again.

The clock waned toward morning, unhurried. Sleep was a struggle. My mind was racing.

The alarm clock jolted me from inertia. I had fallen asleep after all, but the time registered within me as just a nap. Trepidations about meeting up with Gabrielle and where our conversation might lead began to harass me. My stomach churned, growling from hunger. Breakfast would be good.

Throwing a bag over a shoulder, I propelled myself out of the door in the direction of the elevator. As usual, I pushed the button in frenzied spurts while rocking from one foot to the other. Waiting drove me nuts! The arrow above the door lit up, its arrival highly anticipated, like waiting for a movie to begin after the trailers played out.

Ding. The doors parted down the middle to slowly reveal the passenger inside. An assuming woman was standing in the center of the box. She took a step back diagonally and landed in a corner. Since I was the only person about to get on, there was no need for such space between us. I gave her a polite smile as I stepped inside the elevator. She returned a nod as unfamiliar people do in tacit recognition of each other's existence.

I turned toward the doors as they closed in front of me. People at my back always bothered me, but elevator etiquette certainly did not allow room for passengers to turn toward each other in such close quarters. I sensed the lady fidgeting and I felt a bit more uneasy.

"Supposed to be nice weather today," I pitched over my shoulder, giving her a sideways glance.

"I heard storms later…"

Now able to stand at an angle, I could see her out of the corner of my eye. She was wearing a black pencil-skirt, beige heels and a flouncy ivory-colored blouse. A bag dangled from her shoulder and chains of various lengths cut between her breasts. Her hair was pulled up in a messy bun and her sunglasses were already on. *She's caught up in thought and on her way to work,* I guessed. Her eyes seemed fixed to a spot on the floor, based on the position of her head.

Motionless now, like trapped mice, we waited. *Eighteen…seventeen… sixteen…* the descent seemed unending.

"Be careful today, storms are supposed to kick up suddenly," she repeated as a second, subtle warning.

"Really? I hadn't heard."

"Yeah, some pressure system moving in. High winds."

Twelve…eleven…ten…

"You know, storms appear out of the blue some days, and always when you have someplace to be. I'm from the Midwest. We never take storms lightly," she said almost apologetically for the angst she was projecting.

"I'm sure it'll be nothing."

Seven…six…five…

From the corner of my eye, without warning, her head instantaneously began to jerk and bob. She grabbed the railing with both hands. Her knuckles turned white from hanging on so hard. One foot screeched as it dragged outwardly across the floor, and her beige heel flung against the wall. Her other leg started to buckle as her body caved in on itself. Upon instinct, my arms tried to catch her, and we both crumpled to the floor. Her glasses shot off as her head bucked backward in the crook of my arm. Drool slunk out of the corner of her mouth. Her bodily twitching shook me even when I squeezed harder in an effort to stabilize the two of us. She felt fragile in my arms but heavy sprawled against my thighs. Kneeling, my feet folded partially underneath the weight of our bodies. More hair fell out of her bun; blond strands stuck to the spittle running down her neck. I wiped it away with the sleeve of my shirt. Hoping to keep her head still, I moved both of my hands gently against her cheeks. Wrists turned inward, one against her chest, the other gawkily bent near her waist. She had lost all control. Her jaw clenched tightly. I felt the muscles straining underneath my hands now. The lack of oxygen was turning her face a catastrophic crimson. The now-frothy drool bubbled from her mouth.

"I got you, I got you, I got you," the mantra kept pumping out of me. My inner thermostat was rising. Flushed, adrenaline-fueled, I kept holding her. *I don't have a clue what to do!*

Three…two…one…

The doors opened. No one was there.

"Help! Help me! Please, please, please!" I cried out to anyone who might be in the lobby but out of view. I was pleading like a little girl. A frenzy of people hurried toward us. My lungs opened up. "Call 911! A seizure!"

The lift filled with two other people, and countless others peered in, as if viewing zoo creatures. Hands covered mouths as cell phones clung to ears — it was human nature to help *and* gape, I supposed. I kicked her bag toward the onlookers. "Check her wallet!" I hollered. "Look for a name! Get her name, hurry!"

"Claire," returned a voice. "It's Claire."

"An ambulance is on the way!" yelled another.

A lobby security guard pushed himself through the group and bent over me. "Make sure her head is turned in case she vomits," he commanded. "Don't let her choke."

"Don't let her choke?" I asked, as if I could possibly control this outcome.

"Do you know her? She lives on the twenty-third floor."

"No," I said, dazed. "No, I don't know her." Yet I felt fiercely protective of her in this moment. Still supporting her body, I reassured her, "I got you. I got you, Claire."

A medic appeared and pulled Claire away from me. I sat still on the elevator floor, staring at her twisted sunglasses and the high heel that had been left behind.

"Ma'am, are you okay? Can you tell us what happened?" a lanky woman wearing blue gloves and carrying a medical-type bag asked me. "Can I check you over?"

"No, no, I'm fine." I could tell I was overwrought with a stunned expression.

Claire's spit had wet my shirtsleeves and the front of my jeans. Her lilac scent was now on my clothes, too. My mind flashed to my parents' house in the country and the lilac bush outside of my bedroom window. My clasped fingers released with a torrent of emotions.

The medic put a tender hand on my back and encouraged me to take deep breaths. "She'll be fine, ma'am," she told me. "We're taking her to the hospital. Are you sure you don't want anyone to check you out?"

"No, I'm just shaken up," I said. "Never saw that before, ya' know. We're neighbors — I mean, I just heard that she lives here, too. I've never seen that before. I'm good. Really, I'm good." I feigned a smile and stood up. The medic wrote my name down and had me sign a release from medical attention.

Deciding to go back up to my place, I gently stepped back into the elevator and pushed the button for the eighteenth floor. The doors closed, the lift started upward.

Four...five...six...

I can't just mosey on to breakfast like nothing happened, I thought. *Another shower will wash the shock of the seizure away from me and give me the chance to reorient myself. Should I still try to meet Gabrielle?*

Thirteen...fourteen...fifteen...

I don't know. One thing at a time. The ride back up to my floor suspended time. I pretended I had the power to undo the ride down, erase Claire from my mind, expunge the herky-jerky movements, banish the whole thing from thought.

Seventeen...eighteen...Ding.

"Damn," floated out of my mouth and into the hallway, accidentally slapping José just as he was emerging from his apartment. "Shit, sorry, man," I told him. "I didn't see you."

"It's cool, Ave. Rough morning?" He chuckled.

"Yeah, rough," I said as I leaned on my door and turned the key. "Be careful, storms this afternoon," I warned, just as Claire had done. "Actually, maybe they're due this morning."

"Thanks. See ya', Ave." He waved his hand and headed down the hallway.

I closed my eyes and cried as the hot water in the shower hit my skin. Water pellets and tears intermingled. I felt relief that Claire hadn't died in my presence as Jax had, that people were kind enough to help strangers when in need, that the medics had come to take the horror out of my hands.

Toweling myself dry, I lit a cigarette while dialing Gabrielle's cell number. She didn't pick up, so I sent a text: "Gonna be late. Can you wait?"

"No, have a photo shoot. Meet you later? Everything good?" she sent back.

"Everything's fine," I lied. "Want to come over at seven? I'll make dinner? I owe you." I sent my address.

"Later it is," Gabrielle responded.

The elevator scene replayed itself in my head as I paced in the living room. Realizing I needed to get to work, I rustled through the closet, looking for a new outfit. All of my options seemed unimpressive. Yet anything that didn't need ironing would have to do.

Grabbing my diamond earrings from the dresser, I caught sight of a folded note. Had I left it there? My eyes squinted, knowing full well I had not. My cigarette burned low, so I snuffed out the butt in a marble ashtray on my balcony, leaving its sliding door open to pull the smoke's lingering effects out of the room. Smoking inside my apartment was unusual — in all honesty, I detested the habit, even if it was my own.

The note came to life as I unfolded it before me:

Dear Avery,

> *A storm is coming. Not so much a surge but more of a gentle downpour that will start to take root in your life. The showers will be kind, cleansing. Though unexpected, they will be a renewal washing away so many old ideations and carrying with it new thoughts and revelations. Don't be afraid to honor your feelings, they cannot be predicted or anticipated. There is no right or wrong way to be happy.*

No signature — but I knew the handwriting, and couldn't deny that Breya was watching over me once again.

"The storm? For Christ's sake, were you in the elevator *with* me, Breya?" The words leapt out of me angrily this time. Was she watching me, lingering even in moments of complete, personal terror? And what — wielding a fucking pen to leave me riddles and notes?

My insecurity was punishing me as my inner-logic tried to find meaning in these letters. Needing to show them to somebody, yet fearing the reaction they would incite, I shoved this one in a drawer where I now kept all of the others. Work was awaiting me, I was running late. I could no longer pretend these letters were figments of my imagination because too many had been left for me. *Three, four letters?* Unexplainable. Undeniable.

CHAPTER 14

Lost and Found

The doorbell rang as I took the pasta to the strainer. Steam rose to the ceiling, the window over the sink glazed with steam. The night had turned cool for July. My cooking skills were average, but I had figured the food would hardly be the center of conversation tonight. I loved the smell of garlic bread toasting in the oven. The single glass of red wine I had sipped while shuffling around the kitchen preparing dinner was starting to hit me. My playlist, a mixture of world music, was thumping drums and vocals in different languages — all foreign to my ear. I really had no expectations for dinner; it was more my way of apologizing for not showing up for breakfast earlier in the day.

I lied — I *did* have expectations. Opening the door, I had to admit this to myself. When looking at Gabrielle standing in the doorframe, I became a giddy teen. She had on her worn leather boots that told a story of world travels, perhaps cobblestoned cities she walked while taking her photos. I couldn't help but notice the boots, since apprehension pulled my stare toward the floor as the door first broke its seal. My eyes floated upward and locked onto hers just as she was about to look away. Her glance flitted back to me, and those green eyes struck me like shards of emerald moving between us. Her eyebrows were two perfect arcs above each eye, dark, matching her long, wavy, unruly hair. Her lips parted, but she said nothing.

"Right on time," I greeted her as the timer hummed behind me. "Come," I insisted with a tinge of luring charm, chasing after the sound of the timer in the kitchen. "Grab the door. Come on in."

From the oven I brought the steaming half-loaves of garlic bread to the basket I had lined with a white cloth on the countertop. "So glad to see you," I couldn't resist saying, but I snuffed out my voice with another sip of wine. "Wine?" I offered, then read aloud the label on its bottle: *"Malbec."*

"Yes, sounds nice," Gabrielle said as a slight smile curled at the corners of her mouth.

Can she tell I'm nervous? I wondered. *I mean, I wasn't, but I am now.* "Sorry about this morning, Gabby…can I call you Gabby?"

"I've always preferred Gabrielle, to be honest, but I…"

"I get it, no worries, I thought…"

"Slow down, Avery. I was going to say that I don't mind when you call me Gabby. It's fine. A dinner always brings friendship to the surface, eh? I'm interested to get to know you better and hear about this morning. Yeah, and why the late visit last night?" She raised one of her perfectly arched eyebrows and smiled.

"Yeah…" I brought her glass of wine. The slight weight of the vintage swished against the glass, radiating at my palm. Mounting marginal adoration grew within me for Gabrielle. Just seeing her sitting in my apartment, looking so gorgeous — and somewhat sinister — seemed unreal. I couldn't explain why every part of me was rapt by her, but it was.

"Tell me about this morning," Gabby asked me while biting her bottom lip.

Is she aware how drawn to her I feel? Does she have the same visceral response to me that I'm having toward her? Maybe it was all in my head — maybe the lip-biting was a habit she had no matter who was in the room. Or maybe it was purposeful — a means to ensnare me, leaving me conscious but rendering me unable to fight off her allure. I laughed as I replayed this syrupy thought in my head. Perhaps I'd had *too* much wine.

"Um, what? Oh, this morning, yeah. Crazy!" I poured myself another glass and turned toward the stove. "Mind if I finish this up while we talk for a few minutes?"

I tossed asparagus into a stir-fry pan I had inherited from my mother, drizzled it with olive oil, and dropped in basil, salt, pepper, garlic, shrimp, cherry tomatoes, and finally the cooked pasta. The potpourri of sweet smells elevated the space into a five-star restaurant and private dining room all at once. The twist and twine of each aroma and the crackling sound of lemon splashing into the sizzling pan further laced Gabby and me together in this quiet moment alone.

The story of Claire in the elevator was shared, as I tossed some salad and we nibbled cheese at the small island partitioning Gabrielle from me. The granite was cold to the touch, and I pulled my sleeves down to protect my forearms from the chill. Of course, Gabby kept one sleeve yanked up, and the little hummingbird stared into the skylight above us, as if ready to perch overhead on the track lighting.

"You must have been scared! A seizure? And you were holding the poor girl?" Gabby asked me with furled brows, one still maintaining its perfect arch, the other much more exaggerated and lifted.

"She lives here in the building, but I'd never seen her before today. Claire, on the twenty-third floor, I found out. It was a moment, Gabby. I think she's back home now. I'll run up and bring her a get-well card or something. So sorry I missed breakfast," I trailed off as I began to serve the food.

"As if you could have helped it," she said, giving me a wink. "Good people do good things. I'm sure Claire was glad to have you with her."

"I doubt she realized. She was totally overcome, eyes rolling back, really in the clutches of the situation. It was hard to watch, but I'm glad she was not alone."

I carried the last of the food to the table near the windows, expecting Gabrielle to follow. She grabbed the breadbasket and tucked the bottle of wine between her body and arm, still holding her mostly empty glass in the other hand. I could see a tinge of maroon painting her glass as she set it on the table. She sat first and pulled out the other chair for me with her foot.

"Nice view, Ave," she said as we gazed at the city below us. "So tell me about the other night and what had you so worried."

Intuitively, I grabbed her plate and started to add the pasta. "Is this good?" I asked, looking up at her.

"Yes, plenty," she said, demonstrating some discomfort with me taking over her space and scooping up her plate. Then her shoulders relaxed, which carried with it the kindness I had intended. She smiled and offered, "Thank you."

"It's not just the photos, Gabby. It's the entire story unfolding between us. We met by total coincidence twice. Breya, who I hadn't thought of in years, is suddenly looking back at me in the prints you submitted for the fall art exhibit. Realizing that you know Breya by virtue of your mother just sort of blew me away. But, Gabby, there's more. It's not just the common acquaintance of Breya. It's my knowing her life experiences that has me floored."

"I can't explain that, Avery. I don't know. There have to be things we're not meant to understand in life, don't you think? Things above us, if you will, or beyond us."

"There's something else." I wanted to tell her about the letters, but their implausibility hushed me. Rendered silent, I just shook my head and looked at her. We ate and let the soft music in the background fill the quiet of the space for a few minutes.

Our words shifted away from the nucleus of what was bothering me, like the mast of a ship seeking a new direction. Sensing my uneasiness, Gabby expounded on the technique of lens-chimping, the process she used to create the Breya prints. It entails shooting through a convex lens, which distorts the image just a fraction, evoking blended prisms of light and reflection. *If she only knew how much more impressed I was with the movements of her mouth than the technique she was imparting on me,* I thought. As in times before, I drifted in and out of the conversation, landing in the midst of hallucinations of her going about her day. Always bathed in blinding light or confounding darkness, she and I seemed to be at the center of each moment my mind created.

The minutes were escaping us; the evening was rushing by. I wanted it to stop so we could just sit talking all night. Opposite each other on the couch, we sat with our legs side-by-side, crossed at the ankles. The snuffling and spurting of the brewing coffee punctured the air, dotting our conversation with accidental punctuation marks. Gabrielle took the cue that the coffee was nearly ready and slid to her feet, offering me a hand. We had been laughing and sharing stories, getting to know one another all night, but had been careful to keep a relative distance between us. On my behalf this was a purposeful decision spurred on by my absolute feeling of inadequacy next to her. My inexperience was palpable — obvious, I was sure. What if I was reading it all wrong and she had no inclination toward women, or even worse, *me*?

Gabrielle took my hand in hers as her other hand hooked the front pocket of my jeans, pulling us together. My breath was virtually siphoning through her body as our noses and mouths stopped just short of touching. Inebriated by the rush of standing so close to her, the blood splashed against my veins, causing my heart to pound like fists on a locked door. A quick inhalation caused a sliver of a gasp to escape me. She stared into my eyes as my breath passed into her mouth. Her head tilted ever so slowly and she bit her lip again. This time, I knew it was for me. Our lips touched, my eyes closed, and our bodies fused together like melting wax.

I never imagined that a woman's kiss would feel any different from a man's, but it did. It was so much softer, gentler, sweeter. I felt her kiss not only at the surface but in every nerve within my body. Though I had been dying to kiss Gabby, I didn't know until the precise moment our lips actually touched whether I could go through with it. I wondered if, when the time came, I would turn away, leaving her anticipating a moment I couldn't deliver. But there we stood, kissing. My hands gently moved through her hair and down to the small of her back. Its curve became the perfect place to pull her closer to me. Any differences between us were now the magnetic poles that brought our bodies together.

For a long time we just kissed. A blaze I hadn't known could erupt between two people had been ignited. And again, I became that girl responsible for setting the curtains on fire long ago in my parents' living room.

We pulled away for only a moment. A quiet peace parted us, causing our eyes to fall still on one another. *Those green eyes*. It was then that I became lost and found, standing in the same place at the same time.

CHAPTER 15

Making Space

The night ended with that kiss — a train of kisses that became like a blur and a fury, a calm and agitated storm all wrapped into one. It literally drained the energy from me. Like a magician pulling scarves out of a hat, it seemed endless until we said our goodbyes. Self-restraint was exhausting! I wondered what it might have been like to move beyond the gravity of Gabrielle's embrace.

Waking up now and welcoming the morning alone, I wondered if I had made a mistake by letting her leave. Her perfume clung to my skin, causing me to procrastinate showering just to reimagine those moments all over again. It was real — she had been here, and we had stepped into a new dimension of knowing each other, a dimension unexplored before last night, one that had left me unable to distinguish up from down. Yet, when next to Gabby, I was anchored and safe — disoriented, but safe.

My weekend held no plans, but I wanted to find Claire, introduce myself, and see how she was doing. I figured the afternoon would be a good time to pop in, but I had no way of calling first. I scribed a note on stationery in case she wasn't home. I wanted to say, "Hello," and offer her my friendship. I wanted to be a person she could turn to if she needed anything, if another episode came over her. Her condition, though, was none of my business. I was a stranger. Maybe it would be weird for me to reach out to her. It felt like the right thing to do, but I didn't know how my gesture would be received. Perhaps I would appear to be a nosy neighbor, intrusive, a pain in the ass who seemed to have wiggled her way into her life when a door was cracked open, primarily and accidentally. Would she feel embarrassed?

Whatever the reaction, I needed to visit her. I needed to show I cared. Sharing a moment like that with someone you have no personal connection with leads to an emergent bond that cannot be denied — at least that was how I came to internalize the experience. *We were now coupled by fate, by circumstance,* I supposed.

While walking to her apartment, I somehow found myself hoping my knock would go unanswered. *Simply slip the note under her door from the hallway and walk away,* I told myself. *Sure, that would suffice,* a convincing whisper swirled against my inner ear.

As I approached Claire's door, music penetrated the air. A crying violin whined and ached from inside her apartment, lassoing my heart so tightly I couldn't turn and walk away. The music rose and fell, rose and fell, plunging like a swing sweeping low across a fresh-cut lawn and then ascending high toward the clouds, followed by a soaring breakaway. My ear turned against the door without touching it. I smiled.

I hesitated before knocking, imagining Claire was listening to the music while relaxing on her couch, legs crossed and propped up on the armrest, eyes closed. With two knuckles bent, I knocked on her white door with vague commitment. The music suddenly halted mid-note, my presence realized. I listened, but heard nothing — no footsteps, no "coming..." Nothing. I knocked again. A voice responded, "Hi, can I help you?"

Certain that she was peering through the peephole, I turned to face the door straight-on and smiled. "Yeah, hi, Claire. My name is Avery. I was in the elevator with you yesterday. We're neighbors, it turns out. I just..."

"Oh, my gosh! Avery, yes, I recognize you!" She turned the lock and opened the door with a quick burst. A violin hung from her left hand, the bow balanced against the wall. She appeared taller than I remembered.

"Was that you playing?" I blurted with surprise. "It was gorgeous! Sorry I couldn't help but hear." My eyes, likely bright with astonishment, connected with Claire's. Her shoulders heaved slightly in a shrug, as if to say, "Go figure?" Then she tilted her head toward the hallway and invited me in. I followed her down the entrance hall, watching her violin sway in synchronicity with her footsteps. She led me into the living room, where a music stand was positioned next to the sliding glass door of a small balcony. The sun streamed through sheer curtains, creating a haze that illuminated floating dust particles. She propped her violin and bow in a small upright metal stand on the floor.

"I'm so glad you stopped by, Avery," she said. "The security guard downstairs told me you were by my side the whole time yesterday. Well, I guess you didn't have much of a choice, huh?" She laughed, exposing her perfectly straight teeth. "I imagine that was pretty scary for you. Shit, you must have felt trapped! God, was a I mess?" Her fast, nervous voice reminded me of a schoolgirl giving a presentation in front of her class for the first time.

"I've never seen anyone having a seizure, to be honest with you," I said. "Yeah, totally scary! I wanted to help, but I didn't know what to do, ya' know?" I sat down on a purple couch and reached across the coffee table to receive the glass of ice water Claire was holding out to me. "Thank you," I said.

"They started when I was a kid," Claire began as she settled into an antique chair posed opposite of me. Its chocolate-colored leather, stamped with time, nestled her body gently. Her feet were bare, her toenails painted perfectly in a soft pink. One leg bent underneath her. She smiled while resting her chin on her hand as she leaned against an arm of her chair. A bracelet of wooden beads slunk down her arm and halted between her wrist and elbow. Her eyes were the color of light blue slate, eyebrows manicured, long lashes. "Again, I'm so sorry you were put in that situation," she continued. "It's been a long time. I take medicine, but it's been years since my last episode."

"No, really, I'm glad you were not alone. I thought my heart was going to literally tear through my chest. I can't imagine what the experience must have been like for you!"

"Partially terrifying, partially incomprehensible, partially like a dream." She gazed off into a place that suddenly took her attention hostage.

I half-expected another seizure to shake her body convulsively. A part of me wanted to run out of her apartment at a staggering speed, but the better part sat quietly, offering her my patience and the tranquility of this moment to finish her inner thoughts. I took her in again, as if seeing her for the first time. *Yes, long blond hair, as I remember.* Her apartment reflected a minimalist persona, and I found myself wondering what she did for a living — so American of me. Why is it we always wonder what people *do* when we first meet them instead of focusing on who they *are?*

Claire shook herself back to our conversation the way a puppy shakes off the rain from the outdoors. She blinked a few times and reset herself. "Tell me about you, Avery."

We chatted for a while, sharing each other's professional interests and hobbies. Claire had recently graduated from Columbia University as a political science major. "Violin takes the stress away," she laughed, admitting she wasn't sure what her next steps would be. Yet I saw a softness and a determination in her that I wonder if she even recognized. "I think I might travel for a bit before settling into a career, before taking on that responsibility," she continued, nodding her head, "Yeah, I could be okay with being a rolling stone."

Noticing her wandering spirit, I saw pieces of Gabby in her. Claire was familiar to me in some odd way — the far-off look, wanting to see places new and different. A craving for the world also raked against me at times — a wanting to grab my passport and jump on a train, like in the movies, and let it steer me through Europe cutting the foothills of mountains and dashing through the golden valleys of wine country. I pictured myself holding Gabby's hand while our feet beat against cobblestone streets in Spain to rhythms birthed in Argentina and Uruguay. *Cart before the horse,* I thought. *Cart before the horse!*

Glasses of ice water led to hot tea at Claire's, provoking the clock to speed up time, it seemed. Her family, she said, was small — mostly just she and her father. She spoke about her parents and an auntie she could faintly remember. Sadness flowed across her face as she recalled her parents' divorce when she was a teen. The sorrow in her expressions didn't match the happiness of her stories at times, but an ache resided behind her blue eyes. I couldn't ask why.

The afternoon escaped us as we grew to know each other. Her apartment transformed as the sun moved away from the window and shadows of the early evening shrouded the wood floor. The buildings outside, modern-day profiles against the sky, dissolved into the horizon. It was still daylight, but one could sense the day winding down.

"I have so loved getting to know you, Claire!" I finally said, nudging toward goodbye.

"Same here! Thank you again for the elevator and for coming by. Stop up next weekend, if you're available. I'll be having some friends over for a dinner party. Feel free to bring someone if you'd like. Eight o'clock."

"Maybe I will," I said as I headed toward the door. A quick embrace sealed our friendship and I stepped into the hallway. She waved from the frame of her door and gently closed it behind me. As I headed for the elevator, a faint smile overcame me, and I chuckled at the circumstances that had brought us together. *You never know,* I thought, remembering a phrase my parents used to always say. *You never know what's around the next corner.*

I took a detour, compelled to find the stairs back down to my apartment. As I opened my door, the melody of Claire's violin suddenly carried on a hum from my lips.

I needed to freshen up before heading to Gabby's. Last night's encounter still fizzled within me like Pop Rocks exploding at each nerve-ending. A pulsing stirred in my stomach. Carbon dioxide bubbled in my blood. *What might come of tonight?* Speakers thumped a club-dance mix over the shower, and I writhed within the tiny boxed-in space as I shaved my legs, rewashed my hair, and lathered myself in soap.

Soon Gabby and I were back in the same comfortable positions as before, but this time on her couch. An allure neither of us could repel pulled us closer together. I could just stare at her for hours — and, for a while, I did. I looked on as Gabby told me about the father she had known for only a short time, and again about her mother's days as a dancer and friendship with Breya before the cancer. Gabby shared fond memories of her father, Luke, that I hadn't heard before. She said he "went away" when she was eleven, but she kept the details of his departure to herself.

Our eyes brightened and filled with tears as we stitched together the patchwork of our pasts. Understanding that certain elements of our lives remained unspoken, we tucked ourselves deeper into the cushions and wrapped our quilt tightly around our shoulders.

For a while we lay still in silence. It has always struck me that the true measure of any relationship is the ability to be in each other's company in absolute quiet. In such serenity one reconciles all things birthed from regret, struggle, joy, and love. Sometimes, the quiet is simply needed to revel in plain *nothingness*. Within me, though, a conflict was rising between my conscience and my truth: *What would it mean if I loved a woman?* I couldn't find peace with the silence just yet.

Learning more about one another's past and hopes for the future brought the possibility of having to explain my lost love. There were things Gabrielle did not know about me. Jax now crept into my mind, and in-between each word Gabby spoke I fought the urge to break down and cry. A longing hung over my face, like an opaque mask starting to dry, leaving my facial muscles stiff with a flat affect I couldn't control. The struggle to hide my sorrow was growing futile. *This part of me — so private, so personal — didn't need to come out yet, did it?*

"I feel like you're suddenly far off, Avery. What is it?" Gabby urged with tenderness. Her fingers reached for my hand, trying to pull me nearer. The knees of her jeans were ripped, her creamy mocha skin exposed underneath. I touched her thigh and excused myself.

"I'll be just a second," I said as I stood and headed to the bathroom, to walk away and catch my breath. Bracing myself over the sink, I could feel my lungs expand and deflate with air so heavy and hot I thought I might hyperventilate. It felt as if the memory of Jax had been lit ablaze, about to burn out of control. The curtains I had set on fire as a child suddenly whirled and whipped around me again, trapping me in a barrage of remembrances. I needed oxygen — more than what was available in the cramped bathroom.

"Come on! Come on! Come on!" burst out in near silent gasps as I splashed cold water on my face. God, was this guilt, was this longing? *What was this reaction escaping me?* Perhaps it was the realization that my heart was being captured again and by a woman. *Why did this matter?* How could I make sense of the emotions reeking havoc on my heart? I thought I had come to some place of acceptance with my affection for Gabby. *But what if it were more? What if it were love? Could I love a woman in this way, the way I loved Jax?* Fear was setting up a home inside of me. I was violated by its presence. I wanted to kick it out of me, reach deep inside and tear it out, as one wants to do with cancer. Radiation, chemo, whatever it might take, I needed to be rid of this fear. But this fear was only a reflection of the truth inside of me. *Could I find a way to make peace with it?*

Clarity started to spread through me like a warm current, and my breathing began to syncopate with a tranquility I willed upon myself. I needed to share Jax with Gabby — not just him, but our relationship, and his passing. This would release me from the invisible ties that kept me bound to him. Maybe this acknowledgment would emancipate me, allow me to love freely, no matter who the next person would be...is. I would tuck my panic away and summon the courage to share the sacred story of Jax and his accident with Gabby. I owed her this much.

Rumbles of thunder shook so loudly my guts quaked. An unanticipated thunderclap startled me as I stepped back into the living room. The lights flicked as Gabby darted to the kitchen to grab a book of matches. The apartment had gone dark. We were blinded momentarily by a power outage that had blackened fifteen square blocks of the city.

"Hhhmmm. What now?" Gabby asked with a smile I could detect in her voice.

"I'm sorry, Gab, I needed a minute. I'm nervous, I guess — not just about this, you and I, but about my feelings. I've never been with a woman before. I've never cared for woman, or even thought of woman, the way I think of you." My throat was dry, and my adjusting eyes could now clearly make out Gabby's face in the darkness. The faint glow of a candle shimmered off the right side of her cheek, leaving the other half of her face a shadow.

"It's okay, Avery. I have no expectations. There's no rush, no need for explanation. I can't say what it is about you — everything, really — but I find myself longing for you when we're next to one another and when we're apart. Maybe you don't feel this way — maybe it goes against every fiber of your being to want me, too — but it is what it is. If you can't be in this moment as I'm in it with you, I understand. I can't talk you into feeling what I feel, but I can't pretend this gravitas between us doesn't exist."

A lone tear tickled down my cheek. Gabby reached up to wipe it away with the tip of her forefinger. Her hand rested against the side of my face, and I tilted my head to push the weight of my heavy heart against her palm. Her wrist smelled of perfume, dizzying me with vibrations of sensual energy. And yet a tide of tortured memories of the day I saw Jax's body lying still on the pavement scraped down the inside of me like the claws of a startled cat.

"Jax — I have to tell you about Jax," I began.

I don't know how long it took for me to tell Gabby about Jax. I have no sense of how my affection for him impacted her that evening. The narrative engulfed me as I closed out the rest of the world for the hours I assumed it took me to explain my feelings, my loss, my despair, and my ascent to her. In the end I didn't tell Gabby about the details of his accident or how I watched as a car sped into him. Simply put, "Jax died suddenly."

When my account ended, dawn appeared to break in hues across the sky, as if a glass of orange Tang and purple Kool-Aid were toiling together. The morning was peeking in on the city. Gabby never let go of my hand, and now she stood and led me out onto the balcony. Behind me, her arms wrapped around my body like a blanket. We stood in the silence and waited for the sun to bless the city below us. Sharing was what I needed.

Sharing and letting go were the authorization my conscience needed to love another. It no longer mattered that Gabby was a woman. Jax would always be a part of me; nothing could ever erase him. But now my heart had the space to accept a new soul, a new light. I wanted to somehow be closer to Gabrielle and now I was prepared to take down all barriers. Like a lone traveler looking for a place to take up temporary residency, I aspired to make space for her inside of my heart, at least for a short time. She felt like home and I wanted her to see me in this way, too.

CHAPTER 16

Torn

Every day seemed to weave our worlds closer together. Like continental drift, the tectonic plates between us converged, diverged and transformed us, creating earthquakes that shook at our core. Some days we seemed to become each other, and other days we were distinct and separate. I could appreciate both needs: to be together and to be apart. We were forging a loyalty to each other — a bridge connecting one shoreline to another, able to sway with harsh winds if need be, yet strong enough to support the heft of a hundred cars. I had no idea its fortitude would be tested so early, but then again, challenges are never easy to predict or anticipate.

Gabby had gone to pick up some groceries, but I stayed behind to sort through some old boxes she had asked me to look at. They were full of photos, drawings and art endeavors of her past. She thought I might find something to compliment her art installation that would soon be showing at the Hive. As I lifted a knot of tangled wire, a mobile depicting the seasons took shape. Shimmering pieces of glass caught the light from the window, sending rays of green and oceanic turquoise onto the walls. Peppered sunbeams reflected against the floor, flittering as each delicate ornament spun from my outstretched arm. Copper, the color of shiny new pennies, and sterling silver sparkled as the mobile's tentacles dangled and lapped toward the floor.

The next piece was a birdhouse with a pitched roof. An oversized blue jay — *cyanociita cristata* — balanced precariously on the roof's edge with a perplexed expression on its face. Peeping into the house through the circular bird-door, I saw tiny trapeze artists bent from thin wire swaying to and fro, reaching for one another.

As I opened each box of artwork, I saw waves of Gabby's creativity fanning into the air around me. Brilliance, both dark and joyous, began to imprint itself upon me in some animalistic way. Her creativity was seeping into my pores. Emotionally moved by the various works of art Gabby had created over the years, I marveled at every single piece...and these were her throwaways, the forgotten lot. *Amazing!* Every medium was represented: pencil, woods, metal, glass, stone, oils, charcoal, clay, ink, digital.

Charcoal drawings of old men sitting on Central Park benches left smeared soot on my fingers. Marking the trail of my hands, ashy fingerprints stained the outer sides of the cardboard boxes. Oil paintings of abstract figures ripping at their own flesh, heavy with dried clumps of paint that rose like peaks and valleys on the canvas. Closing my eyes and running my hand over the images was like reading Braille. The figures came to life underneath my touch — standing upright, bending over, lying down, sitting, even lurching out at me, it seemed. Flashes of deep reds — pomegranate, merlot, cherry wood, scarlet, raspberry jam — bled from one side of the frame to the next.

Another box was half-full of leaflets announcing a variety of galleries Gabrielle had either visited or exhibited her work at. The Vancouver Art Gallery showed abstract features of women; the Gargosian Gallery in Chelsea, New York, had an exhibit of black-and-white photographs titled *Days Gone By*; the Lemongrove Gallery in London displayed novels made into modern art pieces; Istanbul's Bienniel Gallery presented *Metals Made Meaningful*; and more. Newspaper articles were neatly piled, as if to be slipped inside a scrapbook one day. Some, aged with time, resembled the faded yellow of an overripe banana. I chuckled to myself, again thinking of how antiquated a newspaper was these days.

Each article — carefully cut to capture stories of Gabby, her art, the art of others, galleries, featured restaurants and travel destinations — lay on the floor before me. I rifled through the soft, thin slivers of paper and pretended for a moment that I was with her, visiting these places, tasting the food, commenting on the art, and sipping hot coffee. "One day," I said aloud, echoing through the apartment like a lonely voice distending out into a canyon. Enjoying my time alone, I was also happily waiting for Gabby's return.

An article different from the others, depicting a vehicle, caught my eye. With gentle shoves I pushed away the other stories to uncover the title of this one. Picking it up, I realized I was clasping a dagger in my hands; *to dare a heart is common, but to taunt one is cruel.* This article spurred malice. My heart had been tried, fractured and broken, but now something new was spreading under my skin. My heartbeat pulsed and pounded, as if someone were trapped in the cavity of my chest, pounding and clambering to break out. A tremor moved through my arms. My hands quaked, causing the words on the page to blur.

I was staring at Jax's death — the accident. I couldn't fathom why Gabby would have saved this article so many months ago before knowing me. I had not read this or any other story about the accident. In fact, I had avoided them at all costs.

Pedestrian Killed by Drunken Taxi Driver. The words leapt off of the page and stuck to me like searing hot glue. Reading the recount of the accident, I noticed words like *trauma, fatal, intoxication, voluntary manslaughter.* I had little to do with the aftermath of the accident — I was too messed up to get involved. Jax's family leaned on one another during the cab driver's trial and shared with me his sentence: the prick got twenty years. It turned out he had a history of DUIs. *How on earth did this monster have a license to drive a cab?* Fury combusted inside of me all over again. My ears were hot, my mouth wet with saliva as I swallowed hard to control the sobs rising in my throat. Lucas Colibrì, 68 years old.

"Fuck you!" I yelled at his picture at the top of my lungs. "Fuck you!"

The door of the apartment swung open. Gabby laughed out loud as she pushed through with bags of groceries in both arms. She glanced at the boxes. "Hey, you got to take a look at my stuff!" I could tell she was happy and excited, unaware of the discovery gnawing at me. I must have looked so pitiful, sitting there on the floor with the articles and leaflets strewed all around me.

"What the hell, Gabby?" was all I could muster.

A blank confused stare met my gaze, her face now erased of all joy. I held out the article in my hand like an offering. Perplexed, she moved toward me, looking down. I became so small sitting beneath her, like an ant about to be crushed underfoot.

"What is it?" Her voice was hesitant.

I started to read from the cutout square of paper in my hand: *"Young man hit while crossing the street…"* Barely audible in quakes of tears and anger, I shared scraps of details snarled from the article. *"The fatal accident was a result of intoxication on the part of a taxi driver."* The words poured forth and hung in the air bitterly, as if sour milk had been used to paint the walls. My stomach was crawling up into my throat, slashing against my breaths as a machete cuts into an overwrought thicket. *"Survived by loving parents Vaughn and Samantha Ryker."* Tears cascaded down the curve of my cheeks, following my jaw line to the tip of my chin. I watched them fall into my lap, forming a wet patch slowly growing bigger on the thighs of my jeans. "Why do you have this, Gabby? Why?" I wanted to throw it at her, shake her. "Why?" I shouted again.

Gabby's body slowly bent down to move in beside me on the floor. Her hand reached for my face; I couldn't help but turn away from her. Her tattoo was out of focus so close to me, but I could see it out of the corner of my eye as a bluish, black blur of flesh. I wanted to shove her into a place where she couldn't be seen and hold onto her all at once. Her hand found the back of my neck and softly squeezed it, as if to say, "I got you."

"Tell me why you have this, Gabrielle," I insisted, as if I had the right to know. "I need to understand." *So arrogant of me, so bold*, I thought.

"Let me read it," she said as she started to pry the crumpled paper from my grip.

"I don't want to hear it!" I snapped. "Let go, for fuck's sake! I just read it myself. I don't need to hear it, too! Don't say his name, Gabby! Don't you *dare* say his name!"

A vulnerability I hadn't seen until now came over Gabrielle. Now she looked like a little girl, lost and scared. I couldn't make sense of what was happening, the significance of the situation, the meaning of the article, and why it had been safely tucked away in *her* boxes.

Gabby started to read in a whispery tone as delicate as a lullaby, *"Long time taxi driver, Lucas Colibri, has been charged with DUI and voluntary manslaughter..."*

"Lucas? Lucas," I repeated with embarrassment and shame. The puzzle was starting to resemble the contours of reason. This was not just about Jax or me. This was bigger. The ground seemed to open up beneath me; a crevasse was creating a lesion separating Gabby from me. The parting was happening before she even had the opportunity to fully know how this crisis was related to me and my life. Remnants of previous conversations between us suddenly lit up the dendrites of my brain and I placed the name Lucas into context.

"He was your dad?" I asked, quite certain I already knew the answer.

"Yes, Ave. Lucas was my dad. I told you, he left my mother and me when I was younger. It was because of the drinking. I knew he struggled with alcohol, but I was shielded from the full extent. It wasn't until the accident that I learned of how tumultuous things had become — drinking, losing jobs, DUIs. He was a mess, really in need of treatment. I had actually learned from an uncle that my dad had started in a rehab program, but it turned out he left. Couldn't hack life without a drink, I guess."

I stared at Gabby, fully aware of the haze that had blinded me. My mind was shuffling through every moment she and I had spent together, exhausting itself to rewind and relive each conversation to filter out anything that might have led me to this understanding. *Had Gabby ever mentioned that her father was an alcoholic?* Maybe she had told me he had gone to jail. No, he "went away." Only recently his first name, Luke, was shared. I cringed, yet never in a million years did I think he was the Lucas that had killed Jax. What now? Do I tell Gabby about the connection to Jax's death, or wait until I have time to process the whole thing myself?

"I need to go," I said through a crackling voice. Like someone drowning, it was as if I had just been dragged to shore. Gasps and gurgles of brackish water seemed to fill my lungs as I stood in her New York City apartment. With my bag slung over my shoulder I started for the door.

I didn't look back into Gabby's face, but the squeeze of her hand around my wrist as I passed by her was the tender touch I needed.

"I don't get it, Avery. What am I missing? I swear we move forward, and then we slide backwards. I really don't get it."

Pausing and looking into her green eyes rimmed with tears, I placed a hand against the side of her face and ran one finger down her forearm. She knew this was my way of saying "I love you," and with a turn I was compelled to walk away. Again, my full confession would have to come later.

The phone rang over and over again that night and throughout the next day — an irritating buzz I ignored until the evening. I didn't have the words to explain the wedge that was now cleaved between Gabby and me. Her father had killed Jax — I knew this, but she did not. At eight p.m., I summoned the courage to call her, though I still didn't know what words would come to me, if any at all.

"Gabby?" I whispered in practice while the phone started to ring.

"Hi," she said. She knew who it was but spoke not another word.

My pulse increased. I'm not sure if it was due to the sense of safety in our distance — the fact that her eyes could not rest upon me — or the sense of guilt for wanting to explain my response to her over the phone. The guilt convinced me to meet with her, despite my cowardice wanting to discuss the delicate details only by phone. The intricate web that bound us together had extended itself far beyond just our feelings for one another. She had a right to know this, too.

"I have to see you, Gabrielle," I began. "There's something about the accident I need to share with you."

"Yes, of course," she breathed into the phone. She seemed anxious. I imagined her thoughts were spinning in various directions, wondering if my reaction was a response to her father's prison sentence or his alcoholism. Certainly, she was wondering why I was so concerned. I had been with Gabby long enough to know she didn't suffer from the same illness. "Do you want me to come to you?" she asked in such a hurried way I could tell she was already headed toward her parked car.

"Yeah, that would be good." I pondered what she would do when she realized who *I* was in this story. Would she cry alongside of me? Would she hush me like a child? Would she run away uncaring, cold? This, I did not yet know.

Rummaging through my closet, my hands reached blindly onto a high shelf that held the secrets I had been hiding. My fingers wiggled beneath old sweatshirts and bags I hadn't used in ages. The smell of old perfume I had worn in college faintly swam in the air. My nails finally tapped against the wooden box I had found under Jax's bed one summer. I fell in love with the intricate leaf-carvings on its lid and its bird-shaped iron hinges. Jax had given it to me for Valentine's Day once, and now it cradled my few and precious memories of him. As I pulled this holder of keepsakes down toward my chest, the scent of cedar and his cologne filled my nostrils. I released a deep, steady sigh. My lips pursed tightly together.

Stepping down from the stool, my strides pulled me to the bed. It had been so long since I had last looked inside this small chest. Every sound around me amplified: the tick of the clock, the hum of the neighbor's TV, the chopping of a helicopter outside. The time-capsule in my hands permeated a stale energy that had been tucked into the recesses of my dark closet. Purposefully shelved memories now awaited my attention, clamoring at the lid's surface, straining to get out.

Opening the box was like setting the last bit of our history free into the room. The ring Jax's grandfather had given him was wrapped in a handkerchief embroidered with Jax's initials. A small drawstring pouch held a diamond ring I later found with a note addressed to me. I don't know when he bought it — he never proposed — and I wondered if he had intended to or if he had changed his mind after our last separation just before the accident. The note remains sealed; to this day I have never read it. Honestly, it didn't matter if he had intended to propose; he had not. Maybe it was better I didn't know, leaving me with fewer broken pieces to put back together after he died.

I picked up a beautiful pen, his favorite. Its ink was dry now, but I liked its weight in my hand. Its shiny silver and blue hues were a part of what appeared to be marble or granite. Although much of his architectural work was done in pencil and with computer software, he always outlined one final blueprint in ink from this pen. I guess ink had a finality that pencils and printers did not, in his mind. A few photos of us together were tucked inside the box, along with a compass necklace I had once given him. True, he was the one person before Gabby who had made me feel like my life had direction. Though only a few small, inanimate objects were couched in this wooden box, they gave me a comfort I cannot describe. A connection to Jax was somehow encased in each item like a varnish that could protect and preserve every single memory I knew was actually fading one day at a time.

The faint echo of Gabby's knock broke the quiet. "Coming!" I yelled out as I leapt to my feet with the box under my arm. As I opened the door, a sense of déjà vu bumped up against me. Gabrielle's demeanor was a little standoffish; the brittle wall between us was difficult to ignore. A forced half-smile was pinned to her face — I could tell she'd had enough of my silent treatment and was tired of guessing what pulled me away from her at times.

Her exasperation met me at the door. "Avery, I care for you, but I'm done with the games. What the hell is going on? You dredge up a painful memory of mine and make it about *you* somehow? I don't get it. Really, I don't." Her eyes fluttered, looking for a place to land that precluded any contact with me.

"The accident," I began with trepidation, "has meaning to me, too." A quiver started to creep into my vocal cords, as if a teeny-tiny person were strumming them like a harpsichord. "Your father, Lucas, the driver — I didn't know who he was until yesterday."

"I don't get how my father has anything to do with you, Avery, or us." She pulled out a chair from the kitchen table and sat. Her leg jockeyed up and down in nervous stomps, the heel of her boot lightly tapping against the ceramic-tiled floor.

"Jax. Christopher Jackson Ryker," I said, waiting to see how the name might resonate with her.

"No..." Her eyes flashed toward me, big, frozen.

"Yeah, Jax is Christopher Jackson Ryker. I had no idea your father was the same Lucas who hit him. Gabby, who would have thought, right?" My hands were folded onto one another. As I sat across from her at the table, my entire body thawed like a bowl of ice cream left in the sun, becoming one with the very chair that was holding me upright.

"I never realized Jax was a nickname. Oh, my God, Avery. What the hell does this mean?" The gears in her head seemed visible to me. "My father killed Jax?"

Her confusion was palpable, each expression overt and fleeting in the same way a water-bug lands and then flits away from the surface of a pond. Her balance was suddenly tenuous, as if she were a lily pad leaning and tilting on a wake drifting near shore. And I was becoming a lonely and desolate island — or, better yet, an anchor sinking to the bottom of the dark water she was floating upon. In this moment, all we had become was evaporating before us. It was all nearly incomprehensible, but nonetheless real.

We said nothing. All words had fallen out of our grasp, and our tongues were cast in iron. As we sat, the space between us became unfamiliar and dank. The apartment felt hollow, though filled with a mountain of things that suddenly had no value, no meaning. A vacuum was consuming the memories we had built together over the last months and pulling them into a place I was afraid would be long-forgotten. How to end the awkwardness? Here we were faced with the measure of what a true relationship could withstand, yet only absolute silence filled the apartment.

CHAPTER 17

Anchor

While we were still reckoning the accident in the silence, the lights flickered, the clock on the oven flashed, and darkness fell as if literally floating from the ceiling down to the floor. Another power outage had just fallen on the block, and a collective sigh reverberated throughout the high-rise. This was the second outage this summer. The first had occurred while I was visiting Gabby's apartment, but now here she was at my place. Again, we were trapped in the blackness. Swimming curtains fell still as the late August air-conditioner softly rumbled to a hush. Heartbeats pumped softly against my inner ear — *fewff, fewff, fewff.*

I got up to look for the flashlight under the kitchen sink. Gabby offered to grab the candles stored in my bedroom. As her delicate footsteps pattered down the hallway to my room, my imagination — running away with me now — assumed this was the last time she would ever walk to my bedroom, down my hallway, or be present with me in my home.

"What timing," I uttered into the stillness, upsetting the canister of Comet in the cupboard as I grabbed the flashlight.

"What?" Gabby shouted back.

"Nothing, nothing," I mumbled, surprised she could hear me at all.

The apartment started to come to life in the darkness as my eyes adjusted to it. Now all of the furniture stood out, clearly resembling giant animals on the prowl at dusk. Gabby, no doubt, was fumbling amid all of the framed photos on my dresser, looking for the candles and matches in a drawer. I heard one open, then close, then another.

"Got 'em!" She approached me, one hand stuffed in the front pocket of her jeans.

"Thanks. Here." I handed her a table-runner with a glass of wine. We set up our makeshift confessional while adjusting pillows on the couch and sitting at opposite ends, careful not to touch or graze each other in any way. I felt alone even in our togetherness.

"Avery," she finally said softly and hesitantly, "what are you thinking right now? I don't know what to say. I am sorry. I had no idea my father had anything to do with Jax. I would have told you long ago if I had made the connection. My father's in prison, and Jax is gone. Can you even articulate what's going through your mind right now?"

"No," I responded solemnly. "I really can't."

I wanted to slap *her* for something Lucas had done. Fear was burrowing inside my mind, realizing that each time I looked at Gabby I would be forced to remember Jax. Wasn't that how it was going to be now? I had finally reconciled my love for her, but how could I make peace with knowing that death was somehow channeling its way through her and back to Jax? Faulting her was wrong, but my soul felt overcome with blame and condemnation.

"Angry," I said tearfully. "I am angry and fucking bitter, right now. We had such a good thing, Gab. It feels tainted, wrecked, ya' know? What *do* we do?" I cried, gripping the pillow in a fit of disappointment. "How do I look at you and not see *him?*"

Gabby sat quietly for a moment and then stood up, pushing herself away from the couch. A part of me wanted to pull her back, pull her against me, beg her to stay forever. My hand impulsively grabbed hers. She squeezed it sympathetically and apologetically before conclusively walking toward the door. "'Bye, Little Bird." She left the apartment, closing the door behind her with the faintest sound.

A dull ache assailed me. Again, as if I were a sinking anchor, the haunting horror of the cold, dark depths surrounded me. My ears seemed to fill with water, muffling the sounds of the city. Floating past me now was Gabby, her lush hair flared out around her face like a lion's mane. She was looking at me but plunging further and faster than I, toward the bottom of this blackened pit. She was waving and falling past the long, sinewy rods of seaweed jutting up from the sandy floor. And then she was gone.

We hadn't spoken in several weeks. I missed her more than I wanted to because I hadn't figured out a way to be with her. My fingers found her name in the contacts of my phone, but I resisted making the call. I wondered about her and longed for her most minutes of the day and night. The Hive exhibition of her Breya photos would be opening in a week. How odd the way our lives had been woven together by chance, historic relationships, tragedy, and love.

The thought of Breya brought me back to the moments when I had fabricated her life, pretending I had known her. Gabby's photos of her mother and Breya captured it all, eliciting the feeling that I was actually there, hiding behind a curtain, many years ago. Like a voyeur looking in on Breya's life, a time machine had taken me to her — or I had been nestled in her backpack. Secretly, it seemed, I had watched her travel the world. This was certainly a far cry from the crotchety old lady who used to pick blackberries and ignore me.

My assistants at the gallery had carried out all of the communication with Gabby for the show. Her work would be up for the public for one month. Surreptitiously, I was rooting for Gabby, excited to see the photos (some taken forty years ago), depicting two women friends jumping from country to country together. How uncanny it was that Breya and Gabrielle's mother were friends — true friends. *How rare a friendship*, I thought.

With anticipation I waited to see the installment in its completion: frames hung, lighting fixed, titles mounted beside each art piece. Gabby was the sole artist on feature for the Hive — a pretty big deal in SoHo. My eagerness to see her work, fully hinged on the possibility of also getting a glimpse of her. Though, I intended to avoid evening showings when I knew she would be greeting onlookers. Our avoidance of each other was serving us well, and I couldn't risk ruining that with a chance meeting that would catch us both off-guard while surrounded by others. Her special moment as an artist could not be stolen from her in this way or compromised by presence. This was Gabby's shining moment — one of many, I believed in my heart.

I rang Claire, hoping we could meet for dinner. She had been a lifesaver in these days without Gabby. In the many moments when I didn't know what to do with myself, Claire and I would talk, watch movies, share book reviews, and listen to the music she was studying. The absence of a romantic relationship helps one to re-evaluate how to spend free time, a luxury that can feel lost when in a partnership. Claire and I had become friends. When she was not traveling playing in concerts, we would meet for dinner, taking turns cooking for each other some nights. This might have been my best relationship in a while — shared cooking, my own apartment, and the ability to drink myself into oblivion, only to walk downstairs and fall into my own bed. No strings, no love, just conversation. Perfectly uncomplicated.

I'm being facetious — we were friends and I did care about her like a younger sister. I loved the way she spoke her mind; it was refreshing, actually! Claire was able to hold up a mirror in front of me and help me analyze my own shortcomings and celebrate my strengths. She was also able to dissect herself so accurately it seemed a bit ethereal for a woman in her twenties. She was witty and introspective — qualities I had not possessed at her age. I was grateful to have her sensibility around me, feeding me, keeping me grounded.

"What about Gabby's exhibit?" Claire winked.

"What about it, Smarty?" I retorted, tipping my drink in her direction one evening.

"You should go, Ave. It would be a kind gesture, if nothing else."

"I doubt very much she wants me there, Claire. We haven't even spoken. Shit, I don't know what I would say if we came face-to-face with one another."

God, that face… I would love to see that face, I said only to myself.

I couldn't help smiling, and Claire just smiled back. The thought swam inside me now, and each nerve tingled, as if little electrodes were sending impulses filled with adrenaline throughout my entire body. Visualizing Gabrielle's face in my hands, just a breath away, made me happy. What else can I say? I loved her and never got the chance to tell her so. I closed my eyes and shook my head, as if it would whip the thought out and away from me.

"What?" Claire asked slyly. "You are thinking of her! I can see it in your face. I knew you still loved her. I knew it!"

"Shut up," I laughed, sloughing off her comments. "Yeah, I really do," poured out of me as I slunk deeper into my seat. "I totally love her."

I could see a twinkle in Claire's eyes, as if this acknowledgment bound us more tightly together as friends. I suppose it did, really. She was the shoulder I had leaned on in these passing weeks after Gabby had walked out. Claire had helped me muddle through the insanity that intricately knitted Gabrielle and me together. Blame had turned into forgiveness, and I had learned that every negative emotion I was feeling needed to be aimed at Lucas, not Gabby. Gabrielle became my scapegoat, and I her nemesis. Was our relationship irreconcilable, unsalvageable? Perhaps there was a way to bring our shipwreck to the surface, haul it to shore, and restore it to its original beauty, but it would take time. It would take patience. It would take a skill that maybe neither one of us possessed.

As I lay on my bed that same night, my mind was lighter and heavier, like a wisp of air on a hot summer day and a bucket of lead at the same time. I was overjoyed with the prospect of talking to Gabby, of sharing how I felt toward her, and simultaneously petrified that she would not be able to summon the strength to return my affection.

As I tucked my arms around my pillow, a faint stab poked at the back of my hand. Jerking back and away, I flipped the pillow to find a sealed letter. I knew this handwriting — it had been a while, but it was evident all the same. "Breya!" My heart sprang open like an unhinged door. My name was clearly scrawled across the front of its envelope. I opened it and read its contents:

Dear Avery,

It seems you have found forgiveness in your heart for the one you love. Hold onto it, run toward it. Do not let it escape you. Trust yourself and the friends you have in your life. They are all

good people. My connection to you, though rare, will flourish
with each heartbeat. Your life fuels my own. I will be your
lighthouse.

Sincerely,
Breya

I slipped the letter into the drawer with the others. A night of rest overcame me like no other. I decided to find Gabrielle. I doused all inhibitions in gasoline, lit them on fire, and let each spark fly where it may. The desire to chase my heart, even if I never caught it, was guiding me.

The leaves in Central Park had assumed their autumn tones. The air was crisp and cool. Gabby's exhibit was opening that evening. Battling within me was the urge to go to the Hive against my initial (maybe rational) urge to stay away. The coffee I made went cold as I pictured her — what she might be wearing, who might attend the exhibit, the expression on her face as others gaped at the creativity of her own art hanging on the walls. Closing my eyes, I felt as if she were next to me, breathing on my neck. I stretched and tilted my head, rubbing the spot where her hot breath had once landed on my skin. Thoughts of Gabrielle's touch and the taste of her lips were incessant. She was never far from me, yet I wondered if I crossed her mind at all. I was growing impatient, as the entire day was still ahead of me, making each minute seem to stretch to the length of an hour. Maybe going to her exhibit would be a mistake. The questioning, the second-guessing, was driving me mad!

Sneakers and leggings pulled on, I headed out the door for a run. Earbuds in, I found a pace that matched the rhythm of the music flowing through me. The morning was bright, but not a lot of people were stirring just yet. Jogging in this remote area of Central Park transported me back to upstate New York as orange, red, and yellow leaves cascaded through the air, coating the fields in a burning bronze blanket. Vendors were already out hawking coffee and muffins, and the birds were chirping their goodbye song before heading south for the winter. My lungs were full, expanded.

"Avery? Is that you?" a voice darted from behind a cart steaming with cocoa and java. It was distorted; my music was too loud. Looking around, I saw no one. "Wait minute, slow down!" the voice called out a second time.

Confused, I pulled away one ear bud and looked around again for the faint call that had come to me. Left, then right, I glanced. No one was there.

"Ave, it's me," the voice whispered from behind with a slight tap on my left shoulder. I turned around. Gabby and her green eyes were standing before me — burning through me.

"Oh my God, it's you," I stammered, totally caught off-guard. *Shit, keep it together*, I prompted myself, for my impulse was to wrap my entire body around her and never let go.

"Yeah, it's me." She smiled and tugged one sleeve up, exposing the bird about to take flight with those in the park. The gray scarf draped around her neck was sweet with her fragrance. I inhaled it deeply as we leaned in for a polite hug. I couldn't resist putting both arms around her and holding her seconds longer than I should have. She seemed a little surprised, and smiled wider as we parted and stood looking at each other, as if lost and now found. "Okay, then," she said shyly.

"Sorry, I didn't expect to see you. I was caught by surprise. A good surprise, Gab." I could feel the word-vomit starting to come out of my mouth and thought it best just to leave, fearing I would become a sappy ex looking into the face of a lover who was only laughing at me on the inside. With a quick step back I turned to go, and then offered, "Good luck tonight, Gabby. You'll be great."

"Wait!"

"I gotta go. Meeting a friend." I lied.

"Don't leave, Avery." Her eyes were wet with tears and her hand was reaching out toward me. Her saunter was cool and calm, but everything about the space between us was hurried, rushed. In a blink, we were embracing. Tighter and tighter we hugged and rocked each other, soothing the hurt that lingered from our separation. My hands held her face while her long, wavy hair fell between my fingers. I kissed her, confounded that this public display of affection did not dissuade me in the least. Simply put, I didn't care who saw us or what people thought. We had a right to be in love.

Our lips parted, and we stared at one another, afraid to break the connection that was tying our souls together yet again. "I woke up thinking of *you*," I admitted. "I wanted so badly to call and come to the show tonight, but I didn't want to ruin this special time for you. I didn't want to get in your head if you had moved on." My hands were shaking, even though Gabrielle was holding them.

"You've *never* left my thoughts, Avery," she said passionately. "Not once! I go to sleep thinking of you and wake up missing you. I've never been so connected to another person in my life. With you, I've shared my fears and goals for the future. I've never done that with anyone. I know what food you like and hate. I already know your annoying habits, and..."

"Wait! *What* annoying habits?" I laughed, tucking a strand of her hair behind her ear.

"Seriously, Avery. I had come so close to saying, 'I love you,' but always resisted being so exposed."

My heart seemed both restricted and open at the same time as I heard Gabrielle share her feelings, like a vise grip tightening around the muscle itself and then splitting open as if to invite more love, more honesty, more gratefulness. My brain was labeling it fate — arriving at this exact place in Central Park at the exact same time. We had accidentally stumbled upon each other on this day, as if it had been meant to be all along. She was my love, and I hers. *Yes, I loved Gabby!* I was able to acknowledge this emotion now, and I wanted to own every ounce of it. I was in love with *her*. All doubts had been exonerated.

"I love you, Gabrielle. I completely love you."

"I love you a *little*, not a lot," she said back to me with a smile and a wink.

The evening at the Hive was ideal, more than I had imagined in truth. The sky, lit of amber the color of spiced rum aged in an old oak barrel, ensconced the city. Streetlights began to flutter to life like fireflies at dusk, signaling it was time for the gallery's doors to open. Gabby and I had planned on taking a taxi, but I called us a limo for the special occasion.

Together, we stepped out of the car, holding hands and matching strides. She was my someone special, and I was hers. This was whom we had become — a couple in love, making our way through the evening. We didn't know how the pieces would all come together for us — we just knew we wanted them to.

CHAPTER 18

Fonder Heart

Weeks morphed into months as Gabby and I came to know each other through stories about growing up, family, work, and aspirations. Ordinary days and evenings became most cherished moments. Making dinners together, fighting over which bottle of wine to open, who had more room in the closet, or which movie to watch gave me a comfort I had longed for in a relationship. She made me laugh every single day and challenged my thinking, too. I wondered if I gave her as much as she gave me. Gabby fueled me with a desire to offer more of myself to the world, to others, to strangers, even. And I marveled at the tender underbelly of all that defined her. She was concerned about the whole of society: the treatment of women, children, and refugees. My own empathy for others was further developing, and I found myself absorbed in issues of human rights and social justice.

Between working at the gallery and creating art pieces that reflected contemporary sociopolitical messages, we volunteered at Reprieve International. The organization offered a rare opportunity for us to highlight grassroots activities in the community and around the world by drawing on artistic images to bring global issues to the forefront of people's minds. A growing sense of obligation crept deeper and deeper inside of me toward the causes we represented. A bifurcation of self yielded both the artist and activist in me. I could be an agent for change; art could reach people, move people to act.

This newfound sense of agency, the urge to have an impact on the world through expressive arts and social justice, started to wage a war in me. I wanted to be more of a voice with the oppressed and stop watching life from the periphery. I needed to find more balance between selfishness and selflessness. Gabby and I became regular supporters of campaigns to combat poverty and torture and to ensure international civil rights. Most individuals eventually come to a point in life when they stop, look around, and ask, "What am I really meant to do? How will I impact another?" This was that pivotal moment for me.

Gabby and I had been living with one another in my apartment for nearly ten months when the opportunity to join a delegation with Reprieve International in Thailand came to me. A group would travel abroad to document how art is utilized to bring attention to human trafficking, especially its manifestation among women and children in the country. Thanks to the United Nations' zero-tolerance policy for human trafficking, the problem has not only been acknowledged as a serious human rights threat but also opened the door for various organizations to create a system of networks to tackle the issue. A curiosity about the progress that has been made in this arena gnawed at me. I contemplated an invitation to join the Reprieve group for six months in the northern provinces of Thailand.

Intrigued at the prospect of traveling to a faraway exotic place also drew me in. I knew I could take a sabbatical from the gallery, since the trip would encompass art, and I would make plenty of contacts that would likely benefit the Hive. My thoughts were buzzing with excitement, the kind that sets your mind adrift at odd moments in the day. Daydreams started to take over my thoughts while sitting on the subway, walking down the sidewalk, or cozying up with a book. Not only did I want to go — I *had* to go. *Here's an opportunity to contribute to a social need, start doing my part,* I thought. Broaching the topic with Gabby would be difficult, I imagined, since she was bound to New York for a while to complete a job she had been contracted for by *Architectural Digest*. Would she support my opportunity to go to Thailand or offer excuses as to why I should stay here? I really didn't know.

Details of the delegation's work, the travel plans within Thailand, and the sheer energy of those I had met who were going on the excursion, convinced me to commit. Planning to talk to Gabrielle after I had made a decision, independent of her input, was important to me. We had been living together for nearly a year, and our relationship was stronger than ever, but ours did not require getting *approval* or *permission*. That might be the toughest thing about being in a loving partnership — balancing the needs of the one you love with your own. So many of my friends had lost themselves over the years by transforming into their partner. *What is it about a committed relationship that can sometimes make people give up their own sense of identity?* I did not want that to happen to me, yet in this moment I was afraid. I worried that this self-made vow might come at a cost.

Praying in the quiet of our bedroom, I sat in a chair with my eyes closed. When I opened them and stared at the hardwood floor, a million faces seemed to look back at me, coming to life as the various knots and wood-grains melded into shapes and shadows, casting little eyes, noses and mouths across the floorboards. Similar to looking up at the clouds and turning shapes into figures, the floor converged to create a jury of onlookers judging my decision to go to Thailand. Some appeared to weep, others to smile, some undecided. My mind was made up for certain, but my heart was unsure. Pushing all doubt aside when I heard Gabby's keys in the front door, I lifted my head to go and meet her.

"Hey, you!" she said, smiling and throwing her bag on the back of a chair. She always greeted me this way, and I loved knowing *you* was me. Her arms wrapped around me and we kissed after looking eye-to-eye for a brief moment. *Those green eyes, I so adore!*

The usual how-was-your-day check-in ensued as she kicked off her boots and started toward the bedroom to change. From the kitchen I yelled, "Red or white?" and pulled two glasses down from the cabinet.

"Red," Gabby shot back, then started telling me about some guy on the train-ride home. Distracted to the point of indifference, my oblivion was obvious, as she whistled to get my attention while sliding onto a stool at the island.

"Shit, sorry, Gab! My mind was elsewhere. What about the train guy?"

"No biggie. What do you want for dinner? I can do chicken and salad.

Sound good?" She sipped the wine I had placed on the island, leaving a lip-print on the glass that caught my eye. I suddenly became aware that it was the small things like a lip-print on a glass I would miss while I was away.

"Babe," I said, "you know the work we've been doing with Reprieve and the art project we've chatted about? I've been seriously considering the impact of going abroad and getting involved for a bit. I've been mulling it over for a while now. I've been unsure of my level of commitment until recently. It's a six-month stay. You've mentioned how amazing the trip would be, but we've never really discussed it seriously. We both always talk about how we value the independence and dependence we have between each other, and I..."

I couldn't look Gabby in the eye. The clinking of pans and the rustling of food in the fridge stopped. I still couldn't look up at her. A delicate hand reached beneath my chin, pulling my face upward. She stood in front of me silently. Her hair fell both in front of and behind her nearly bare shoulders. Her eyes were glistening and aglow, but she was smiling.

"We got this," she said. "I know you've been thinking about going. If it calls to you, go, Babe. I'll be here when you come back." She winked. Her arms swaddled me as if I were a baby, and we rocked from foot to foot in the kitchen. This was another reason why I loved her. She gave me a sense of freedom and belonging I had been unsure really existed before knowing her. I couldn't believe she had met my decision with such enthusiasm and support.

As we cooked dinner, Gabby chatted about the details of her *Architectural Digest* gig, confiding that it would make it impossible for her to visit while I was away. "We'll probably be able to message each other every day, so it won't even feel like we're apart," she tried to convince herself.

"I don't think the rainforests in Northern Thailand are fraught with cell towers, but I like your positive attitude," I teased her. But my heart was singing with the vibration likened to that of a choir. *Unbelievable! She is really unbelievable,* I kept thinking.

The rest of the night we looked up different places in Chiang Mai, Chang Rai, Phayao, and Nan. We laughed about the many cultural nuances I would have to learn, so as not to offend anyone: avoid touching anyone's head, keep feet pointed away from others even when sitting with legs crossed, and so on. Gabby shared the few Thai words she remembered from a visit to Bangkok she had made several years ago: the words for "hello," "thank you," and "bathroom."

Thailand's northern provinces were green with jungles and rife with Buddhist temples called *wats*: Wat Pray Singh, Wat Chedi Luang, Wat Rong Khun. The intricate ornaments and carvings that outlined the images of temples we found online mesmerized me. The Office of National Culture Commission boasts that more than 34,500 temples speckle the countryside, along with mountains and rice-fields, while limestone cliffs and islands dot the Gulf of Thailand at the southernmost tip.

Yes, I was going! The allure, the adventure, the work were all summoning me, and I was ready with absolute abandon. Gabrielle would be with me every step of the way, metaphorically speaking. She was ingrained in each of my thoughts.

The morning sun warmed the glass as I pressed my palm against the window, trying to memorize the view from our apartment. Gabby and I had been living with each other happily, and our plan was to consider our time apart as a work endeavor. *Six months would pass quickly,* I kept telling myself. The time to leave was upon us, and this afternoon I would board a plane to Chiang Mai. Two suitcases and a backpack lined up neatly near the front door gave me a brief chill. The scene, taken out of context, looked more like an ending instead of a new chapter.

I breathed in the stillness, aiming to awaken my every sense before leaving my comfortable life behind for a short while. My coffee tasted extra sweet as I basked in the quiet, secretly hoping Gabby would wake up. It was impossible to stop reviewing the list of items I needed to pack. Resisting the urge to shove extra things into the lonely bags at the door, the luggage locks were clamped with a final click. They looked like little soldiers standing at attention.

My last day with Gabrielle would end in three hours under the eyes of public spectators checking luggage and standing in torturous airport lines. Our hug would be long, but our kisses short, in a place that would not be our own. This morning would be my last chance to feel her face against mine, cheek to cheek, and press our lips together for some time.

No doubt my heart would remain here at home with her, tucked inside a safe built of our loyalty and commitment. Our goodbye was really a "See you soon," but it hurt just the same.

"Love you a little, not a lot, Little Bird!" Gabby said in her own special way. She wiped the tears from her cheek with her sleeve and hugged me hard.

It was nearly impossible to let go of her. "Love you, too! Be back before you know it." My heart was undeniably manacled to her.

CHAPTER 19

Dust and Distance

My flight would last twenty-two hours with a two-hour layover in Singapore. The seat was as big as a recliner, enough room to lay back and relax for sleeping. My Reprieve International group totaled seven people, including myself. We had all met and worked together on previous projects in New York, but none of us really knew each other well, yet. In our six months in Thailand we would share housing, travel together, and work together on everything — photo shoots, interviews, focus groups, dinners — so that our lives would weave into one collective experience.

Reality told, no matter what we experienced together, these moments would never really be a true collective. Each of us would have our very own distinct takeaways from Thailand. The memories would be unique to each one of us, depending on where we had come from and where we would be going afterward. Undoubtedly, they would reshape how we saw the world and, perhaps, how the world saw us.

As the Bangkok airport doors opened, a wall of humidity assaulted me, melting the cotton shirt onto my skin. A drop of sweat dripped down my spine as I became drunk with the sweet scent of *phuang malai* flowers corseted together, forming a *Thai lei* around my neck.

"*Sah-waht dee, kha!* Welcome to *Thai-lan*," a young woman said, ushering our group into a snow-white minivan. "Your driver name,

P'Tang. He take you to hotel, and tomorrow we go *Chiang Mai* by train. Good nigh."

Her infectious smile was now pinned across the face of everyone in the group. We were simply awestruck by the everpresent feeling of being somewhere so steeped in history, so ancient and different from what we all knew. The smell of the air was distinct, the vehicles unfamiliar. The roadside, even in the dark of night, looked unusual.

I sensed that this would be an unforgettable time for me. If the whole of my life was contained on one roll of 35-millimeter film inside an old camera, I knew that this frame, Thailand, would stand out from all of the others. Gabrielle flashed into my mind, and my heart knew sadness as subtle as a blink yet as painful as a pinprick. Already I was missing her. I think that is how real love is internalized: it is experiencing something new or beautiful and wishing that special person was beside you taking in the same moment. I wished Gabrielle were here with me to see every new sight that baffled me, surprised me, astounded me. A part of me wanted to share this time with her so that, years down the road, we could say, "Hey, remember that time in Thailand when..." Yet another part of me was glad to call it all my own.

The van ride did not allow us nearly enough time to recalibrate our internal body clocks, which would take days. Fluorescent blue lighting sprang from the van dashboard setting P'Tang's face aglow. At two a.m., Bangkok was buzzing. Food stands dotted the curbside, wafting in the intermingled aromas of barbeque chicken, pork, and beef. Sour, pungent smells mixed with the toxic stench of exhaust fumes. P'Tang rolled up the windows, exchanging the night air for the air-conditioner, a much-welcomed relief from the hot, stale air encapsulating the city. "Thank you," a few of us echoed.

"No problem," he replied with a grin. I could see his eyes darting back and forth from the road to the rearview mirror, trying to get a look at each of us. As his eyes met mine, his friendly smile widened. "You all from U.S.A?" he asked in a soft voice. "Welcome!"

He actually knew where we were from; he was merely trying to engage in polite conversation. P'Tang was a driver with the United States Embassy. Our visit with Reprieve International was a partnership between the Thai and United States consulates. P'Tang would be our guide for the duration of our trip, shuttling us from village to village, interpreting the tongue of every Thai we encountered, while channeling our thoughts and words back to them. *He'll be a gift,* my intuition told me. The honking of horns and flashing of lights suddenly overtook me as the city boomed with the din of cars, sirens, music, and yelling voices.

Gold-framed temples reflected lights, illuminating the dark skies. Fountains sprayed water into the air, forcing traffic to maneuver in circular patterns around the base of the structures. There seemed to be no rhythm to the flow of taxis, buses, motorcycles and *tuk-tuks* as one cut off the other and bobbed from lane to lane with no signal, no warning, no rationale. I couldn't help but marvel at the sheer chaos of it all, and yet the lack of incident or accident.

At last the hotel came into sight. P'Tang said it overlooked the Chao Phraya River edging though the city. The moon was full, a giant flashlight in the sky. Looking down from the bridge, I could see chocolate waves swishing and meandering through the grassy shoreline below the steel and concrete of the city. Palm and banana trees lined the hotel drive, while tropical flowers popped in shades of bright orange and red around a lit walkway. Running water trickled from nearby fountains. This opulence would starkly contrast the places where we would be staying and visiting up north in the coming days. My body was craving a shower, sleep, and stillness. Morning would soon be at our doorstep, calling us to the train headed for the jungles of Chiang Mai.

My room was cool from the air-conditioner. Crisp white sheets clung to the bed in perfect corners. Towels lined up with precision hung in the bathroom. Fresh flowers stood in a clear vase, half-filled with water on the nightstand. My heart was full and hollow at the same time. Excitement about the adventure ahead fueled me, yet a longing was stripping something from me. Adjusting to days without Gabby would take some time, some getting used to, I supposed.

The hotel room phone lit up and rang all at once. I answered it. "Hello?"

"Hi, Avery. We'll be meeting for breakfast downstairs at eight a.m., then we'll head out to catch the train at ten. Sound good?" It was Darion, a woman from London who was leading our small delegation through the six months. She and I had worked together on a couple of gallery projects back in New York. She was a total gem!

"Yeah, sounds good. I'll see you then." My voice was a little scratchy from a lack of water on the long flight, and sleepiness was starting to overcome me. After a cool shower, I fell into bed and tucked into the sheets without loosening them. They wrapped around me tightly, as if securing me to the bed so I wouldn't roll out. I let the night sink into my bones, rendering my body heavy. My eyelids closed, my lips parted, and a long, soft sigh blew toward the ceiling like a summer breeze. A woman's face came to me like a mirage, and her stunning green eyes met mine. A small hummingbird fluttered between us, and I knew then that I would feel Gabby's presence no matter where I went or how long I would be away.

Breakfast allowed our group to rejuvenate, chat, and plan for the day ahead. Darion, Mark, Steffen, Madison, Aubrey, Ethan and I shared where we grew up, discussed family, and revealed our motivations for coming to Thailand. Darion, Madison, and Aubrey all had careers in human rights. Madison and Aubrey were lawyers specializing in refugee rights and asylum. Ethan and Mark were involved in nonprofit or nongovernmental organization (NGO) project management.

Instantly I connected with Steffen, a photographer who had spent twelve years with *National Geographic*. He saw the world as one giant canvas — "an artist's studio," he said. Like Gabrielle, Steffen saw people and landscapes through a camera lens, which transported others, including myself, to places we may not have otherwise visited. There seemed to be a bit of magic in people like him and Gabby, turning destitute places and people — who sometimes had seemed to have lost all hope — into reflections of ourselves (or vice versa). The human spirit resides in all of us. Sometimes it is lonely and quiet, perhaps only an inch from despair; other times it is joyous, peaceful and inspiring, like children laughing and playing in the spray of a fire hydrant on a hot day. I wondered what kind of human spirit would penetrate our work here.

"It is time," P'Tang announced as he stood, his bowed hands meeting at his chest as if to pray. "We will drive to train station to head to Chiang

Mai. It is a long journey, and we will sleep on train tonight. Many hours and very hot. Please bring all bags, we meet in lobby in thirty minutes. My friends, our trip is just beginning! Bring bottle water and good book. We arrive in Chiang Mai at four a.m. tomorrow."

"P'Tang," Darion began in her soft but committed voice, "should we bring food or mosquito nets?"

Smiling, as always, P'Tang responded, "We will have for you, Ms. Darion. Let me share, we will sleep once in Chiang Mai and then gather for three days to learn about culture, good care, and help others. We learn some Thai language and make plan for the stay for the months ahead. Okay?"

"All right, ready!" Ethan chimed in.

A sense of relief came over all of us as we realized we would team together to sort out our stay, to work, and to contribute to the causes we were investigating and representing. It would be imperative to gain a sense of the culture with guidance from the Thai nationals.

General calmness intertwined with slight nervousness as we all looked half-sideways at one another, as if to say, "Here we go!" Huddling into an elevator, we headed to our rooms to collect our bags and gear to meet with P'Tang in the lobby. The leather bracelets Gabby had given me slunk around my wrists. I fiddled with them, pretending she was next to me in this incredibly small space — an abstraction, I knew, but to me I was touching *her* arm, not mine. The comfort these bracelets brought to me was golden. *So very far away,* streamed through my consciousness into an inaudible whisper.

Arriving in my room, I grabbed all of my items from the bathroom, put them in my bags, and zipped up the pockets. A Snickers bar and a book lay atop the smallest backpack; I shoved them inside a front compartment for easy access. Turning to leave, I made one final sweep of the room, and noticed a letter leaning against the lamp on the side bed table. *Avery* was written across the envelope. My heart sang. It had been so long since I had received a letter from Breya, I began to wonder if I imagined their existence. I opened it and read:

Dear Avery,

The wonderer wanders. Here you are so far from home and yet right where you need to be. I envisioned walking with you,

always, but sense that I may not be able to keep up much longer.
Oh, I do not know the rules, the answers to these riddles, I just
walk the path before me. It seems to be leading me into a fog.
I cannot see too far ahead, but the haze is bright and seems to
be calling. Maybe it is my time to succumb to another life that
awaits me, a space where I am not stuck in the in-between but
exactly right where I should be. I do not know, but it is this
uncertainty that tells me I may not be able to reach you again.
I believed my connection to you was as unbreakable as iron,
but perhaps I misunderstood. I do not want to let you down.
Forgive me if I can no longer reach you, it is not my hope or my
choice. I will look for you always and hold you dear to my heart.

Always,
Breya

As I sat at the edge of the bed, my head dipped low and my chin quivered. I remember feeling fear and confusion when I first started to find the letters Breya had left for me, and now I had begun to look forward to them. I sensed her looking over me at random moments in my life — a guardian angel of sorts. *She can't leave me, not now.* I tucked the letter into my backpack, convincing myself that another would surely find its way to me one day soon.

Breya had become a conduit to what I dubbed the afterlife, yet it was a secret I kept all to myself. Images of those days when I was a child and watching her pick blackberries came to me. Her stained fingertips flooded into my mind, but now she seemed kind…waving to me. Like a slow-motion film, there she stood with her white, white hair, but she was smiling a sweet smile never noticed before. My little girl self waved back and smiled, too. And I watched as she turned and made the long, slow walk back to her tiny home.

"Avery, I'm headed downstairs," Aubrey's voice boomed through the door. "You comin'?"

Startled, I responded, "Yeah, yeah. I'll meet you down there!"

My throat was dry, my body trapped between sorrow and longing. A sense of finality was creeping inside of me, but I wasn't sure if it was real or something I was unintentionally making up, based on Breya's letter and this vision. *Was this goodbye? Was she leaving me? Where was she going — to heaven, to hell, to guide another?* My mind whirled, hoping she would be okay. Bags in hand, I strode to the door and closed it gently behind me.

When we were all gathered in the lobby with our bags in tow, P'Tang lead us to our van so we could head to the train station. Our insides shook with excitement! We really were off! Flashes of orange lit the corners of my eyes ablaze as Thai monks in bright citrus robes with silver metal bowls in hand walked down the sidewalks in a pensive line.

"What are they doing?" Mark asked.

"Collecting rice, breakfast," P'Tang said.

Madison shared what she had read in her *Lonely Planet* guidebook: "Over ninety percent of the Thai population is Buddhist. The religion first took root starting in the fifth century."

"What about the collecting of rice?" Aubrey prodded. "I see the monks being beckoned by people as they pass by. The Thai people are waiting to meet them in front of their homes, it looks like."

"Alms," P'Tang interjected. "Each day, monk walks barefoot to show humility. No need for all the things so many of us can live without. When monk is offered food from villagers, he take with grace and thanks. This is only meal some days — one. Monk do not cook."

"Imagine the peacefulness of their lives," Ethan said in a hushed mutter, staring out the window with his forehead pressed against the glass.

"Everything is so distinctive. We've only seen the tip of the iceberg!" I chimed in. "Completely unmatched by anything I've ever experienced. I've traveled to a handful of other countries but this place exudes mysticism. Every sight and sound creates an ambiance of allure."

"You sound like a real romantic, Avery!" Mark quipped from the last row of seats in the van. "I wonder if you'll feel the same way when you're balancing above a squat-toilet, trying to splash water on your ass!"

"We'll see," I responded, shooting a wink over my shoulder in Mark's direction.

Mark and I had been pals for a while. I had met him through Gabby, actually. They had met at Columbia University and had only recently reconnected through Reprieve International. They had lived in the same dorm their freshman year on South Lawn. One too many times they recounted drunken stories that had unfurled outside of Butler Library from their days together as artsy outcasts. Gabby loved to reminisce about the time they had convinced their resident assistant, Rachel, to go downstairs to the union lobby at one a.m. in her skimpy T-shirt to check the sprinkler system because it reportedly was a "fire hazard." When she got down there, Rachel found herself surrounded by her entire dormitory floor, only to be hosed with shaving cream and handfuls of confetti in celebration of her twenty-second birthday. She was a graduate student studying biophysics and the study of formation — whatever the hell that was, I didn't know. But Gabby was always sure to share that detail whenever she told that story, so it must have had some significance.

Neither Gabby nor Mark ever told me they had been romantically involved back then, but I could glimpse the residual energy between them. It was quiescent, dormant like a sleeping volcano, but slightly detectable. It didn't particularly bother me, but I wasn't blind enough to believe that passions between two lovers couldn't be reignited, given the proper circumstances. Yes, Gabby and I now loved each other, but I have always seen love as a very fluid emotion — sexuality, too. Love can come and go, change shape and function. I am not proposing I wish this to happen; I am just honest enough with myself to recognize that it can. Despite the lascivious past Gabby and Mark had shared as college friends, I have seen a deep and respectful friendship form between all three of us, which I cherish and trust.

The drive to the train station took about an hour, given the city traffic. I was thinking about the letter from Breya and realized my right hand was instinctively protecting it, pressing firmly against the small turquoise backpack on my lap. The others had been kept in a drawer at home, untouched, for some time now. I needed to be sure this one was kept safe so I could add it to my collection. They were proof, in my mind, of an *after* I couldn't explain — an after-*what?* After-*life?* None of it made sense. However, if I didn't have those letters to hold onto, my sanity would be in serious question. It scared me, haunted me with a wondering I dared not share with anyone. Breya was like an invisible thread connecting various points in my life together. She was my watcher. At times she was the very stitching that kept me together, even when I was threadbare. Breya had become a binding agent, allowing me to be whole and introspective, as opposed to worn and frayed.

"Avery? Avery?" Darion said in her precious British accent. "Your train ticket, Love."

"Oh, thank you," I said, snapping out of the caged thoughts rattling in my head.

P'Tang parked the van, gathered us in a circle, and gave us a quick rundown of the train's amenities: a shared bunk area with one other group member, bottled water, and a bag of snacks. "Remember, keep bags close," he said. "Inside of bunk against wall of train. Try to take in the scenery but get sleeping. Move about as much as you like, we have long ride. Have fun! I am Bunk 24, if need me before Chiang Mai. We arrive in fourteen hour." He motioned with his hand that his bunk was down the narrow aisle a short distance.

The bunk areas were half of the size of a small room on a cruise ship. *Cramped but only temporary,* I told myself. The train lurched, chugged, revved. I could see little boys in flip-flops running outside beside the tracks with baskets draped on their shoulders. I couldn't tell what they were selling. Their small hands waved feverishly like windshield wipers. "'Ello, 'Ello, 'Ello!" they yelled and hooted. Dust swirled in the air around their speedy feet like a cartoon. Their demur bodies faded away among the clay dirt as the distance from them steadily increased. Soon I couldn't see the boys at all, but their soft, high pitched, voices shouting, "'Ello!" continued on until they fell silent to the train's hulking lumbering.

"Goodbye, goodbye, goodbye," I yelled back from our bunk's open window, smiling.

PART II

Gabrielle

CHAPTER 20

Returning

Gabrielle sat up in bed, unable to let sleep seize her fully. A full moon was framed in the top left corner of the white windowpane, casting the fluttering shadows of the curtains onto the ceiling. Some nights were lonely, like this one. Avery had been gone for five months, and the anticipation of her arrival in just a handful of days made sleep a lower priority this evening. She would be coming home early but the details were hazy as to why. Internet connection had been pretty spotty, and often the Skype calls she and Avery had shared were interrupted, brief, leaving her with a mouthful of words she was unable to express. Why Avery was coming home a few weeks early didn't matter so much to Gabrielle — the important thing was that she would soon be back in New York City. Gabby envisioned walking in Central Park together, matching each other' stride the way little kids sometimes do.

Gabby thought the days would fly by while Avery was away. Immersed in work herself, she anticipated having little time to miss her. This did not quite turn out to be so. Keeping busy, she came to realize, did not replace longing.

The days were fine. Gabby selected jobs that would take her to one end of the city and then the other on photo-shoots. For a month and a half she drove to New Jersey, Connecticut, Massachusetts, New Hampshire, and Maine for a project on the history of lighthouses along the northeast coastline. The nautical serenity inherent in the work brought a wave of tranquility to the secret lonesome that had taken up space inside of her. But she missed Avery the most when the stillness of nightfall tiptoed in. Perhaps she especially missed the silly banter that ensued between them while getting ready for bed. Or maybe it was Avery's foregone warm body pressed against her, transforming them into mirrored silhouettes like the arc of a bow. Avery would snuggle close from behind and talk into Gabby's ear. Thinking of the tight wrap of Avery's arms around her now made Gabby curl up into a ball like a frightened caterpillar and weep.

As Gabby made her way along the New England shore hunting for lighthouses, she was taken aback to find some were dilapidated, forgotten. These treasures had fallen out of the *bag* of American history, much as grain might have spilt from the corner of a torn burlap sack in 1910. Framing the beautiful and neglected in her camera lens offered her a sense of purpose. She sent Avery a photo of each lighthouse and a handwritten letter each week. Both seemed to be a lost art this day and age — real photographs to hold in one's hands and handwritten letters scribed in ink.

Gabrielle imagined Avery riding on an elephant through a rainforest in northern Thailand while reading her letters, fanning herself from the exhaustive heat with whatever weekly lighthouse photo happened to be enclosed. In reality, Gabby knew that the weekly letters sent by airmail actually piled up in a one-room post office in villages scattered throughout northern Thailand. It was P'Tang, the driver, who gathered the letters and hand-delivered them to Avery before the group moved on to a new village every few weeks.

But that didn't matter. Gabrielle held onto to the adventurous momentum these daydreams brought her, imagining Avery sitting high on a stool in the middle of a watery rice field, reading about how she was missed, adored and remembered while far from home. The achy loneliness that swallowed up Gabby at the end of each day was about to come to a close. It would not be long until Avery filled the apartment's empty spaces again. The time between now and then made it easier to start counting the days — twenty-eight to go. Even Claire had started to get excited at the thought of her neighbor and friend returning to the States. She, too, had corresponded with Avery but mostly through Facebook. She checked the Reprieve blog to stay abreast of the issues and uncoverings of her friend's trip, too.

With Claire's help, Gabby decided to redecorate the living room. Inspired by Southeast Asian flair, they left ample wall space for Avery to make her own once she returned with the artwork she had been creating. Many of her photos for Reprieve International told destitute stories of abandoned children, addiction-bound communities, and the human spirit hanging on by its fingertips to promise and potential. Despite the social and political shortcomings emblazoned in Avery's photos and letters, hope was etched on the faces of the Thai people. These, Gabby imagined, might adorn the transformed living room. Children smiling with arms slung around the shoulders of friends or siblings, a mom holding the hand of a son walking to school, a farmer sitting cross-legged and looking up at his wife standing beside him — these were some of the samples Avery had posted online.

It was surreal to know that Avery would soon be standing across from her again, leaning on their kitchen island. They would return to sharing stories and discussing everyday life's mundane routines. The *ordinary* suddenly seemed so special. Gabby planned to have dinner at Claire's to get away from the overpowering odor of the freshly painted walls they had just rejuvenated. It would be a nice respite from perseverating on Avery.

As the spongy new towel drank the water from Gabby's skin, the phone rang above the voice of Cheryl Wheeler singing "Almost" from the speakers on the living-room mantle. She tugged on a pair of sweats and a shirt. Gabby shuffled her feet toward the phone, expecting to see Claire's name and number reflected. A name registered as Unknown flashed, and the country code of Thailand appeared.

"Oh, my God, Avery!" Gabby was flush with excitement, for phone calls between them had been a rare gift. "Hello!" she said, aghast with excitement. "Hello," she repeated into the silence. "Avery, are you there?"

The dull, low tone of a male voice she recognized came to her ear: "Gabby, it's Mark."

"Mark, hi. What's up? Where's Avery?" Salty saliva pooled in

Gabrielle's mouth. "Mark, what's up? Where is Avery?" she repeated in a voice teetering between quiver and quake. It made no sense he would be calling her.

"Gabby, you need to sit." Mark cleared his throat, only to be gagged by an obvious paralysis of the vocal chords. She could hear his breaths through the phone and the clearing of his throat. She wanted to hang up, quickly, and stop the moment altogether, before words could be said that she could not unhear.

"Gabby," Mark said again.

A barely audible, "Yeah?" pushed through an intuitive fear building inside her chest.

"I, uh…" Mark started to stammer. His voice was suddenly stuck in the same place as hers now, somewhere between that of a lost youngster and a scared adult.

Gabrielle lowered herself to the floor and let her hand fall to her lap. She looked down at the phone, which projected Mark's voice, as he was…13,378 miles away. He seemed so small, so very, very far from her. But his voice could still be heard, even as the phone sat on her lap.

"Gabby? Gab?" Mark pinged over and over again.

She raised the phone, laying it to the side of her face. Tears glazed her eyes. The room turned blurry with the sudden swelling water level, as though she were slipping underwater. Mark's voice, muffled, rendered a nearly imperceptible hum in her ear, even though the receiver was again close to her head.

The news pelted against Gabrielle's body like icy hail in a winter wind. Jagged edges stung and cut her, no matter what direction she turned. The details were foggy; she did not have the strength to listen to them, let alone absorb them or make sense of the matter. Only fragments of the conversation streamed into her consciousness. She tried to organize the snippets she heard: in two days the delegation would be gathering at Reprieve's headquarters in New York; Mark was driving a motorcycle; Reprieve would be meeting with Avery's family to share details; he was sorry; Avery was not alone when she died.

The pressure in Gabrielle's head was explosive, causing her breaths to pump out in short quips of air. "No, no, no, no, no…" screeched in quick syllables, her tongue tapping the roof of her mouth in rapid succession.

Her grip on the phone intensified to a near-crushing strength. "No, no, no, no, no…" was compulsively and rhythmically ensnared on repeat.

Mark's voice was suddenly gone, and a long dial tone took its place. He had hung up. Mark was coming home. Avery was not.

Gabby's anxiety was muddled her shock like a bitter toxin. The trappings of denial and anger pressed down on her, as if the ceiling itself had dropped, literally resting upon her chest. She punched at the wall until her knuckles felt as if they had turned to a fine powder.

"No, no, no, no!" she wailed into the quiet afternoon. Drool slipped from the corner of her mouth as she shouted and screamed at everyone and no one. Her throat was raw from the yelling by the time her neighbor, José, and a security guard banged on her door.

"Ms. Gabrielle? Are you there? Can you let us in?"

"I'm here too, Gabby. It's José. You all right?"

The sound of a key turning in the door clattered but the deadbolt was also locked. Gabrielle had installed it herself.

"Gabby, open up!" José banged on the door. He sounded rattled for sure.

Confused, dazed, shattered, Gabrielle approached the door, wiping the tears from her face with the back of her bloodied hand. She looked as if she had been beaten, assaulted. Before she could crack the door open herself, it was kicked inward. José fell toward her, grabbing her with outstretched arms.

"Holy shit, Gabby! Holy shit! What happened?" Instinct drove José and adrenaline jetted through his veins like heroin. Pulling Gabby into the hallway and shielding her with his body, he scoured the apartment for a would-be assailant. "Who did this, Gabby? Who?"

"What? What do you mean?" Gabby's face was contorted, as if she were attempting to decipher a complex code. "No one. There is no one," she said, trying to wriggle from his grasp. "What the hell, José?"

"I heard you screaming, Gabby. Banging, punching, crying. Christ, your hands are covered in blood. What was going on in there? I thought you were being attacked! It sounded vicious!" José's eyes were the size of quarters and they kept darting between Gabby and her apartment door.

"It's Avery."

"Avery? Avery did this to you?" José said, bewildered, disbelieving the prospect of Avery lashing out in any way. Gabby could tell he was trying to surmise how she and Avery could ever be in a position such as this. They were always so gentle to each other.

"No, no, she isn't here, José. Avery is gone."

"I know, Thailand, right?"

"She's dead, José. Avery is dead. I lost it, that's all. I lost *her*. I got a phone call...I don't know..." The words were so incredibly vile Gabby started to vomit in the hallway. The scene was graphic: busted-up hands, blood smudged on her face and the wall, and now puke on the twentieth floor of the opulent apartment complex.

José had no idea what to say next. There were no words, really. The security guard stayed with Gabby after taking a look at her hands, the wall, and the last phone call received on her cell. The men cleaned the wall, wiped her face, and wrapped her hands in ice. It was a kindness Gabby did not expect but graciously accepted.

"Let us help you get settled in," the two insisted.

"I should go to Claire's. She was expecting me for dinner and she's a friend of Avery's, too. I'll be all right." Gabrielle appreciated their kindness but she needed to be near a friend when she fell to pieces.

José walked Gabby to the elevator, and together they rode in suffering silence to the twenty-third floor. His arm felt awkward around her waist and the strong smell of his cologne now stuck on her. She knew he meant well.

Claire, answering the door in complete unawares, became the catcher of Gabby's hurt, pain and loss that evening. Claire did not ask a solitary question but instead took Gabby in her arms like a caring sister and waited for her to talk when ready.

The evening was an assault on time — the entire world had been claimed by an immeasurable pause. The TV had been muted, the street lights refused to go out, the sun delayed its rising. Hot tea, pacing, and reliving the phone call received from Mark — the snippets now permanently impressed into Gabrielle's mind — fed the evening. Claire gently patted Gabby's back as she watched her friend finally cry the sun awake. It was hard for Gabby to make sense of death, to find a purpose in its existence sometimes.

CHAPTER 21

Discovery

The days immediately after Avery's passing seemed not to have happened at all. Erased from Gabby's short-term recollections, she remembered nothing of them, no matter how hard she tried to summon the minutes, the hours, the days. The entire month was a collection of only splintered thoughts. Pieces of reality intermingled with blackouts and visions birthed from sadness.

Gabby understood that she would receive a copy of the accident report from Reprieve International through certified mail. The power of attorney rights she and Avery had exchanged before the trip were materializing. Gabrielle had not joined Avery's family for the debriefing at Reprieve's headquarters and sadly fell out of contact with them soon after. Yes, the broken pieces of her life created an ugly mosaic, which she knew she must reconcile as her new reality. It was difficult for her to fully accept that Avery was really gone, vanquished from the earth.

What happened to bargaining, depression, and acceptance? Gabby wondered. She thought of a blogger, Megan Devine, who had once written in the *Huffington Post* that the stages of grief — first explored by Elisabeth Kübler-Ross — were "meant as a kindness, not a cage." In other words, the stages were intended to help people make incredibly fucked-up circumstances bearable. They were not meant to be a guidebook in dealing with the shit the world throws at us. The aim was not to make people feel they were grieving the *right* way or the *wrong* way. However, the stages have done just that, for many. Gabby wondered if she was grieving the right way, the wrong way, or just *her* way.

The phone rang, but Gabby got in the habit of ignoring calls and listening to the voicemails instead, and selectively choosing who and when to call people back. *Privacy is a funny thing,* she contemplated. More and more people were squandering their privacy these days. Every minute detail of their lives — the personal, the mundane, the ordinary — was becoming food for fodder on social media. The lines among trusted friends, acquaintances and strangers were blurred, rubbed out, obliterated, leaving most people with no sense of privilege when it came to hearing another's story. Gabby, too, lost site of the boundaries by which she had kept the people in her inner circle close while keeping others at an arm's distance. Most of her relationships were gradually evaporating.

Cognizant of the voicemail alert on her phone, she reluctantly entered her pin to listen to her messages. Anticipation tugged at her open wound, so she halfheartedly lent an ear while neatening the living room, straightening pillows, putting dishes in the sink, and organizing unopened mail.

"Hey, Gabs, it's Mark. Just calling to check in, see how you're doin'. Call me. Love you. Miss you." These messages came often from him, but Gabby rarely picked up, or even called back.

In her mind, their friendship was now tainted, damaged in ways she did not know how to repair or restore. Unfairly, she acknowledged, she was holding Mark accountable for Avery's death. He seemed never to mention Avery or the accident when they did talk, almost as if it never happened. Perhaps his trauma was so great he needed to forget. Yet Gabrielle's was so great she needed to understand. *And why the 'love yous'?* Gabby wondered. *For Christ's sake, he isn't exactly the touchy-feely type. We haven't shared an 'I love you' since college. Exaggerated guilt, maybe.* Whatever the reason, Mark's calls came often and always ended the same way, clenching Gabby's intestines into a knot every time.

A claim ticket landed in Gabby's mailbox on a Tuesday in the form of a yellow receipt for pickup at the local UPS store. The items were described as two three-by-four-foot boxes from Thailand. She needed a taxi to get them home, especially in the rain. Stuffing the slip into her jeans pocket, she hailed the first cab moving through the drippy streets.

"305 West Broadway," Gabby stoically said to the driver, shaking the droplets off her hands and wiping them dry across her lap.

"Uh-huh," grunted the man behind the wheel.

He made eye contact with her in the rearview mirror and continued to stare at her for a few more seconds. A decorative elephant charm dangled from the mirror, creating sparkling flits of green, blue and pink as it twisted and turned on a beaded steel chain. Gabby considered its significance to the man: *Is the man, in this sense, the elephant or its driver? Does the ego control him or does he control the ego?* Gabby decided that the man must be the driver of the elephant and, of course, the taxi. Their eyes met again. They exchanged smiles.

He only slightly resembled the man in the ID card on the dashboard. The long black beard that had once outlined his chin no longer sprouted from his pores. And a Yankees baseball cap replaced the turban that had once covered his head, making him appear younger than his picture suggested. Gabby guessed he is, or once was, Sikh. *How long did his hair fall before cutting it?* she wondered. *And why would he do such a thing?* Something in her wanted to put a friendly hand on his shoulder. She looked again into the rearview mirror and saw his eyes concentrating on the traffic, darting left, right, left, then straight ahead.

A deep sigh escaped her like the emissions of an exhaust and pressed outward, creating a torrent of hot breath. The smell of the taxi's ocean breeze air-freshener intensified in her nostrils, burning a little. Gabrielle realized this was the first time she had been in a cab since her father hit the man she would later find herself inexplicably connected to. Summoned memories of Jax — ones Avery had shared — whirled inside Gabby's mind, along with the box of keepsakes Avery once showed her. Gabrielle ran one finger over the tattooed hummingbird on her arm and thought of her lost Little Bird. Unaware of the irony of the situation — as Gabby was now remembering *her* Little Bird — she was thinking of the lover who had first dared to claim Avery as *his* Little Bird.

The rides were quick, both to and from the UPS store. Gabrielle needed to make two trips to her stoop: one to collect the box from the trunk, the other to grab the box from the back seat. The driver just sat staring at his phone while Gabby struggled to move the boxes. "Come on," she muttered under her breath. The cab driver was watching her from the side mirror now, with no intention to get out and lend a hand. "Prick!" she murmured in his direction.

He got out, only to extend his hand for the cash. "Eighteen dollars, thank you."

In truth, she felt impatient and annoyed at the driver's lack of assistance and dearth of chivalry. She gave him a small tip with her payment but hurried away, feeling a little embarrassed. The unknown items waiting to be discovered inside of these boxes caused a tense tremor to travel up both of Gabby's arms. Slinking its way into her stomach, her eagerness turned to stone and sat heavily inside her. The return address read *Chiang Mai, Thailand* in a typed black font in English, then in Thai Sanskrit.

The rain had waterlogged the boxes a bit so she rested them on an old towel on the floor. Her hand shook while she wedged one side of the scissor's edge between the box and the brown packing tape. The seal broke along each side with an unobtrusive pop, and she turned the box to sit squarely in front of her. Kneeling, she raised herself above it and pulled one flap, then another, then a third, then the final up and outward. She figured the box would contain some answers about how Avery died. The detailed report that Darion said would be sent to her was here. But Gabby doubted she would ever have the stomach to read it.

Sure enough, a manila envelope addressed to Gabrielle, stamped CONFIDENTIAL in partially faded block letters, sat right on top of the box's foam stuffing. Perhaps it *was* time for her to decipher the details of what had happened the day she lost Avery. She nervously opened it and pulled out a forty-eight-page document. Skipping the names of the investigators, the volunteers, the mission of the organization, and the reason for the group's stay in Thailand, she flipped to page fifteen, where the specifics of the accident and injuries began to be outlined. She ran her finger below the text as she read.

The accident, she learned, had taken place in the small hill-tribe village of Pai in Mae Hong Son province, population 2,284. While traveling the winding mountain road on a motorcycle, Avery and Mark had been hit by an oncoming Toyota truck — "sideswiped," she remembered Mark divulging. Gabby had once read in a travel magazine that Pai had become a popular tourist destination, affording trekkers beautiful waterfalls and up-close encounters with elephants, but Route 1095 was known for its treacherous curves, narrow pathway and ambivalent drivers. Avery and Mark had been on their way to meet the rest of the Reprieve group to investigate the town's recovery after devastating floods and mudslides had swept over the hill tribe village in 2005. Paramount to the group's work there was researching and reporting, through art and images, evidence of police misconduct and the drug trade. Known drug routes connecting Burma and Thailand had scarred the people of Pai.

Gabby recalled Avery's pre-departure discussion about the Thai War on Drugs, declared in 2003 by Thai Prime Minister, Thaksin Shinawatra. Avery had wanted to learn more about the laws allowing the killing of 2,000 people who were accused of involvement in the drug trade. Like hunting season, imaginary permits had been issued, and ordinary people had started to seek out and shoot anyone suspected of perpetuating the drug problem in Pai. Avery had found the deaths to be such an injustice to human rights they had started to keep her up at night: void of any defense, regular citizens were literally given permission to shoot any supposed drug trafficker, seller or dealer with no repercussions. Vigilante law had been accepted for a brief time but had quickly become a source of mourning and a blemish on the Thais of Pai. Those related to the slain people had discovered that it was their own neighbors and friends who had taken the lives of their loved ones. *How does a community recover from this?* Avery and Gabby had both wondered.

A picture of a red 1983 Toyota pickup truck with notes about its make, model, and license plate number stared back at Gabby from the report. Also detailed was an image of the motorcycle Mark was driving, notes about the road they were on, distance in kilometers outside of Pai, and the weather conditions and time of the accident: sunny, cold season, 63° Fahrenheit, 17.2° Celsius. 3:10 p.m. It seemed like an ordinary day. *The same thought might have even crossed Avery's mind,* Gabby realized. Mark's injuries seemed inconsequential, and Gabby had no patience for his suffering. *He lived, didn't he?* She skipped to the boldface text: *Jolen, Avery, deceased, age 43.* Her injuries read like a grocery list in simple, concise bullet points, but Gabby couldn't go on. "Not now," she whispered. "Not now."

She pushed the report aside and removed the box's foam stuffing to reveal Avery's small turquoise backpack, emblazoned with red tape marked with the word EVIDENCE. The bag appeared to have been gently raked across the rim of an opened tin can, leaving one side shredded with lacerations and the other side fully intact. Dark grease stains traversed the 'I Love NY' patch that Gabby had sewn on before Avery's departure.

Gabby lifted the backpack out of the box and cradled it in her tattooed arms as delicately as she would treat a newborn baby. Goosebumps transformed the texture of her skin, its surface like bubble wrap. The fine hairs of her forearms stood up straight. "Ssshhhhh," she whispered to soothe her escalating sorrow. The bag did not make a sound. It did not move. The stillness with which she stared down at it reflected the same stillness that haunted her nightly in the bed she and Avery formerly shared.

She pictured Avery cold, alone, dead beneath the earth. This thought rankled any sense of peace Gabrielle had managed to make of this senseless loss. She was afflicted with this torment, the vision of Avery trapped beneath the moist ground. Gabby's own thoughts invoked a living hell, toured only in the quiet of night while lying in bed. Sometimes, Gabrielle would sit in a corner-chair in their bedroom and just stare at the vacant place on the mattress that Avery had declared was *her side*. *Her side* — now empty. Gabby herself was near to catching fire when she glared at the unoccupied mattress and perfectly creased comforter; to her, it seemed like a decrepit floating dock on a dark, dark lake.

Gabby let her head roll backward while closing her eyes to guess the weight of the backpack she was clasping in her arms. "Ssshhhh, I got you," she said again. Four black zippers safeguarded the pack's contents. Gabby slowly tugged at one zipper, which felt cold to the touch like the tab of a refrigerated soda can. *Zzzzzzzz*, the zipper lashed into the apartment's stale air. Then her fingers slipped inside the square pocket and pulled out a set of keys: the apartment key, a key to Avery's car, and three others she did not recognize. The lighthouse keychain Gabby had sent her from Maine instigated tears — soft tears, the kind that brush over cheeks lightly, feathery. Avery's favorite navy-blue signature pen with white polka dots pushed against the outside lining, showing its form. A pack of gum and a Chap Stick also rested in the pocket. All were anticipated items, but sad to see.

The backpack's next section was bigger, with a mid-sized pocket in the middle. *This is the cream of the Oreo,* Gabby thought. Again, the zipper belched out a string of *Zzzzzzzzz.* Opened, the pocket was a diminutive pit of black, like a pocketful of midnight without a moon. She tilted the bag toward the light from the window to peer in. Inside was a brown leather journal filled with Avery's handwriting. Blue ink created rivers of cursive writing across nearly every page. Tempted to read the journal, Gabby found herself unready, set it aside on a table low to the floor, and plucked rolls of 35-milimeter film, a small case of SD cards, and Avery's prized, robust Canon Rebel and its three lenses from the pocket's shadows.

A book with the paper jacket removed carried its title imprinted in gold lettering across the front: *What is the What,* by Dave Eggers. This was Gabby's most beloved book, which she had given to Avery as a going-away present. She cracked the binding open; the book appeared to have been dunked in a puddle. The pages were wrinkly but had long since dried.

What is the What, a Dinka myth birthed in Southern Sudan, offers the opportunity for one to contemplate the unknown. God offers a man and wife the choice between a cow (a certain source of sustenance for their family) or the *what* — the unknown. The book reveals the constant choices people make, drawing specific attention to the choices rooted in predictable outcomes and the choices that hinge on chance — the unpredictable, the unplanned, the unknown.

Life's biggest question, Gabby thought. *Do we accept the sure bet or take the gamble?*

When we come to a fork in the road while navigating life, we envision the *what.* We try to imagine the possibility of the unknown and balance that against the likely. Some of us might call the *what* hope; others might call it greed or indulgence.

Gabby thought of the *what* as possibility. She cherished this book and its painful story of Valentino Achek Deng, a Sudanese Lost Boy who walked thousands of miles to Ethiopia seeking refuge amid civil war. His salvation was finally realized in the United States. Gabby wanted Avery to experience this book, not only to learn about Valentino's struggle, but also to offer Avery the chance to explore how the question, *What is the What?* had manifested in her own life.

Reaching back into the center of the Oreo, Gabby discovered hand-sanitizer, sunblock, and an envelope with Avery's name written across it. The seal was torn open, and a letter waited inside. Pulling it free and unfurling it, Gabrielle read the letter aloud:

Dear Avery,

The wonderer wanders. Here you are so far from home and yet right where you need to be. I envisioned walking with you, always, but sense that I may not be able to keep up much longer. Oh, I do not know the rules, the answers to these riddles, I just walk the path before me. It seems to be leading me into a fog. I cannot see too far ahead, but the haze is bright and seems to be calling. Maybe it is my time to succumb to another life that awaits me, a space where I am not stuck in the in-between but exactly right where I should be. I do not know, but it is this uncertainty that tells me I may not be able to reach you again. I believed my connection to you was as unbreakable as iron, but perhaps I misunderstood. I do not want to let you down. Forgive me if I can no longer reach you, it is not my hope or my choice. I will look for you always and hold you dear to my heart.

Always,
Breya

Like a rainbow-patterned kite fluttering against a light blue sky, Breya's signature summoned every ounce of Gabby's attention. The mere word *Breya* was more than just the center of her focal point; it was the sum of it. "Breya?" The name felt familiar on her tongue but strange in the way a person struggles to detect a faint herb that has been added to a favorite dish. "Breya?" she said again to no one.

Comparable to a helium balloon slowly rising as it is inflated, the realization of who Breya was rushed to Gabrielle. Could this be the same Breya whom she had come to know through her mother's stories and photos, who had become the focal point of her exhibit at the Hive? She had studied her face for years and infused the old photos with modern techniques and care, literally transforming her into art. But how could it be *this* Breya? It couldn't be. The letter appeared to have been recently written — fresh ink, clean, crisp white paper.

Gently pushing the backpack away, Gabrielle stood, wrapped her hand in her T-shirt, went to the fridge, retrieved a cold beer and opened it. It was too bitter. She sprinkled a pinch of salt into the bottle, creating an erupting fizz that bubbled to the top and over the lip. She returned to the shipments and sat down, perplexed by the letter, the name, and the mystery encircling her. Indisposed to unpack any more items, she scooped up the 35-millimeter film, SD cards, journal, book and letter and carried them into the bedroom. She placed Avery's soft leather journal on the nightstand so it could be read in bed in the stillness of the evening. The other items she decided would be safe in one of Avery's dresser-drawers.

Avery had an antique bureau dating back to the early twentieth century. She and Gabby had found it one weekend at an artisan's market on 21st Street in Chelsea. The detail of the walnut wood melding into herringbone patterns had caught their eye instantly. Taken with the foliated molding and its charm, they had been absolutely sold when the woman who had restored it told them the price. Close up, the knotted, burled wood still smelled earthy. Gabby ran a hand over the smooth planks at the side and inhaled Avery's perfume still sitting atop the dresser. It was as if Avery were suddenly standing beside her.

She remembered that Avery had reserved the top drawer for random collections: movie tickets, business cards, letters from friends, bookmarks. Pulling the heavy wooden drawer open, Gabby saw pages of letters covering the small treasures she expected to find. As if reaching into a grab-bag, she pulled out the sheets of paper one at a time and scanned them. The handwriting was that of the Breya letter she held in her hand. The signatures were identical. Somehow, the drawer contained other letters from Breya. Although it felt like an invasion of Avery's privacy, Gabby had to read them — morsels of them, at least — to make sense of the words and find meaning for the sake of her own sanity, if nothing else.

Avery, there is more to this life and all that comes after it than you could ever understand. I have watched over you and my attention has cloaked many decisions you have made, both good and bad. Perhaps, our souls merged the day you saw me in the snow. You saw me and now I see you. I am but a guidepost without judgment...

Gabby knew this story. She could visualize Avery sitting in a chair in the living room with one leg propped over the arm as she told it to her one evening. The account of the clumsy moon boots on her feet, the snow falling, the blood-stained snow. Avery had seen the flannel robe and the "old lady next door" with the blackberry-stained fingers face-down in the snow. *It seemed to have tormented her, actually,* Gabby remembered. She shuffled the papers, and another segment of text leapt off the page:

... I squeezed your hand and felt your existence vanquish for a brief moment when he hit the pavement. You stood still as stone. I watched you stare at your apartment door, Jax on the pavement, and I felt you buckle inside. Death was deafening.

It can't be, Gabrielle said to herself. *Jax? Breya saw Jax perish? She was present, it seems.* The vision of the car barreling into Jax while Avery stood helplessly on the curb watching was eerie enough. But to conceive the presence of Breya there that day was accepting a ghostly phenomenon Gabby had never embraced before. Still trying to reconcile that the letters really were from the Breya who had traveled the world with her own mother was challenging, but to now imagine that Breya was leaving Avery letters from somewhere beyond the living seemed outlandish — an implausible reality. Gabby read another:

It seems you have found forgiveness in your heart for the one you love. Hold onto it, run toward it. Do not let it escape you. Trust yourself and the friends you have in your life. They are all good people. My connection to you, though rare, will flourish with each heartbeat. Your life fuels my own. I will be your lighthouse.

A timeline of sorts started to materialize in Gabby's mind, bringing with it a flurry of various conversations she and Avery had shared since they had first met. *We fought about the article, the car accident,* Gabby replayed.

The forgiveness of which Breya spoke was meant for Gabrielle — she knew this. Palpable regret over the misunderstanding when Avery had discovered the article and they had parted for a short time flooded back to her. *A misunderstanding,* she thought. *Half of the damn mishaps and missteps in life are affixed to misunderstandings, aren't they?* Thankfully, they had reconciled, despite Lucas, her father, being the bane of Avery's loss.

Gabby sat on the edge of the bed to read these letters again in their entirety. The closing of one of them particularly stuck in her mind:

> ... *Forgive me if I can no longer reach you, it is not my hope or my choice. I will look for you always and hold you dear to my heart.*
>
> *Always,*
> *Breya*

She placed the letters back into the drawer and pushed it shut. Gabrielle did not know what feeling was taking up residency within her heart, but her hands were quivering the way a leaf flutters in the cold before it falls. She stood still before the old dresser, the surface level with her shoulders. For a moment she rested her crossed arms on the ornamental ridge and bowed her head. All of her weight leaned onto the bureau, holding her upright. She could hear voices of her neighbors through the walls. They were laughing.

"Why didn't Avery tell me about the letters?" she spoke into the empty room. A sense of betrayal began to creep into her thoughts, but her inner monologue scolded it away: "No! No, she *couldn't* tell me. I wouldn't have believed it. Letters from a dead lady, come on!" A crazy kind of laughter spurted from her mouth. "I wouldn't have been able to hear it!"

But now what to do? she wondered. A wild crack in all rational thinking seemed to split her in two. She hurriedly pulled on her boots, snatched up the letters from the drawer, placed them back in the small turquoise backpack, and jetted from the apartment, her compass aimed in a very specific direction.

Claire stared at the backpack on Gabrielle's lap, then interrupted the stillness: "Can I get you something, Gab?"

Gabby noticed for the first time the sterility of Claire's apartment — few pictures, beige paint on the walls the color of desert sand, and some unpacked suitcases after a recent trip to play violin at a concert in New Haven, Connecticut.

"Tea," Gabby said. "Tea would be nice." She wanted to tell Claire about the newly discovered letters from Breya but couldn't even find the words to explain the phenomenon. *Really, how can they be explained?* Instead, she focused on the returned items from Thailand; the elusive Breya would have to come later. She felt her face warming, her interlaced fingers sweating.

"Can I see the backpack?" Claire timidly asked. Not knowing if her asking would provoke anger, she braced for what might be a torrent of insults stemming from the hurt enveloping Gabrielle.

"Yeah," Gabby simply said as she sniffed and handed the pack to Claire across the coffee table.

"It looks pretty beat up. Fuck, was Avery wearing it when she was hit?" Claire asked, lacking all sensitivity.

"I think so. The Reprieve report outlined what both her and Mark were wearing, injuries, weather conditions, possessions collected at the scene. I haven't looked at it that closely yet. Officials told the family that they considered the accident just that — an accident by an oncoming pickup truck. The roads are so damn narrow in Pai the investigators didn't feel they could charge the truck driver with reckless driving."

Claire took another sip of her tea. "Tell me," she said with sad eyes. "What else did you find in the bag?"

Gabrielle listed the contents she had discovered so far — Avery's journal, sunscreen, the book she was reading — until her attention was abruptly consumed by the item Claire was pulling from the backpack: Avery's small Sony camera with its thin, black, broken wrist-strap.

"You look shocked!" Claire said. "Did you see this?"

Gabrielle said nothing for a moment as she reached for the scuffed Sony. "No. No, I didn't! I guess it blended in, being black. The weight of the bag didn't even register; I guess it was too light, too small, and uh...My mind isn't right, Claire! It went unnoticed. I never even noticed it. I can't look at the pictures by myself. Come over and sit with me." She sounded like a scared little girl.

The women scooted tightly together on the oversized chair, and Gabby turned on the camera. The photos in the viewfinder looked so real, so relevant — only a hair shy of the actual living moments. Brilliant green foliage framed the Pai hillsides, beautiful Thai faces beamed with smiles, and red dirt roads cut through the village, ascending toward the sky in winding twists. Gabby smiled, and then began to cry silently. As a close-up of Avery filled the viewfinder, Gab's chest heaved with a breath of surprise and heartbreak. Avery's smile was brightly blinding and kind. For a moment Gabby blinked feverishly while laughing and sobbing at the same time. It was her Baby, her Love.

Claire squeezed Gabby's knee and put an arm around her trembling friend. "It's okay," she whispered. "It's gonna' be okay, Gab."

According to the Reprieve report, Avery had been sitting behind Mark on the motorcycle taking pictures as they traveled Route 1095 the day of her death. She had often spoken of taking photos while riding on the back of the bike and the freedom it had born. She and Mark had been assigned as riding partners for the duration of their work.

The next round of photos on the camera became a silent movie. Gabby held the advance button, the photos moved in a swift progression, displaying a series of moments one right after the other. In slow motion, the details of Avery's accident became animated, galvanizing themselves in Gabrielle's mind.

Following the scenic shots of Pai, a sporadic barrage of ill-angled pictures appeared. Some were in focus, others were blurred. The sky was the color of a robin's eggs, with strokes of cirrus clouds. Mark's profile, his right shoulder, his back, and his gray T-shirt were crystal-clear, and a single stream of bright red blood trickled down the back of his upper arm. A small gash was visible.

"What the hell happened to Mark's arm?" Gabrielle asked, as if Claire had been present when the photo was taken.

"I don't know," Claire responded softly.

The red Toyota pickup truck, its muddied front grill, and its license plate came next in the barrage of pictures. Then came the dirt road, its grassy edges browned by the heat of the baking sun, even during the cold season. The motorcycle, still moving down the road with only Mark on it, was off-angle, and it appeared he was riding up the side of an invisible hill. The underside of the truck, its axles and frame coated with rust, looked like a labyrinth of metal. A tire's rim was frosted in coal-like break dust. Then appeared the turquoise backpack, Avery lying under the truck exposing her hand and wrist (adorned with the leather bracelets Gabby had given her). Also in the frame, Mark's boots stood near the truck, the rusty underbelly of the Toyota in the foreground.

"They were both on the bike and hit by the truck, Mark had told me," Gabby said, looking at Claire. Gabby pulled up the photos again and flipped from the grill of the Toyota, Mark's profile and back, the undercarriage of the truck, and Mark on the motorcycle. "Mark said they were hit by the truck, that it came out of nowhere. He said he was able to turn quick enough to suffer only a sideswipe but lost control, lost his balance."

"Then why is he still on the bike and Avery is under the truck?" Claire looked confused, befuddled. "How is Mark on the bike, Gabby?"

"They were both thrown from the bike when they were sideswiped. Did he lie? He fucking lied... Why? I have no idea what *really* took place on that road, do I?" Gabby looked defeated, beaten up by circumstance.

Claire interjected in a docile attempt to rectify what seemed to be a wrong she didn't want to acknowledge: "It can't be what it seems."

"Avery was thrown from that bike, suffering beneath that goddamn truck," Gabby continued. "And Mark — what the hell? He's riding away? He stops to approach *my* Avery underneath that piece of shit truck. We can see his legs. He's *standing* there! He told me he broke his left femur, cracked ribs when they were hit. When *they* were hit! The bastard even described the snap he heard. He's a liar! A fucking liar!"

Enraged, Gabby threw elbow-jabs at the back of the oversized chair. All of her bewildering thoughts about the Breya-letters were instantaneously replaced with this new revelation concerning the accident. There was horror in acknowledging that the shards of information Gabby thought she had known about Avery's fate were untrue.

Claire hugged her friend, the kind of hug meant to calm a person. Her arms gripped tightly around Gabrielle's upper body, making it hard for her to move, only wiggle. Her heaving body undulated but after some time together they regulated their breathing.

"Stop, stop! We'll get some answers," Claire assured Gabby. "We'll find a way to make sense of what we're seeing. We *will*."

CHAPTER 22

Like Being There

Gabrielle had spent the last two hours trying to contact Darion, who was in London with Reprieve International. This meant a five-hour time difference between them, and it was too late — the offices in London would be closed and Darion would already be home. Gabby did not have her personal number. She felt the need to speak with Darion before calling the New York offices or the police. Gabby needed time to process the mess and muck seeping into the convolutions of her brain.

She grabbed Avery's leather journal from her nightstand and began to look through it. The entries were familiar — not so much by the words as by Avery's cursive handwriting. She had her own style, much like that of a calligrapher; the sweep of her letters was uniquely hers alone.

Gabrielle thought of the little notes Avery would write and carefully fold into tiny squares barely the size of one side of a die. Gabby would find them tucked into the nooks and crannies of her days. Sometimes they were secretly placed in the front pocket of a pair of jeans. Once she found a miniscule note among the spoons in the silverware drawer, and another time she found one tucked into a very small crack time had wedged itself into; a crack running vertically along the wooden bookshelf in the dining room. They were like petite fortune-favors scrolled by hand, each crafted by a gesture specifically meant for Gabby.

The leather journal in her hands was smooth to the touch, like a rose petal. It was the color of amber sap. A scratch in the lower-right corner made it look as if a kitten's claw had scrambled to turn the pages. Avery's sisters had given it to her as a parting gift, as a safe place to keep records, to account for life's adventures, mishaps and wonderings. It was such a private thing Gabby debated whether she had the right to trespass and read the thoughts hidden here. *Would Avery want me to read the journal?* she asked herself. She supposed that she would, and cracked open the worn binding. The inside front cover read:

To our big sister,

No matter how far apart, we are all with you.

Always with love,
The Girls

But the rest, every word thereafter, was Avery's. Her moments in Thailand were contained within these pages. Would they shed light on the pictures Gabby had discovered with Claire? Would they offer answers or insight? As badly as she wanted to know, Gabrielle's spine turned to jelly, nearly forcing her to set the journal back down. But this time she didn't. She couldn't. Her fingers kept feeling the edge of the cover until each fingerprint had nearly been erased of its ridges.

Her hesitation left her stuck, undecided if she should continue to journey further into the pages of Avery's narrative. What if the recesses of Avery's mind held thoughts she didn't want to know about? Instead, maybe she would find small, dazzling nuggets she would want to string on a necklace to keep with her for always if she could. Gabby's urge to know rose within her like a pot of slow boiling water until she could no longer think about it; she was simply moved to venture forward, one page at a time.

The first page noted the date, a small heading. Day one, she realized, of landing in Thailand. Initial reactions to the intense heat radiating from the pavement, the sounds, the smell of foods, and the van driver P'Tang were all described in vivid detail. Maybe this initial reading would be best absorbed if Gabby skimmed the pages, floated through the experiences

Avery had brought to life. She leafed ahead, always pausing at the date of each entry. She noticed the names of the others in the travel group: Darion, Madison, Aubrey, Ethan, Steffen, and her "old buddy" Mark. These names were peppered throughout, provoking a smile from Gabby each time she saw her own name looking back at her.

Fucking Mark, she said to herself. Their time at Columbia University seemed so long ago. Like twisted, poetic justice, her long-ago boyfriend was with Avery as she lay dying. "My Catholic grandmother couldn't have written this script," Gabrielle mumbled past the cigarette she had lit and pinched between her lips. The smoke barely rose, but instead hovered like a screen between her and the journal.

The entries were laden with descriptions, reactions to the people and culture, and funny stories about the Reprieve cohort. A tear trickled from her eye to the corner of her lip as she took in the amount of times Avery wrote about the way she missed her, loved her. She sniffed and wiped the side of her cheek with the sleeve of her sweatshirt. For a moment she paused to fiddle with the leather bracelets she had given to Avery, now back on her own wrist. They had been returned, wrapped and tagged as evidence inside the boxes from Thailand; some were built with braids, others had turquoise beads. *They traveled from here to there to here again,* Gabby thought. *Such a long way.*

As the entries went on, it was Mark's name that frequented the pages most often. They had become friends, too, so this wasn't surprising. Hell, she had asked Mark to keep on eye on Avery, to watch out for her. But at a glance, Mark was at the core of most of Avery's final entries. A pit started to gather like a wad of gum inside Gabrielle's stomach. *Mark, Mark, Mark* seemed to come at her in 3-D, over and over again. The details of those entries were teasing her, begging for her attention. Nervously, she began to read the final entries with a new sort of intensity:

> *...There are times when he just stares at me. I can see Mark out of the corner of my eye watching. Doesn't he know I can feel his eyes on me? I never noticed this in New York. Not at dinner, not hanging out with friends, nothing. Have I given him the wrong idea? Shit...*

...I thought the awkwardness would subside but it has not. Am I imagining things? He waits for me at every bend like he is my freaking chaperone. We've been paired together but come on! Breathing room would be nice. A little respect, think of Gabby. How could he not? They were friends. Close friends.

...Mark is not the person I thought I could count on. I don't see him the same anymore. Nothing overt. There is just a feeling I have...

...I am perplexed at the aloof attitude he demonstrates toward me some days, like a switch has been flipped. I must have mistaken his interest. Mark is almost rude to me but has a constant interest in Gabby. Is he moody? What did she ever see in him? Hot and cold...

Avery somehow knew, or sensed, that Gabby and Mark had once been more than just friends. Now Gabby couldn't resist feeling guilty for never actually telling Avery herself that she and Mark had been involved. Maybe Mark had told her. The words in the journal were starting to reach out like fingers wrapping themselves around Gabby's wrists and pulling her into the moments described. These shackles made it impossible to put the small book down. *He was our friend*, Gabby thought. *Our friend.* The weight of imagining that a person *she* had brought into their lives made Avery uncomfortable stabbed at Gabby like a fork between ribs. She read on, threading the various entries together like a tailor:

...I see it now, the social complexity of love lost. Mark could care less about me, but I am sure now that he still loves Gabby. He has not told me, not even when he has been drunk and more talkative than usual. But it is in the way he looks at me, partly with disdain, partly with a wanting to be me, to be close to Gabrielle. God, does she know?...

...Tonight he said it. He told me he loved Gabby, that he always had. A rage filled him as he spoke; a sleeping evil was suddenly awakening as I looked him in the face. His admittance made

me nauseous, his sense of ownership over Gabby, a little scary. Backing up against the wall of the small hut he stood over me, silently seething. I felt his hatred. His sour beer-breath insulting. I could not tell if he hated me for loving Gabby or hated Gabby for loving me. No, he does not hate Gabby...he loves her. It is me who is unwanted. I am a breathing barrier standing between the two of them, that is how he sees me...

...Our pairing has become a nightmare. We travel to photo shoots in pairs, usually on motorcycles. It's not our choice. The groupings were established the first week we arrived in Chiang Mai. At the beginning, our assignments were awesome. We were friends, after all. I'm afraid to broach the topic of getting new partners for the remainder of the trip. I am not sure how to ask more about his feelings for Gabby. Since he told me, drunk, it has not come up again. His shitty attitude permeates every moment we spend together, but really, do I want to bring attention to the matter? Do I want to try and discuss his jealousy, the fear that swells whenever I am around him? Not really. I'd rather avoid the drama, be professional. Soon we'll be back home...

...I am freaking out, rocking, holding my knees like a goddamn child in my own bed. The rain is rare. It is dancing on the tin roof of the one-room hut I have been staying in for the last three days. Where the fuck did he go? The throbbing in my eye won't stop. My cheekbone feels like it has exploded from the inside out. Where the hell am I going to find some ice? This is too much...

...I am going home early. Tomorrow I will leave, back to New York. I have not shared these details with Gabby. I cannot tell her from afar that Mark is a spiteful, delusional fuck. She will die to hear about the things he has said, the things he has done. What a fucker! I did not tell Reprieve the details either — I cannot bare an interrogation right now, not until I tell Gabby.

I need her to lean on for this. Will she believe me? Oh my God, what if she doesn't believe me? Her Little Bird is coming home…

… P'Tang will be driving me to the train station so I can later catch my flight in Bangkok and head home. Without anyone in my cohort knowing the truth about my circumstances for leaving, I feel I am abandoning my team. I will have to make peace with my time here in Thailand. I have tried to see the beauty in this place and look over and past the torment that Mark has brought to the experience. He is sick. I know this now. I head out in an hour via Route 1095. My heart is breaking without Gabrielle.

This was the last entry. Stupefied, Gabby sat on the edge of the bed, processing the entries she just read. It was like crawling through the opening of a chain-linked fence, naked, jagged metal scraping against a bare back. She felt exposed, cold, and raw. Her hands trembled. Her exhalations were loud, breathy, phlegmy.

Naw. No. Mark? The Mark I trusted, we trusted? She chewed on her tongue as the lukewarm water from her kitchen faucet filled a glass. The details of the accident messed up enough! To now discover this requited love bullshit, and that he put his hands on Avery!

"All of it is just too much!" Gabby yelled into the hollow walls of her apartment. Her anguish kept building, multiplying with each new facet of the trip discovered. She knew Avery's words could not be lies. *How is it that Mark and Avery ended up on a motorcycle together after what he had done to her?* she thought. It made no sense.

Gabby had known all along that Mark had been on the motorcycle with Avery; he had called her and told her so. But that was before she knew he had loathed Avery and loved *her*. All of the details were becoming soap bubbles cascading about her head, each one popping as it rose toward the ceiling, spilling out more bubbles, more details. She needed to move beyond the minutiae of the incident to uncover the heart of the whole. Now it was becoming clearer to Gabby that she was obligated to uncover for herself which aspects of Avery's accident were worth believing and preserving.

A surge shot into her. She ran to the living room, where the Reprieve report had been flung just feet from the half-unpacked boxes on the floor. She picked it up and leafed through it to find a section titled *Summary Account*, which detailed that Mark had been assigned to drive Avery to the Chiang Mai Rail Station near the Ping River after P'Tang's van had gotten a flat tire. Gabby could only imagine the emotions that must have flooded Avery's senses — to be sitting in a van in the middle of nowhere with a flat tire, and to see Mark ride up as her rescuer. "Oh my God!" Gabrielle's heart sank like a rock thrown into the abyss of an ocean. The taste of puke hit the back of her throat thinking about it. She swallowed and sucked in the sides of her cheeks. He had beaten her! He had put his hands on her, and then she had to ride on the back of a bike with him? *No fucking way...He was her only way out! Her only way to reach the airport. Her only option,* Gabby realized.

Overcome with the desperation that undoubtedly must have paralyzed Avery, Gabrielle understood complete helplessness in a manner she had never known or dreamed of before. Alone at the bottom of the deepest well, it seemed, Gabrielle contemplated her urge to kill Mark. Closing her eyes, she felt the rapture of squeezing her hands around his neck until the blood vessels in his eyes popped and his lips foamed from searching for a breath of air he would not find. This thought brought her momentary tranquility — accomplishment, actually. But did it make Gabby just as twisted as he?

The section titled *Coroner's Report, Summary Report of Autopsy* came at her as if the words were floating off of the page, hovering closer and closer. Might these words suffocate her? Might they cover her mouth and nose like a hand from behind in a dark alley? Gabrielle feared that the finality that would come from reading Dr. Sankrapoon's assessment would be like personally digging Avery's grave. *It was Mark,* she thought, *who deserved to be buried beneath the heavy soil.* "The injuries, the injuries..." she said as she searched. "What really happened to *you,* you little bastard!" she shouted at Mark, as if he were standing quietly in the corner of the room with her.

The index indicated that Mark's injuries would be found more as a preface to Avery's autopsy details. A nervous laughter grew in her like a boil and burst into the air. She became freakishly giddy as she tore through the pages, looking for what she knew would be Mark's pitiful injuries, as compared to Avery's.

LaPonte, Markus Kevin, age 46. Gabby half-anticipated the broken left femur and cracked ribs Mark had described. Neither were listed. Barely a scratch was noted, actually:

External Examination

- Hematoma to the left elbow
- ½ inch laceration to left triceps caused by maxillary central incisors (upper front teeth)
- Excoriated neck and right cheek caused by fingernails

"That's it?" she shouted. "Really? What happened to the broken bones suffered by the sideswipe, damn it? A vicious liar!" *It was confirmed,* she thought. Stunned, she flipped the same page over and back, over and back, looking for another explanation. Gabby knew the accident could not have possibly happened the way Mark had described it. There was no way he could have laid down a motorcycle going 70 kilometers an hours without more serious injuries. She needed to do the math. "What the hell is the conversion on that?" A hair over 43 miles an hour, she figured.

She wondered now about the photos, which also told a different story. *How could the investigators have missed this camera?* Gabby tried to rationalize why she had missed it in the pack herself. She had an excuse: shock. Grief easily disguised the dark black cube nestled in the bottom of the darkly lined backpack. But did everyone else who had passed a trained eye over the accident scene miss it too? Grabbing the turquoise backpack again, she realized that the petite point-and-shoot Sony camera that appeared camouflaged, as if at the bottom of a murky pond, was different from the other items she had pulled from the pack. No red *Evidence* sticker. Not a single eye had discovered the picture-show she and Claire had just witnessed. No one had seen this camera, or Mark on the bike alone, or Avery under the truck, or his lanky legs approaching her like a stalker as she lay dying.

What seemed to be a tragic accident had morphed into gruesome acts of violence. It was all coming together, as if a kaleidoscope had been adjusted to let in the light, creating a new display, a new horror. She read Avery's autopsy notes:

Jolen, Avery, deceased, age 43.

External Examination

- Craniocervical cyanosis: Intense purple facial congestion and swelling with hemorrhagic petechiae of the face, the neck, and upper chest (broken blood vessels; purple spots on epidermis and dermis).
- Skin tissue underneath fingernails; right hand index and middle fingers

Internal Examination

- Subconjunctival hemorrhage: Bloodied eyes
- Broken maxillary central incisors (upper front teeth); #8 and #9
- Traumatic asphyxia: Hypoxia (oxygen deprivation), hypercapnia (high carbon dioxide) and acidosis
- Blunt chest trauma
- Severe thoracic injury: Spinal fractures, mid-back
- Compound skull fracture
- Subarachnoid hemorrhage: Bleeding between brain and surrounding membrane

At once, Gabrielle was transported by the particulars of Avery and Mark's wounds, and she was standing beside the dirt road in Pai with the prickly brown grass beneath the soles of her boots. Birds, bronzed drongos, perched in nearby trees, innocently singing hymnals. Their sweetness felt so out of place. Bob Dylan's "In My Time of Dyin' " sank into the belly of her ear. The notes rose and swelled until they poured out onto Gabrielle's shoulders and ran down her back, sides and chest, pooling like a puddle around her feet.

A rumbling, the hum of a motor, and the crumbling of rocks beneath tires grew in a crescendo. Nearer and nearer the motor's vibration approached her but the road still remained vacant. Her internal organs agitated from the rumbling. A hazy cloud of dust appeared around the corner before the red pickup, as if to announce the truck's arrival.

From behind Gabby, the crunching of rocks cracked louder, and a grumbling moan growled from a motorcycle muffler. Avery's blond hair appeared to glisten with gold-leafed flecks, much like the pressed gold flakes worshippers stick on the sleeping Buddha in the temples throughout the countryside. Her hair fanned out around her like a peacock's train, emulating shivering feathers. The bright blues and greens shone brilliantly. The intricate fan extended larger and wider the closer the bike came to her, as if magnifying in circumference, hovering high above both Avery and Mark. The iridescent eyes that adorned the feathers appeared outlined with black eyeliner. And then it dawned on Gabrielle that a hundred watchful eyes suddenly looked down on the scene. Were they judging eyes? Kind eyes? Eyes of a voyeur simply taking pleasure in the impending pain soon to spill forth? *Schadenfreude?*

Avery was smiling and looking out onto the countryside through the viewfinder of her camera. The turquoise backpack sat on her back. Mark was feverishly scanning the view ahead, swiveling his head from left to right. A gush of wind swirled from the passing motorcycle and assaulted Gabby. Specks of dirt cascaded all around her. Grit settled between her teeth. Mark's attention was lured to his side rearview mirrors, looking both at Avery and for approaching vehicles.

His stare connected to Gabby's, and he winked. Mark blew her a kiss and raised his left arm like the wing of a bird. A studied, well-timed pause kept him frozen in this position until the red Toyota broke the bend in the road. They were traveling toward each other, like teenagers running toward center-court in a bloody game of dodgeball. But this time the balls were replaced with grenades, weren't they?

As the truck came closer to the motorcycle, Mark pulled his elbow across the front of his body and then jerked it back with so much force the bike nearly tipped off balance. A gasp seized Gabby's lungs as she imagined the scene unfolding: Avery caught the pointed force of his elbow in the mouth. Flaying, stunned, she groped at him in a desperate attempt to stay on the bike. Blood streamed from the corners of her mouth as she gagged and sputtered. She choked for a moment. Fear flooded her eyes. With outstretched arms and fingers flung wide apart, she clawed at the air as the bike sped up and moved out from under her. Mark screeched to a stop at the side of the road, turned, and watched.

Gabrielle remained fixed in this trance, watching, too, as if she had really been there. Like all those times she actually did pass car accidents on the road and cursed the gawkers who refused to look away. Now she rebuked herself. Though all of it was in her mind's eye, she couldn't stop watching. After all, the undoing of her life would demand her testimony.

"Avery!" she screamed in a long, drawn-out bellow. "Avery!" Gabby's heartbeat quickened, and her mouth went dry. "Avery!" But she couldn't move. It was all a mirage, and Avery was out of her reach, unprotected. Avery's body met the dirt road with such force her back arched in pain as she looked up at the sky. Compacted from years of vehicles and feet trampling upon it, the road's surface had turned to hardened cement. Like a paddle with a ball tied to it, Avery's head bounced once, twice against the ground. Her mouth was sprung open, her jaw unhinged, but no sound was emitted. Blood was spat into the air, and then wailing erupted — first low and quiet, then a high-pitched squeal.

The driver of the red pickup truck was not even looking at the road. His head was turned while talking to his buddies in the cab. One of the men pointed, another braced his arms against the dash, and the driver tried to swerve. The tires turned, locked and skidded, leaving trails of blackened burnt rubber. The disfigured road folded in on itself, swallowing her love in one gulp.

Gabby could not help but close her eyes at this point, exactly like when a sneeze overcomes the senses: no matter how hard one tries, the eyes cannot be forced open. The room was silent except for the whistling of the vents.

Waking from the vision that had taken over her senses, Gabby clutched the report until its edges felt crinkly and bent against her palm. She no longer needed to intuit what had happened in Pai. The facts, though revolting, were as clear as a freshly frozen ice cube. There, on the living room floor among Avery's things, Gabrielle lay down and wept into her hands until the evening lay upon her like a woolen blanket.

She felt both hollow and full at the same time — full of regret for not warning Avery against a Mark she had never really met herself, and hollow of understanding or comprehending why the lives of the two women she had come to adore — her mother and Avery — ended too soon. Was there ever a *right* time for death? Perhaps for some, there was. Perhaps, for some, death was a respite, a relief, a gentle hand to the forehead, a whispering of peace before the lights went out. In this case, though, death was like a jarring slap to the face. The door of the cage had been left open, and her Little Bird had flown away.

CHAPTER 23

Full Circle

Sunday morning came quickly. Six-thirty a.m. sat still and quiet on the face of the clock. Shuffling to the bathroom, Gabrielle brushed her teeth and stepped into the shower. The hot stream relieved the kinks in her back from the hardwood floor she had spent the night on.

She wondered what to do next: confront Mark, ask what really happened, thrust her conjurings onto him, and make him answer for pushing Avery off that motorcycle? What about the physical abuse? She needed to report it to the police, all of it. The pieces were falling around her like crystalline snowflakes, yet each was unwilling to melt or vanish. Instead, they glistened like broken glass, crashing onto the cold tile of the bathroom floor. Mark's jealousy, the extent of his actions, was psychotic.

"And to what end?" Gabby asked herself out loud.

She knew well to what end, because she was living with it alone in her apartment without Avery. *Should I call Darion or the investigators in Thailand?* she wondered. Maybe it was futile at this point. The investigation was closed, evidence overlooked, the findings completed. But still, Gabrielle needed to talk to her family and Claire about the inferences she was drawing and projecting. Another point of view was needed.

After dressing and towel-drying her hair, she let it fall damp down her back as usual. The nape of her sweater became wet, and a chill caused her shoulders to shudder for a moment. Her mind wandered to Avery's journal and the book *What is the What.* Earlier, Gabby had focused only on a smattering of Avery's entries, painting a picture of Mark's evolution from ally to antagonist, friend to foe. Maybe Gabby needed to find a ray of hope in the journal, a sparkle of joy Avery had discovered, to help her pave a path to light.

Before Avery had left for Thailand, she and Gabby had discussed *What is the What,* and Gabby had found it to be such a gem, something of a small treasure that stayed behind within the reader long after the book ended. She gave it to Avery, hoping it would provoke new curiosities in her, propel her to answer the question, *What is her what* — the unknowns, the choices she had made that were a leap of faith. What of those choices turned out well? What turned out poorly? This, or that? Door number one, or door number two? Gabby was compelled to know if Avery had come to some understanding or realization about this question. For some reason, her speculation was like an irritating sliver she could not expel.

As Gabby returned to the journal, just the sight of Avery's handwriting roused a smile in her. A vision of the many lighthouses Gabrielle had visited and photographed while they were apart, and the letters they had exchanged, warmed her, as if the sun were beating down upon her face. Hot and inescapable, the heat filled her, softened her.

Gabby opened the leather journal and turned to the pages Avery had earmarked. The corners of these pages neatly folded over offered discrete bookmarks, reminders of special thoughts. Trepidation cannot be discounted, but beneath it all, she found a momentary sense of peace as the flipping pages produced a breeze as gentle as a butterfly's wings on her face. She succumbed to this inquisitive awareness and perused the entries on a mission to find Avery's interpretation of the book.

The fanned pages wafted the faintest smell of Avery's perfume — basil, vanilla. Mellifluous memories vividly appeared in color deep inside Gabrielle's imagination. She concentrated on the dog-eared pages, searching for what might have resonated with Avery, provoking the placeholders. Like a game of search-and-find, she relied on her own intuition and the mutual understandings between the two of them to find the meaning of each passage. She searched for droplets of significance in each paragraph or sentence.

Some ideas walked off the pages; others left her perplexed and wondering. The daunting awareness that some of Avery's thoughts may never be understood had to be reckoned with. Maybe that was how it was always meant to be. After all, even those we love the most have the right to their innermost thoughts, secrets, delights, and torments. This cannot be argued or denied. The journal, though, felt like a connection to Avery that moved beyond this time and place. It was a route, a path, backward. Maybe it would also become Gabby's path forward.

Finally, she came to the page she had hoped to find. It was dated and titled, *What is the What*, in black ink. A tired exhalation made the pages move underneath Gabrielle's breath…

> *What is my what? It is this… I know love and have love in my life. She is a woman, an artist, my friend, my heart. My eyes focus on her face every morning and I think to myself, thank God for her. Thank God there can be an us. I do not need to look for the 'what' I do not know. I am not searching for greener grass because I am able to walk through life holding her hand.*
>
> *The true weight of air makes sense now. It is the delicate balance of all the variables in one's life. It is the perfect amount of pressure on the inside pushing out, as the external pressures outside pushing in. Inner thoughts and demons counterbalanced with love, acceptance, and kindness.*
>
> *There is no wonder of 'what' is on the other side, because my side is whole and quite lovely. If I have found only one half of happiness then I must reconcile the fact that anything more would be beyond that which I could possibly bear. Let the leftovers be for those who have nothing.*

As if swallowing a salty wave, Gabby tasted her own tears. The naissance of Avery's interpretation overwhelmed her. Tucking the journal into her worn satchel, Gabby was seized by emotion, figuratively impaled. She knew she had been irrefutably loved. She felt its joy, its purity, its unconditional fortitude. The oxygen in the room was so thin it was as if she were drinking it through a pinched straw. The love she coveted so deeply was affirmed. But it was also achingly lost.

"Lost..." She considered what *lost* implied. "*Misplaced?* Have I *misplaced* Avery or our love?" A dialogue ensued, but no one was present to answer her. "Nothing was lost," her singular voice continued in a one-sided debate. "Not lost at all. Simply stolen. Love was stolen."

"Come in!" Claire yelled through her door. Gabby could hear the clicking of the lock on the other side. She opened the door to receive Claire's warm greeting. Her arms were bent upright at the elbows, like a surgeon after scrubbing in before surgery.

"I'm baking." She smiled. Flour coated her hands. "Pies. Want some coffee?"

"Yeah, that would be perfect."

"I couldn't sleep last night. My mind just wouldn't stop racing after you left yesterday. Those pictures kept playing over and over in my mind. I mean, the shots, the sequence, Mark standing there beside that truck. It just didn't add up, ya' know?" Claire always baked when she was anxious. "I keep trying to puzzle it all together."

"I read her journal. Parts of it, anyways."

"And?" Claire responded with some hesitation in her voice.

"I, uh, I can't really talk about it right now. My head is whirling. I keep tossing between anger and rage, then..." She drew in a quick sniff and shook her head.

"What, Gab? Then what? I can't imagine what you're feeling, but you can't keep it locked up inside you." Claire stirred some cream into a coffee cup and handed it to Gabby.

"At moments, I want to push away the bad and just latch onto the good we shared, ya' know?" Gabby sipped her coffee with a slight slurp.

"Everyone comes to terms with death in different ways. And this is so messy, Gab. It really is." Claire pushed her hair over her shoulder with the back of her hand, leaving flour on her cheek. "My grandmother used to say that people carry on after death — their spirit, anyways."

"I have a new found respect for that possibility," Gabby said through a half-smile.

Breya's letters now seemed like the lesser of strange things. How could she start to begin to describe the events she had just discovered through Avery's journal and the Reprieve report? Should she come out and just say Mark was an abuser, a killer? Pretty hefty accusations, but she was confident it was the truth. Gabrielle continued to sip her coffee and added some agave to sweeten it. She decidedly settled on the lighter side of her thoughts for the time being: the letters. "What makes you think people carry on, Claire?"

"My grandmother," Claire said, waving the recipe card she was glancing down at, as if to signal it had come straight from Grandma's secret drawer.

"Uh-huh." Gab gave her the nod to share more.

"She used to tell me stories about traveling when she was in her twenties and thirties. That's probably where I get my love of music and cultures. She immigrated to the United States when she was in her thirties, I think it was." A smile appeared on Claire's face, and a sudden, far-off look settled in her eyes. "Grandma Abaroa was born in Spain but later ended up here in New York, upstate. She used to tell me our surname meant *refuge*. Once I was old enough to understand what a refuge was, I found it to be so fitting of her. She was my refuge, my safe place, my haven. I only visited her on occasion because she lived so far outside of the city. So when I saw her in the country, I would stay with her for a full weekend at a time. Gram used to go on and on about these oral traditions, stories, that were passed down from village to village in Spain among our ancestors. They always seemed so unreal to me, just stories, but I don't know, Gabby. Sometimes I think they're more than made up tales, ya' know?" She shook her head. "Why am I telling you this, again?"

Gabby sat upright on her stool and tilted her head. "Come on, you were trying to explain how people carry on after death."

"Yeah, I remember Grandma Abaroa telling me about the times she traveled with her best friend. They were like sisters, I suppose. Gram was the older and wiser of the two, the way she always told it anyways. They once caught a free ride on a train leaving from Madrid, Spain. Together, she and her friend wooed the ticket-taker on the Eurail, and nine hours later they were stepping foot in Bordeaux, France, and sipping wine from the Gironde estuary. 'Right bank — heavy on the Merlot, light on the Cabernet,' my Gram used to say."

Claire raised the pot of near-gone coffee, as if asking if Gabby would like some more.

"No, I'm good," Gabby said, putting a hand over the mouth of her cup.

"Of course, the Eurail was intended for non-European citizens, so my grandmother, a bit of a rebel, used her American cousin's passport to board. Can you imagine those two, my Gram and her friend? Two young women traveling with reckless abandonment through Europe!" Claire laughed, throwing a hand-towel down onto the counter. A puff of flour rose and floated back down to the granite top.

"My mom traveled with a friend, too," Gabby said. "She and your Gram were cut from the same cloth, I suppose. Tell me more about those stories she used to share, Claire. What makes you doubt that death is final?"

"Gram used to say that some people go to heaven, others to hell, while some rest in the *in-between*. I guess this in-between space was for those whose forever-after place was undecided." She raised an eyebrow. "This in-between space is not permanent but could last a long time for some, Gram used to say."

"What's a long time? Years?"

"I guess," Claire said as she lined the pie tins and gently placed the doughy piecrust inside of them. Setting a plate atop the open pie dish, she trimmed the pastry with a butter knife. Her fingers delicately pinched the edges of the circular pan, and she dipped a brush into melted butter. The small peaks and valleys, now laden with her thumbprint, glistened with a yellowy sheen. "Never mind." Her voice trailed as she tried to shrug off the last ten minutes of the conversation, as if it hadn't happened at all.

"Wait a minute, Claire. Never mind? Where the hell were you going with all that?" Gabby retorted, her frustration apparent.

"I'm just saying that sometimes death is not final. It sounds stupid, I know. Forget it." Claire turned on the oven to four hundred degrees. A whoosh emanated from its base as the pilot-light caught.

"There's something I haven't shared with you, Claire." Gabrielle reached into her satchel and produced the letters. Each one left for Avery, over the span of several months, now sat in a pile on Claire's countertop.

Confused, Claire asked, "What are those?" She stood on the opposite side of the kitchen island and averted her eyes, focusing more intently on the mixing bowl before her.

"They're letters. Letters sent to Avery from a woman she once knew. The lady died long ago."

Gabby was still unsure of how Claire might react to these seemingly impossible messages from the *in-between* space Claire might actually acknowledge or accept. But Claire seemed neither surprised nor disturbed, leaving Gabby to question her own response to them.

Gabrielle read parts of each letter to Claire as she listened, calmly and unshaken. Gabby looked on, pensively waiting for her to posit some type of reaction to the ludicrous findings or show some sign that they were, indeed, a bit unnerving. As Gabby bit her nails, nerves curdled in her stomach like sour milk as she watched Claire's facial expressions.

"What? Christ, say something, Claire!"

"I don't know what you want me to say, Gab. It is what it is." Claire sipped her coffee and continued to whirl about the kitchen, baking, as if all were right and normal. She grabbed an oven mitt from a drawer.

"It is what it is, Claire? Let me clarify — they are letters sent and received *after* Breya passed away. Does that not strike you as strange? Should I not be concerned or worried? What about the fact that Avery never confided in me about the letters? I just found them. It's fair that some kind of response is elicited, right?"

"Wait — Breya?" Claire asked with a tinge of surprise. Her hands stopped stirring the mixture in the bowl as she fixed her eyes on her friend. "Did you say Breya, Gabby?" Now Claire's face read as not just curious, but also awkwardly emotional.

"Yeah, Breya. She was the friend who traveled with my mother in Europe but..." Gabby felt as if a peach-pit was caught in her throat and she was willing herself to swallow it. *Okay,* she thought, *Claire finally understands the absurdity of it all!*

"Breya?" Claire repeated in a daze. She stared off into the living room, but her gaze seemed transfixed on nothing. Her eyes became joyful, squinting with the curve of a slight smile on her lips.

Fearing she would lose her nerve to explain her connection to Breya and the letters, Gabby forced herself to continue. "So, believe it or not, my mother, Havana Colibrì, traveled with this Breya when they were young women." She shuffled the letters on the counter.

"Uh-huh."

"They went through Belgium, Switzerland, Italy, France, and Spain. My mom was a dancer; that was what initially drew her to Europe. She was just a kid from the Bronx, right here in New York, but she always had a dream to see the world. She wanted to put her feet in the same place and position as the revered Pierre Beauchamp of the Ballet de Cour of the 1650s. So the poor girl from the Bronx did exactly what her father had begged her not to do. Mom was determined to run off to see the world!" Gabrielle raised her coffee cup as if toasting to her mother's gumption. "God, I loved my mom," she continued with tears and a short laugh. "She had guts, ya' know." She sniffed and wiped her tears on the sleeve of her shirt. "Uhhh," she exhaled, "Where was I?"

"We were trying to make sense of life and death," Claire reminded her. "Clear as that coffee you're drinking, right? So what happened to your mom, Havana, and this Breya you mentioned?"

Claire seemed to be baiting Gabrielle. She sensed Claire knew something of this story but could not really fathom how she could possibly know any of its details. Maybe Avery had confided in Claire at some point about the letters she had received from Breya. Perhaps these letters weren't news to her at all. *Could Avery have told Claire before telling her?* she quietly wondered. She had to ask: "Did Avery ever tell you about Breya?"

"Not a word." Claire mixed a cup of white sugar into the bowl and gathered a lemon from the refrigerator.

Caught up in the sweet memory of her mother and the sickening feeling of losing Avery, Gabby suddenly imagined she had fallen into the tumbler of a washing machine, her back banging and breaking against the rotation of her feelings and the anxiety of wondering if Claire had really known about the Breya letters long before she herself had. In the end, this really didn't matter, she supposed. More important matters were occupying her mind.

A memory of the ghostly figure Avery used to describe popped into Gabby's head. She envisioned Breya's slight silhouette standing at the fence between her and Avery's yard. The images of her frail body and translucent skin, even her stained fingers from the blackberries she gathered each summer, were vivid. What a contradiction to the Breya her mother had traveled with in Europe! The Breya that Gabrielle had become intimately acquainted with through her mother's photographs. Breya, then, looked to be a vivacious, daring, vibrant woman.

"Tell me more about who Breya was to you, Gabrielle?" Claire asked as she shaved the rind of a lemon into the mixing bowl.

"To me, Breya was my mother's mentor, an older sister of sorts. To Avery, she was her neighbor while growing up. Can you believe it? Deer Lake, upstate New York — you probably never heard of it. A tiny town. Breya died there as an old woman. While walking home from school one day, Avery saw her dead, face-down in the snow. A heart attack, I think it was. Avery used to tell me it looked as though the snow was bleeding, but it was the red flannel robe Breya was wearing. Can you imagine seeing that as a kid? No one could. In fact, she told her mom about 'the bleeding snow' but no one believed it. Therefore, no one checked until the next day."

Claire listened but remained constant in her baking oblivion, partially hearing the recount and partially absorbed in the task at hand. Plunging a wooden spoon into the mixture, she stirred the contents while holding the bowl between her forearm and rib-cage. "And the letters from Breya?" she asked.

The inquiry is so insistent, Gabby noticed. "The letters are interesting." She paused to sip her coffee. Hesitantly, she looked up at Claire.

"Come on, Gab, the letters?" Claire chided.

"They came from Breya, handwritten, addressed to Avery. I assume that some had been left for her before the trip. But one was left in Thailand, I guess." Gabby's voice shook now.

Sure, Claire had spoken about her grandmother telling tales about the *in-between* space, but come on, to *hear* and to *see* were two different things. To *see* these letters on her countertop was quite another thing entirely. This would be a true test of where Claire's beliefs really stood.

Gabrielle timidly unfolded a letter like a tri-fold accordion, and turned the signature toward Claire. "Take a look. The letters from Breya came *after* her passing."

Gabby paused. A stopgap lingered in the air, allowing Claire to really process what her friend had been telling her.

"The letters talk about what Breya saw — witnessed, for Christ's sake — right alongside Avery. She'd been like some goddamned guardian angel from beyond or something."

Claire just nodded, still seemingly unphased, while Gabrielle spilled her confusion out and into the kitchen: "But where the hell was she the day Avery needed her the most? When she was on that fucking motorcycle in Pai? Where was Breya *then?*" She sobbed.

Claire stopped her baking frenzy for the first time since answering the door, walked around the island, and reached out to hug her friend. "It's okay, everything is going to be okay," she said. "I'll finish up here, and then I'll tell you more about my grandmother. I think you'll find some comfort in hearing about her."

Gabby inhaled the lingering sugary aromas coming from the warming kitchen. Vivaldi tenderly vibrated on the Bluetooth speaker in the living room. Each note made Gabby think of her mother dancing and Breya, who introduced her to his music in Europe.

Claire went to the sink to collect the strainer that had been running under cold water and placed the last ingredient into the mixing bowl. Fresh blackberries, dark as the night sky, were tenderly stirred in with the sugar and poured into the pie tin with the prepared dough still brimming with the buttery glaze. Lemon shavings were sprinkled on top — specks of sunshine.

Claire winked at Gabby and said, "Grandma Breya left more than just stories behind." While closing the oven door, she cocked her head toward the pie and then toward the stack of letters.

Gabrielle's eyes moved from Breya's letters to the pie recipe to the blackberries, and back to the recipe and the letters. The handwriting, the wisp and curl of each word were all the same. *A match*, her mind muttered.

CHAPTER 24

Retribution

Snowflakes sprinkled outside, on this cold night in late winter. The city looked frosted with cream cheese, yet at closer glance footprints and puppy-crap defiled the walkways. Gabrielle stared, unaffected, out the window as two young men duked it out in front of a bar under the glow of a neon sign. They slipped and stammered in the snow, twisting to stay upright while hurling punches at one another.

"The city... a charming catastrophe!" Gabrielle admitted with sarcasm. She and Claire were sharing one of their routine evening tea sessions. "She is still with me. I feel her," she reminded Claire, as if it weren't already obvious.

"She always will be," Claire nodded in agreement. "Avery will always be a part of you, a part of me, a part of anyone who knew her."

The friendship between Gabby and Claire was as strong as a massive chain mooring a ship to its dock — that of sisterhood. In a roundabout way, the universe had given Gabrielle the sister she had always wanted. They were fused together, not by DNA, but by the unbelievable bond her mother and Claire's grandmother had shared years ago...and by the indescribable, undeniable fact that Claire's grandmother, Breya, somehow, someway communicated with Avery long after she had died. No one else would ever believe it, so no one else was ever told.

"We could not *make* this up!" Gabrielle said with the shake of her head.

"Oh, I know. I know," Claire agreed.

However, in the shadows of their sisterhood was the menacing outline of mortality. Gabrielle was ready to share the unclaimed evidence with the authorities at Reprieve International. A deep-seeded determination became the catalyst driving her. It forced her to stay up late into the evenings and rise before the dawn as she inferred the timeline of events that must have taken place between Avery and Mark. The vision she had of the accident, the details drawn from the photos and Avery's journal entries, all added up to the truth so many had neglected. These details pointed to the proper ending she was certain Mark deserved.

Mark needed to answer for what he had done, be made to relive the day in its entirety. His calculated cruelty could not go unrecognized. Gabrielle would make sure he felt a pain that surpassed that which he had brought to Avery. She wanted to bring him down to the lowest level imaginable, to make him suffer in unkind, hurtful ways. Guilt for these thoughts dropped away from her and rolled back up into her chest like a yo-yo, away and back, away and back. At one point Gabby had to come to terms with her own humanity, flawed as it was. When the guilt dissipated, she reveled in the means to make Mark's end.

The grotesque scenes her mind conjured pinned Mark tightly at its center. He was the main attraction — rendered destitute, fearful, pitiful. A deserted soul in a dry desert, Gabrielle imagined Mark slowly thirsting to death as scorpions riveted their telsons, rife with venom, into his face again and again. Shame and embarrassment for these thoughts should have plagued her, but they did not. His screams of agony would be recognized with a smile, not a frown. These thoughts brought her deliverance from the loss she could not shake. *After all,* she often admitted to herself, *they're just thoughts, right?*

At times remorse would slap Gabby upside the head, erasing the sinful thoughts that crept inside of her for just a moment. During this awakening — the parts of the day that were filled with fake "I'm doing fine" and "Everything is good" statements about herself and her life — she fastened together a somewhat normal existence. The authorities ceased all artifacts Gabby received from Thailand, except for the letter from

Breya. This, Gabrielle decided, would be best honored in her safekeeping. The police, Reprieve International, and the U.S. Embassy aligned to collaborate and transfer the charges Mark would face to New York — a rare occurrence Gabby had learned. First-degree murder fit Mark like a tailor-made suit. His act of pushing Avery off that motorcycle in Thailand was deemed both malicious and premeditated. The trial, though long and arduous, created a second chance for Gabrielle to reconnect with Avery's family. In them, she was grateful for the glimpses of her.

The cinderblock walls resembled the color of bile — the floor, the ceiling, the whole place. The constant hum of the ventilation system buzzed in the ears, a kind of white noise that aided and abetted drowning out the inner audio-loop that played within most inmates' minds. Each footstep was padded by the irritating squeak of an orange rubber sandal, the kind that cost five cents to make at the hands of an impoverished child in a country few Americans have visited. The lighting bathed each face, not in a glow, but rather a dinge that resembled dirty yellow piss. The overall stink of the place assaulted the senses and turned the stomach most days. Either the stinging odor of ammonia or the nauseating pong of puke lingered in the atmosphere.

Three hundred seventeen miles north of New York City, a mere twenty miles west of Vermont, sat the rural town of Dannemora. It was close enough to the Green Mountain State to catch a glimpse of Lake Champlain and the majestic mountain range if the goddamn windows were low enough to see through. But they were not. So the only time the sun warmed the skin was during the one hour of isolated recreational time. The Honor Block was reserved for inmates charged with lesser offenses, not the hardcore shit.

"I'm doing my time, but I get to roam — do laundry, work the mess hall, stuff like that," Gabby overheard an inmate telling a visitor sitting next to her one Saturday. She had come to understand that life on the inside was very different, depending on the crime one had committed on the outside. Some prisoners were treated like dogs: kicked, beaten, fucked, shanked. They barely had the opportunity to speak to others, touch another. Yes, it struck her as callous at times. *You reap what you sow!* she supposed. *We all make choices.*

Some inmates considered the tumultuous Lake Champlain, which separated New York and Vermont at the border, to be a place of baptism. Many closed their eyes, picturing their future escape and the frigid swim across the forgiving lake. The washing away of sins, stroke by stroke, a shedding of the past like unsheathing from a wetsuit that had been pasted to the skin; immerging on a new shore to be saved, reborn; the undoing of all things rotten, dirty, regrettable. North to south, the body of water canvassed one hundred seven miles tip-to-tip and plunged to depths of four hundred feet. Its dual-citizenship claimed both the United States and Canada as home. But very few had the guts or the brains to really conceive of a plan to get out of this shithole. Few had the resources to set any plan into motion at all. So, instead, they rode out their sentence as if standing on a conveyer belt moving through an abandoned airport — no flights in, no flights out.

The officers at Clinton Correctional Facility typically gave Gabrielle a simple nod when their eyes met. Impassive at best, they ran through the usual routines, barked orders, and escorted her from place to place until she had signed in. She was searched, patted down, rubbed between her inner thighs, under her breasts, and down the length of her arms, back and ribcage. It felt like a violation, and she was pretty sure the correction officers in these positions derived pleasure from moving close enough to feel the heat between most visitors' legs. Each time they did this, she felt repulsed. They, on the other hand, glanced at her with crooked, creepy smiles. *Get it over with*, the internal dialogue ticked in her head.

She had grown accustomed to the procedures, the prerequisite steps required for the few visits it would take to remove her mind of incessant thoughts, the thoughts she could not rid herself of, the thoughts that had staked themselves into her consciousness. Gabrielle herself would *become* retribution. An appeasement for the things Mark had done, and her hate of him for doing them, was the fuel that had brought her here for the last two months. Gabby had listened to the tenets of forgiveness; she had tried to climb the metaphoric mountain that was supposed to assist her in finding some place of exoneration. But the resolve never came to her

— not in prayer, not in meditation, not in friends urging her to "give it a little more time." She was incapable of pardoning Mark.

One by one, the men in their dark green jumpsuits walked into the heavily guarded room. Each visiting-station allowed two people to perch upon round stool-seats, appearing to grow like branches from a center stem beam bolted to the floor. Small tables bruised the elbows of those anxiously awaiting and leaning on propped hands, biting their nails. The visits within these walls were reserved for the Honor Block inmates. No bulletproof glass divided the conversation. Visitors and inmates sat closely, a breath apart, eye-to-eye, closely, intimately, intimidatingly. It would be the shackles of metal handcuffs and anklecuffs that kept each prisoner in check. No leashes were on these men; no chains restrained them to the table. An element of trust was afforded each inmate, in turn creating a hint of apprehension on Gabrielle's part. She waited patiently. Each visit had become longer than the last one but could never exceed the allowable time of one hour. Gabby was up to forty minutes.

It was hard to look him in the face. After all, he had changed over the years. She had not remembered him being as tall as he was or as bald. His gait was confident, even in those freaking chains. "What a waste," she said under her breath each time he sauntered into the room.

"Gabs," he started, as if they were old friends.

The metal stool, always cold through her jeans, made it impossible for Gabby to find a comfortable position to sit in. Evidently he did not dwell in the past, leaving her to wonder if he had any remorse at all. "Hey," was her usual welcome. A hard shell encased her; the very shell Avery had worked so hard to chip away at had somehow reclaimed its hold over her.

"Thanks for coming," he said exposing his teeth under a half-smile.

"Yeah," Gabby said with a lack of empathy. She wanted to believe she could care less about the man sitting across from her.

"Glad you came. I was looking forward to seeing you. A bit nervous, though," he managed as he cleared his throat. His large hands, fingers interlaced on top of the table, brought back a memory of him holding her hand long ago. Smudged fingerprints shone on the silver cuffs at his wrists.

"Me too," she admitted. "I thought it would get easier. It doesn't," Gabby admitted. Her worn leather boots bounced underneath the tabletop, and the faint tapping of her heel against the tiled floor sounded like a nearby woodpecker. A ring on her finger spun underneath the pressure of her thumb as she anxiously considered the difficult topics she wanted to discuss. *Where to start?* she wondered.

"Let me begin," he ignited the conversation.

A sigh of relief, a way to cope with the unease of the situation, escaped her, and she decided to just listen for a while.

"Gabrielle, I'm so sorry for the many hurtful things I've done over the years." Remorse played on his vocal cords like vibrating guitar strings, each word shook beneath the heft of his breath as he spoke.

A piece of Gabby wanted to touch his hand, sooth his pain, but she refrained.

"I've always cared about you," he said.

She could tell by the lonesome tear settling in the corner of his eye he was being honest. *He does care*, she realized while wondering to herself if that was enough. Her eyes fixed onto him: his strong jaw line, the stubble peppering his chin, his green eyes a hue betwixt mint and pistachio. And suddenly, there in the cramped visiting room with all of the other men and women around her, she sensed a coming home, a return to the past.

"I have to share something with you," she started. "I need to be honest and just say what I need to say before I lose my nerve." Her heart raced in her chest as she contemplated the conversation.

Gabrielle laid bare, in staccato elements and broken fragments, her thoughts. This manner of approaching the conversation was an intentional attempt to avoid any obvious exchange. Talking in code was exhausting, and any morsel of privacy had to be earned. It took time.

This visit she stayed until the hour was up, the buzzer rang, and the guard walked him away. The back of his jumpsuit had a long white number ironed on it. The guard directed him through a barred glass door with one hand on his shoulder, the other on his arm. He looked back over his shoulder at Gabrielle and tenderly whispered, "I got you."

His orange sandals squawked as he was led away, and Gabby wondered if she would ever return to the correctional facility. She believed she had gotten what she had come for. His image through the glass door grew smaller and smaller until it vanished around a corner. The walk to his cell was long, navigating from one unit to the next. The right cuff dug into his anklebone, but he kept moving to match the pace of the guard.

"Hey, how was it?" the guard chimed in, regarding the visit.

"Good. Real good," he responded, casting his eyes forward down the narrow hallway.

"Yeah? Been a long while since you had a visitor, eh?" asked the guard in a hopeful tone.

"Yep, some guests are worth waiting for, I suppose," he said in a daze, his distraction evident.

"Well, good for you. A visit can change a person, fill them with purpose, ya' know."

"Yeah, purpose..." he echoed back to the guard. "Purpose..."

In the quiet of his cell he prepared for his laundry detail, made his bed, and brushed his teeth. The afternoon would be spent sweltering over a pressing iron among baskets of newly washed clothes. The few pictures he was allowed to have were of Havana and Gabrielle, which were stuck to his wall with a gummy paste.

"Colibrì!" a guard shouted down the block. "Laundry!" The footsteps of heavy boots clomped loudly as he plodded nearer. "Ready to go?"

"Ready," he said simply and stepped outside the cell to lead the way to the laundry room. The palms of his hands felt greasy with sweat, and his heart seemed to flutter swiftly against what would have been a chestplate had he been preparing for battle. The walk would take him through areas of the prison seldom visited by most inmates of the Honor Block. He passed the thieves and the punks who beat on women. He moved between the pedophiles, the molesters, and the rapists who either sat solo and sullen in their cells or hung on the bars shouting filth at those traveling the highway parting the two rows of human cages. He cast his eyes forward, avoiding all insults and outwardly stretched arms until he came to the last cell on the block.

The guard behind him had stopped to tie a shoe, offering him a rare opportunity he would later find a way to expand upon.

"Hey, Mark, I'm coming for you!" he threatened. "I'm fucking coming for you!"

The man inside the last cell stood at the bars with a calm, contemplative look on his face. His knuckles were exposed to the outside walkway as he stood grabbing the bars with both hands. From within this last cell Mark lifted an eyebrow, but otherwise did not flinch. "Who the hell are you?"

"You can call me Luke," he said in a deep low hush.

"Move on, Lucas!" the guard ordered as he stood back up. Irritation gave way to a dismissive wave. "Move it!"

The voices behind Lucas — the curse words, the shouting, the sound of heads slapping against walls, hands banging on the bars — all seemed to quiet down. It was as if he were walking through a forest on a sunny day again, sun streaming through the branches, giving way to warmth on his face and his shoulders. The flapping of tiny wings caught his eye as the streak of a small hummingbird flew among the rafters above him. And he, too, felt a return home. As if pulled from a frozen pond, a father's love had been resuscitated. *Now* he carried an obligation– not a chore but a duty to rectify a wrong. And deep within his core, Lucas sensed the exchange of any and all remaining decency slip away and out into the tortured air of the prison.